# Clearing
# in the
# Woods

Phyllis M. Newman

This book is a work of fiction. Names, characters, businesses, organizations, places, events, and incidents are either the product of the author's imagination or are used fictitiously. Any resemblance to actual persons, living or dead, events, or locales is entirely coincidental.



ISBN: 9781701629363

Cover design by SelfPubBookCovers.com/vikncharlie
Interior design by Liv Birdsall
Author photo by Kathie Houchens

To my mother, Effie Lee Prince Millsap, because she had the strength to stay

## CHAPTER 1

Once upon a time, she teetered on the brink. She didn't know what tipped her over the edge.

Maybe it was her husband. "Honey? Where are my green shorts?"

"No clue," she hollered upstairs. "I don't wear your shorts." Elbow deep in the garbage disposal clogged with a mass of onion skins that she'd repeatedly told her daughter Laura not to put down it—that and stringy celery—Roberta pushed the mass of chestnut curls off her face with the hand not full of slimy vegetable matter.

"Are they in the wash?"

"Maybe. Just look for once," she muttered. Brad thought the uterus was a homing device.

"Will you see?"

She'd rather slice off a finger digging in the InSinkErator than take the time to facilitate her husband's golf outing.

Or her unhappiness could have resulted from something else earlier in the week.

Sunday morning, she'd walked into the dining room and been startled to discover her grandmother's delicate handmade lace tablecloth missing. She didn't have to wonder for long where it was. Laura had worn it across her shoulders to a Saturday night party and left it in a heap on her bedroom floor.

Late for a Monday dental appointment, Roberta had opened the garage door to find her car gone. Wresting Laura's car keys from the pockets of a newly acquired son-in-law who was asleep on the couch, Roberta learned the battery was dead. That explained why Roberta's car was absent, but not why Laura was so inconsiderate.

And Tuesday, Bradley Jr. tracked mud through the house, left his smelly shoes in the middle of the kitchen floor, then dumped a boatload of stinky camp clothes in the washer. He'd actually pushed the start button but left them to sour.

It could have been that salesclerk on Thursday, folding the darling dress, all slinky stretch fabric and sequins, that Roberta had found in a trendy shop and thought so appropriate for her eighteen-year-old niece. Beaming at the billowing, blush-colored tulle skirt, the clerk said, "This item is lovely. Lots of our over-forty customers look great in it."

Long ago, Roberta would have been flattered. Now she almost swallowed her tongue. *Does she imagine me wearing a girlish, figure-hugging, mid-thigh-length, nylon net tutu?* She'd abandoned the Fairy Princess look long ago. Then the second shockwave hit: *Do I look like I'm over forty?*

As if the nail tech at the beauty salon, Curl Up and Dye, hadn't already clued her in. The pearly polish she suggested for her last weekend was The Party's Over Pink.

Or then again maybe it was the moist, overheated breeze that blew, swirling through the impossibly green leaves, making the rusting zinnias dance and the garden gate swing back and forth, slapping with a dangerous rhythm. Her head throbbed as if keeping time. Frustration bubbled up like carbonated discontent.

The cupboard was stocked with half-empty cereal boxes, their wax paper linings torn open and their contents stale. The dishwasher was full of clean dishes while dirty ones piled in the sink. The microwave beeped. The stove beeped. The refrigerator, coffee pot, and dryer beeped. The constant summons tolled like the limitless, insistent forever.

Stepping onto the back porch as she dried her hands on a dish towel, Roberta peered upward into the infinite sky. The half-moon shone with ethereal brightness, the dark side black against navy heavens. That is how she felt, like part of her was missing. No, not missing—obscured. Her pulse raced. She felt small and inconsequential, but also connected to those who came before and those who would come after. She imagined an endless procession of women—in buckskins, calico, factory coveralls, and pantsuits—standing in this spot: women who lived tedious, unsung lives, women so completely buried they must have hardly known their beds from their graves.

She thought of her mother, the woman after whom she'd modeled herself: little Martha, the last of six children, who slept in the makeshift bedroom in the attic where unwanted things were kept. Roberta ached for her now that she was gone, but also nursed a growing resentment of her mother's long-suffering tolerance and quiet patience. She couldn't remember her mother ever having anything of her own, no passionate interests or consuming desires. She didn't collect thimbles or gather sea shells or study the intricacies of quilt designs. Roberta was shocked when she once found a picture of her mother on horseback: it was so far beyond her understanding of her. Martha's only focus appeared to be her husband, Roberta's father, whose every gesture was like an impatient snap of his fingers. Her mother jumped like a servant, handmaiden to his every whim. Roberta gritted her teeth.

Sitting in the darkened kitchen after the dinner dishes were done, she could see her mother in shapeless housedress and dispirited slippers, looking slightly blurred like a figure in a tapestry. Roberta could almost hear her, trudging up and down the stairs with laundry, the vacuum sweeper, or dishes left under the bed. The truth struck with an agonizing clarity. Roberta was but a reflection of her mother, repeating the unfortunate past. She would be yet another unhappy woman, sitting in the ashes doing the dirty work while the undeserving went to the ball.

Her mother had unwittingly prepared Roberta for a life of servitude. Roberta's early socialization had beggared her existence. The insidious, seductive, all-encompassing soup of traditional values she'd been steeped in during her formative years directed her own unfortunate family dynamic. She was stuck in the groove of 1950s' expectations in a twenty-first-century world of opportunity.

A pang of regret pierced her heart. Laura and Bradley Jr. might look back upon their own childhood with resentment or anger. Roberta remembered her own youth with mixed feelings and not because of anything her mother had done, but because of her own wickedness. She remembered the first time she screamed, "I hate you," at the only person who was always present in her young life. Children always knew the vulnerable spots and where to sink their daggers.

Even at this distance, Roberta felt ashamed. Her mother's face had drained of color hearing her exclamation, and she blinked back tears. The hostilities were over a movie Roberta wanted to see with friends, but her mother didn't think the horror flick Cujo was fit for twelve-year-olds. Roberta had had another kind of fit, which ended in a stony standoff. She remembered feeling like an evil being, pieced together with shadowy secrets and dark threads. How could she be so hateful to her quiet, patient mother? But Roberta had wanted something from her: anger, some swift emotion, something more than resignation. Forever afterwards, Roberta felt those words woven into the fabric of their relationship. She was unable to take them back. Now her heart sank. It was entirely possible that she had also spoken in ways that would haunt Laura and Bradley Jr. all their lives.

Roberta was saddened when recalling the misery she'd caused, although eventually she understood her mother provided the only safe place for her outrage. Her father was never enlisted in their battles. Despite the bitter combat, there was trust between mother and daughter, and Roberta was free to hurl verbal abuse without fear of punishment from her dear old self-centered dad. Now Roberta felt left behind, abandoned before she had the opportunity to be the daughter she should have been.

Lying in her room later, Roberta stared upward as passing cars threw parallelograms across the ceiling and down the walls, disappearing with the hum of their engines. Distant traffic whispered like metallic surf. Longings and disappointments bared their teeth at night. Fears growled in the darkness. The cat, slinking in the corners, was a living shadow, a sentient being without commitment. She felt equally untethered, as if something loosened the ropes of love or devotion, the ties of kinship or loyalty, and found herself to be just one more lonely, disaffected female.

She burrowed under the covers. What had happened to the woman she'd been in her earliest imagination? Her novella was merely a series of scrawls in one of her children's discarded grade school notebooks. The poetry she composed on the backside of Brad's cast-off work product languished unfinished. The enlightening trip to Florence she'd saved for had never materialized because both kids needed braces.

Staring at the blank wall across from the foot of her bed, she was reminded it still wanted decoration. She'd fancied herself an artist at one time. Years before, she'd taken up watercolors, believing she might at least control ten- by twelve-inch pieces of paper, turning them into scenes as delicate as Venetian glass. But her brushes had blended the tubes of color into unappetizing shades and indecipherable shapes, the combination failing to metamorphose into art. Her artistic endeavors revealed a despairing thought. Her life, like the wind captured in a painting, could only be measured by its effects, the shadow cast or the leaf turned.

But no one seemed to care about what she created or why. Without enough time or money to study properly, she was reduced to creating her own Christmas cards and decorating gift bags. As for the writing, everyone said she composed charming, heartfelt notes to commemorate birthdays and anniversaries. Terrific. It was as if a mean-spirited troll blocked the bridge to accomplishment, and she didn't know the magic word.

Roberta was always the only one who knew what was for dinner or where to buy Brad's favorite brand of tighty whities. She never had more important problems to solve than stains in the carpet or a leak in the roof. She might have been a damned rocket scientist like Brad if she'd been given half a chance.

With mounting pressure, anger burned deep in her breast. She had no idea how she'd ended up here. Perhaps it was Karma. Or some ill-considered past life. The happenstance collection of decisions that directed her fate was lost to shadowy history. Who knew what chances had come and gone for her, how many discarded paths had led to other could-have-beens.

Through a slow and steady osmosis, she'd absorbed the elements of her eventual undoing. She was a willing dupe. Having fallen thoughtlessly into the grooves created by her childhood experience, she'd allowed the past to pave the way toward a distant, diffident husband and selfish, entitled children. Although she chafed at the thought, she knew she was trapped in a cage of her own design. Her imprisonment was self-inflicted, embraced for fear of losing the faint promise of a fragile, happily ever after. She stared at her limp arms lying on the white coverlet, mute testament to her uselessness.

* * *

She sat at the computer the following morning, trying to find a recipe for corn pudding she'd copied to her desktop. The screen froze. Roberta hit 'escape' again and again and again, but she was still there.

That afternoon, birds fell through the summer sky, the air thick with unnatural warmth. As she composed the grocery list, the scratch of her pen on paper sounded like whispers. The sycamore trees stood silent, their mottled leaves hanging in the stillness of the day like the hands of the newly dead.

All evening, she moved with languid limbs through the heavy atmosphere. Eventually the swollen skies burst forth with an angry storm, the fat raindrops bursting against the window glass like kamikaze. She didn't think she could take it anymore.

The unknown lured the disappointed as surely as the adventurous. Her energy attracted some mysterious cosmic force, a tricky wind that swirled and settled in her vicinity. Her heightened emotions strung her nerves so taut she imagined their vibrations were heard only by wild animals. Standing in the kitchen the next Saturday, she stared at her reflection in the toaster, the image so like her mother, and dropped the wet sponge into the potato salad.

That week of heat, moist air, and incessant beeping ended with Roberta sunk in the backseat of a taxi speeding toward the airport. She didn't look back at the house she had tended for twelve years, white on the outside, beige on the inside, surrounded by weed-choked flower beds because while Brad would mow, he would not weed. She made her getaway well before the noon sun beat down upon the derelict swing set and rotting backyard deck.

* * *

Roberta had no idea where she was going until she looked at the departures board at the Indianapolis International Airport. With her mother in mind, she chose the farthest point she could get to without a passport: Juneau, Alaska.

A lone traveler without luggage might seem out of place and attract attention. No one questioned her, however, a middle-aged woman of medium stature and a broad, pleasant face, and carrying nothing but an over-sized mint green summer purse and a funerary urn containing her mother's ashes.

After the TSA satisfied themselves as to the contents of the urn—with Roberta standing discreetly a few feet away—no one spoke to her, perhaps imagining her on some sentimental mission to fulfill a last wish. Although she hadn't expected it, the urn had become a protective shield, separating her from her fellow travelers. Until the layover in Seattle.

"Hi," said a dark-haired girl with smudges under her eyes and a gumdrop nose.

Roberta startled, blinking. "Hello."

She was immediately on guard. Another young one, wanting something, perhaps money. Or advice. Roberta hadn't much of either. Although she'd failed to teach her own children respect or responsibility, she might just as well start with the tough love right there. Her purse held exactly $12.39, a credit card, and a thin gold bracelet with a broken clasp. She was holding on to all of it.

"Got the time?" the girl asked.

Roberta glanced at her watch. "It's two-twenty. But that's Eastern." She thought for a moment. "It's eleven-twenty here." It was surprising to realize she'd been traveling all day but it was still morning where she was now.

She'd sent Brad a cryptic text: scattering Mother… don't know where yet.

Roberta made no excuses but embraced this current effort on behalf of the mother who had worn herself into oblivion taking care of everybody else first, always cheerfully accepting the broken cookie or the dregs of the coffee pot. Her mother, a victim of broad traditions and narrow circumstances, would escape her confines at last.

"You going to Juneau?" asked the girl.

She seemed to be settling in for a conversation. Roberta sighed. Can it really be two more hours until we board? She looked for a way out.

"Yes, Juneau," she said.

A skinny boy sidled up behind the girl. His cargo pants and striped shirt hung off his bony shoulders and hips. The girl was equally thin and hollow-looking. They both seemed ill. Her mothering instincts kicked in.

*I should buy them a meal.*

"This is a nice airport," Roberta ventured. "Did you see a place to eat?"

"Yeah," the girl said, looking at the boy, who then sat down. Both of them had large backpacks.

*Hikers?*

They had that tattered, stray-dog look of people who lived on the trail, but their muscles were slack, their skin sallow rather than sunbaked.

"Yeah," the boy agreed. "Back there." He tossed his head. "A Tim Hortons."

Now that she was sitting eye-to-eye with them, Roberta saw he was actually a man. His hair was thinning at the temples and he had a two-day stubble on his chin. The girl was maybe in her late teens, not as young as she'd first thought. They looked like people whose only reason for being was to retain their existing organic structure.

"It's two hours before we board. Would you join me for a cup of coffee? I hate to sit in a restaurant alone."

They looked at each other. The girl allowed herself a smile and they both stood. The girl was taller than Roberta expected. Walking single file, the three of them made their way down Concourse B toward the diner.

They found a littered table. Roberta reserved it by plunking her mother's urn in the center. The three of them approached the nearby counter.

Roberta turned to her companions and said, "I'm happy to buy you lunch. Anything you like."

The young man carried a tray for them all laden with two Cokes, one coffee, and three flatbread breakfast paninis.

"I'm Roberta, by the way," she said with a smile. "Roberta Blankenship."

"Oh," said the girl. "I'm Carrie. This is William."

*No last names.*

Roberta had eaten half her sandwich before the girl tore off a bite of hers. The third one sat untouched in the middle of the table.

"And who is Martha May Princezna?" The girl nodded at the urn.

"My mother." The urn was inscribed with the name along with the date of death, March 15, 2009.

"You going to bury her ashes in Juneau?"

Roberta said, "Yes," without admitting she hadn't decided. She didn't want to conjure up her mother's ashes wafting on the wind or sea. Images from The Big Lebowski floated into her head.

"You waited a long time. 2009." William spoke again, his voice hoarse.

Roberta was unsettled by his wolfish grin, his yellow, uneven teeth. "I didn't have the heart, or certainty about where or what, exactly…" her voice trailed off. She didn't quite know why she hadn't taken care of the ashes years ago. Nothing she could think of before seemed to honor her mother's memory. Maybe that's why Roberta was making this splendid effort at an exotic end. The disposition of her mother's ashes should symbolize something, tap into a deeper meaning. Her mother should have had more adventure, more excitement—more of anything.

"Alaska. A good place to end up." William smiled.

Roberta finished her sandwich and coffee while they sat in uncomfortable silence. She was surprised Carrie ate only half of her panini, while William hadn't yet taken a bite of his.

"Did you see a ladies' room?" Carrie asked.

Roberta checked the time, then glanced down the concourse. "It's over there."

"Go ahead." William pulled his still wrapped sandwich toward him and nodded at the urn. "I'll watch Mom."

Roberta accompanied Carrie to the restroom, thinking perhaps William was embarrassed to eat in front of her. She watched Carrie's shoulder blades, small and sharp, move beneath her thin T-shirt as she walked ahead of her.

Roberta scrutinized herself in the mirror while she washed her hands. The harsh overhead lighting was unkind, throwing unattractive shadows under her eyes. *I look like a ferret.* She tilted her chin up and tried on a smile. No better. The day of travel had left her clothing limp and wrinkled. Her face had followed suit.

She looked like her father, another point upon which Roberta's mother should have been aggrieved. Her only child bore no resemblance to her, Martha Princezna with her exotic features and thick black hair, nor to her delicately-boned, patrician family. Roberta had a decidedly Magyar face, framed with the paler tresses of Eastern Europe.

Carrie exited a stall and, after washing her hands, turned to Roberta and said, "Do you see something in my eye? I feel something in the left." She rolled her eyes upward as she stood under the light and leaned forward. Roberta held her breath and pulled gently on the lower eye lid to examine the pale blue orb. "No. I don't see anything. Pull your upper lid over your lower lashes, see if that helps."

"I remember that." Carrie smiled. "Mom tricks." She tried it and blinked, then splashed water in her face. Turning to Roberta once more, she said, "It's still there. Will you look again?"

Roberta poised her fingers along the delicate cheekbone and stared closely once more. Recalling a sudden image of Laura in the same posture, she suppressed a wave of homesickness.

"Nothing there, dear. You've probably irritated it by rubbing."

Carrie blinked and said, "Thanks. It's better now."

Roberta shrugged off sentimental thoughts of her kids, pushing them to the back of her mind.

They ambled toward Tim Hortons once more, where William was now standing. The urn still sat in the middle of the table which had been wiped down, cleaned of both food wrappers and wayward crumbs. He'd either eaten the sandwich or stuffed it in his backpack. When Roberta reached for the urn, William said, "Let me." He carried the urn back to Gate 23, where Delta flight 1462 to Juneau would board in thirty minutes.

Roberta consulted her boarding pass then looked at her companions. "I'm Zone 2. You?"

Carrie looked sheepish while William stared at his feet. "Umm…I don't think we're on this flight. I think ours leaves in an hour," she said, glancing at William.

"What?" said Roberta.

"We don't board yet."

Roberta was puzzled but did not press them. For all she knew, these youngsters lived at the airport, bumming food from strangers and sleeping in the restrooms. Disconcerted, she stood before they called her zone and headed toward the long line forming to the right. "Well, it was nice to talk to you. Safe travels."

"Yeah," said Carrie. "Thanks for the sandwich."

"Yeah," said William. "Thanks."

Roberta hoisted the urn in one arm and hung her purse on the other. She felt Carrie and William watching as she made her way toward the gate. Glancing at them, Roberta felt a motherly urge to warn Carrie that life is no fairy tale. If you lose your shoe at midnight, you're probably drunk.

# CHAPTER 2

Feeling achy and bedraggled, Roberta got off the plane in Juneau. During the flight, she'd worked herself into a fit of pique, the epicenter being Brad. She didn't know when she began to think of him as a hairball on the busy carpet of her life.

Harsh lights overhead illuminated shadowless strangers making their way toward the baggage area. Having checked no luggage, Roberta exited the building to board a hotel van going into the tourist area of the city. As she watched the kaleidoscope of scenery whiz by, she considered life with her husband. He seemed always to be elsewhere, doing whatever he pleased, while she filled the emotional voids in her existence all alone. Beyond the drudgery that was homemaking, she'd fashioned a social life of sorts. There was the book club, for instance, where ladies of her own class plumbed the merits of Gone Girl, oblivious to the jabs at popular culture, or The Goldfinch, a reimagining of Great Expectations about which they hadn't a clue.

She competed with the neighbors over decorating efforts at Halloween and Christmas, vying for the neighborhood honors. An image of Marybeth Harrison's Easter cake popped into her head. It had been an elaborate foot-high, pink and green rabbit-shaped confection donated to the church bake sale. Never mind that the shredded coconut tasted like toenail clippings. The cake was the talk of her circle, and Roberta recalled being envious as well as disappointed in her own concoction, birds' nest cookies made of Chinese noodles and jelly beans.

She was still mad at Gracie Ford, Marybeth's younger sister-in-law visiting from Muncie. Roberta was known for making the best coffee. All her friends would praise her, saying, "Nobody makes coffee like Roberta." Having joined them after the PTA meeting, Gracie took one sip of Roberta's brew and announced, "Cinnamon! My grandmother used to do that, add a pinch of cinnamon." Thereafter, Roberta's secret was out and she felt guilty and small, like she'd deceived everyone.

By the time the van came to a stop, Roberta decided she hated Gracie. She resented the interest Gracie had showered upon Brad at the Fourth of July picnic, laughing at his jokes and trading quotations from The Princess Bride like it was a secret they shared. Roberta had been irritated, so much so that when they got home, she took Brad by the hand and pulled him toward the bedroom. She quickly undressed him. They made love passionately, almost angrily, she recalled. It was funny to think about that now. No doubt Brad thought it was all about him but actually she was getting back at Gracie.

"Screw Gracie," said Roberta aloud as she was deposited on the curb in front of a row of motels. So what if she seemed to be around for every holiday, looking like a cross between a high school prom queen and a Ferrari? So what if her cool voice sounded like it was allowed out only on special occasions, all rounded o's and crisply enunciated t's? So what if she was soft and fresh? Roberta felt as if she could suck the life out of soft and fresh. The last time they were in the same room, their thin-edged smiles crossed like blades.

Feeling like a whiny jealous wife, Roberta couldn't think of one single achievement to claim as her own since she'd married. She was pathetic. But she and Brad were together. Surely, that counted as a success. So many of their friends had divorced. Since she and Brad never argued, didn't this mean their marriage had been a good one?

"But maybe he doesn't care anymore," she spoke aloud once more, now standing in line at the reception desk of the Goldrush Hotel. Or perhaps he simmered as she did, resentful, angry, and unfulfilled.

Really, she didn't think she'd done it so badly. She'd been more thoughtful than most. Her best friend in high school, Jeannie, had begun a whirlwind courtship with a busboy at the diner where she waitressed the summer after graduation, and they married before Thanksgiving. They had three children in five years and lived the hapless life of the habitually careless, with no aspirations or expectations. Jeannie, with her ragged yard and cluttered home, somehow had avoided the wretched excess and obsessive neatness Roberta embraced. She envied Jeannie—with whom she still exchanged Christmas cards—and her joyful, messy life. Maybe Roberta had been too cautious, trying to live up to some abstraction with an impossible standard.

Marriage. Such a union should change like the seasons, moving from spring to winter, with shifting weather and transforming landscapes. She had hoped, in the beginning, that Brad would be among the evergreens of her life but, alas, he was proving to be deciduous. Sadly, he had fallen, like a leaf, short of expectations.

She sighed. Now their relationship was over. Done with. Discarded. She mentally brushed off her hands. She would move on to something entirely unexpected. They would no longer just plod along together toward retirement, which to her meant half as much money and twice as much husband.

She rented a nondescript room faded by time and lack of attention from the youngish innkeeper, a woman whose hair appeared to have been styled with an egg beater and who wore enough lip gloss to wax a kitchen floor. She looked like a throwback to another age. In fact, all of Juneau seemed to be stuck in time. The boardwalk, wooden storefronts, buildings painted in discarded sale-bin colors, and peeling signs gave it a Wild West quality. She decided the image was cultivated for the tourist trade, probably supported by zoning laws passed by commercially minded city council members. The sightseers seemed to be everywhere in their sweat suits and T-shirts embroidered with grizzlies or eagles, easily distinguishable from the locals, both male and female, who sported cuffed Levi's and faded flannel shirts. Roberta's aqua slacks and matching top made her feel like a petunia in a corn field.

As she relaxed in her room with a glass of tepid water from the groaning bathroom tap, she opened the color brochure provided by the management and learned there were no roads connecting Juneau to the rest of Alaska or to any part of North America. The only way to get there was by water or air. Most of the people she saw on her way in were day trippers from the cruise ships that lined the harbor. Being so isolated gave Roberta a sense of comfort. Still, there was the phone, the electronic leash that tethered her to her family.

She had three text messages from Brad: **Where are you?**

**When will you be home?**

**Do we have more cat food?**

And two from Laura: **Do u have my car keys?** (Roberta realized that, indeed, she did) and **When u coming home?**

Nothing from Bradley, Jr.

Since she'd forgotten her charger, she turned off her phone to preserve the battery. They could fend for themselves for once.

Roberta hadn't yet formulated a plan, so she hoisted her mother's urn onto the closet shelf and walked the streets with a heady sense of freedom. She drank in the peculiar atmosphere of the city, an odd blend of old mining town and new technology. The local inhabitants, in their scruffy boots and well-worn cowboy hats, were holding cell phones to their ears and driving Priuses. She'd strolled past an independent burger joint, a mom and pop grocery store, and a couple of neighborhood taverns before she came to a Volunteers of America thrift store, reminding her she had no extra clothing.

She went through the racks of somebody else's discards and picked out a simple black dress in a cotton blend, a pair of worn jeans with an elastic waistband, and three faded T-shirts, the only ones she could find with no stains. In the dressing room, Roberta reviewed her full-length image. She'd begun to look as if eternally positioned in front of a funhouse mirror. Angling her body sideways, she viewed her freakishly narrow shoulders and bulbous hips, the result of her last box of Valentine's Day chocolates. She could never figure out how a two-pound box of candy could put five pounds on her thighs. Either she needed a total makeover or to accept the inevitability of aging gracelessly. She gave silent thanks for the fact that wrinkles didn't hurt.

Before she checked out, she found a funky nightgown to add to her stash. Total cost of her new wardrobe: $16.43. She found a Sears a few blocks away and bought underwear and socks encased in plastic. The wooden floors were creaky and the fluorescent lights buzzed like insects, reminding her of her childhood. Some of the stock consisted of brands she'd never heard of before, Elkadent toothpaste and Gard hairspray. It made her feel as though she were in another world, or another time, where nothing was familiar. The elderly lady behind the cash register must have come of age in the '70s judging from her appearance: whitish lipstick, black-lined eyes, and brows drawn in thin arches of perpetual astonishment. Her white hair fuzzed delicately about her face like a dandelion gone to seed.

Heading toward the hotel, Roberta hesitated. Overwhelmed with a sudden sense of unease, she stood at the corner and scanned the streets. The colorful cars weaved past her like leaves in a stream. Business people and ordinary folks flowed about like rivulets of water, and individuals scattered here and there crossed the intersection or popped into doorways or cars. She saw nothing out of the ordinary. Windows reflected the blue sky or the brisk, busy passersby. Still, the back of her neck prickled as a tingle of apprehension crawled up her scalp. She mentally shook herself. It was nothing. Only her nerves, her overwrought imagination playing tricks on her.

By the time she reached her hotel again, the sun was fading. Roberta used her old-fashioned brass key to open the door. She heard the toilet running before she stepped onto a carpet soaked with water.

She summoned the desk clerk, who appeared at her door almost before she hung up the phone. Leaning behind the commode to turn off the water, he said, "I'm so sorry, ma'am. We'll fix this right away. We'll move you next door if that's okay. We regret the inconvenience."

He used his master key to open the door to the room immediately to the left of hers. "Do you need help with your bags?"

"No thanks." She'd already stepped to the closet, her shoes squishing in the water-logged carpet and her purse and the plastic Volunteers of America bag hanging heavily on her right arm, to retrieve the urn. Within moments, the clerk returned to give her the key to her new room, and she settled into a space as shabby as the one she'd left to contemplate her next move.

Although it was early evening in Juneau, in Indianapolis it was almost ten. Exhausted after a full day of travel, Roberta showered and slipped into the used nightie, hoping it had been washed and not too pawed over, and crawled between rough sheets smelling of Clorox and damp. Thinking how she would begin the next day, she fell into a fitful sleep.

* * *

In a place between wakefulness and dreams, Roberta tossed about, struggling with the sheets. She was aroused too often by the drip of the bathroom faucet or the rattle of the useless fan overhead. As the stuffy room caused congestion in her sinuses, she breathed through her mouth. Hair stuck to her damp forehead while she floated just on the edge of consciousness.

What time is it? Roberta startled awake. She heard furtive movement and for a moment was paralyzed with dread. Then she realized where she was. The Goldrush Hotel, Juneau. Strange sounds would be a given.

She sat up. The clock radio displayed a glowing 2:14. The sounds came from next door, the soaked room with the broken toilet.

*Surely, they aren't fixing it in the middle of the night.*

Roberta strained her ears and peered into the darkness. Unfamiliar shapes materialized as her eyes adjusted—dresser, mirror, chair. Another thump came from next door. Sound traveled, so maybe it was from upstairs.

No. A shoulder or hand was sliding along the wall in the room next door. A sting of fear pierced her chest. She calmed herself with a shuddering breath and crept to the door. Placing her ear to the jamb, she slid the security chain into place. Silence.

*You're being silly. Go back to sleep.*

* * *

Roberta roused again at five-thirty and stared at the ceiling. Freed from the pull of responsibility that weighed upon her at home, she let a flood of memory engulf her. On the day her mother died, she'd awakened at the same time and with an uncanny sense of knowing. Before the phone rang, before her Aunt Ginnie said, "I'm sorry, Roberta," she knew. Perhaps her mother's death caused some cosmic shift or subterranean tremor, infinitesimal yet detectible by some deep part of Roberta's heart. Or, most likely, her mother was with her in spirit when she passed from this earth, a homeless breath evaporating with the morning dew.

It had happened less often of late, but for months after her mother passed away Roberta felt a lingering presence deep in the night, something that yearned to speak, tried to touch. She would snap awake to find indistinct apparitions of thickening fog or shadows like frosted glass hovering just above the floor. Surely a dream or wayward memory, these visions were neither menacing nor peaceful, but inherently uneasy. She'd tried to fit them into a semblance of the woman she'd known, wanting to believe it was her mother's spirit and that she was still here.

Roberta wasn't sure what she wanted from her mother, what sign she expected, but sadness always gathered at her memory. It sometimes still shocked her to realize her mother was gone—irrevocably and relentlessly gone. She conjured the feel and smell of her, recalled the tilt of her head and the set of her mouth. The intense longing Roberta lived with since her death welled in her breast and washed over her.

She sat up in bed in the frail light and buried her toes in the sickly green carpet laid out beneath her feet. Roberta knew it was more than just missing her. Something had always troubled Roberta about her mother. Some secret—a dark, disquieting tragedy—harrowed the life of Martha May Princezna. She was the black sheep. It appeared that her own family found her difficult to love. She left home as a teenager and, once her father died, she had no more contact with her own mother or her four sisters except for Aunt Ginnie, her oldest sibling, the only family member who made a point to keep in touch. Then Aunt Ginnie passed away, taking the truth with her.

Swallowing tears, Roberta bounced off the bed and drew the curtains wide to the weak sunshine, shaking herself out of her sorrow. She was in Juneau. Euphoria was all she should feel now, being on her own with no responsibilities and no one to take care of. Merely to be alone was a luxury. It had been far, far too long, perhaps in her college days, since she'd been able to spend time in any way she wished. Roberta glanced at her phone and decided not to turn it on. She had reassured Brad she was okay. Let him and the kids stew. Brad had a Ph.D., for heaven's sake, and both kids were out of high school. Laura was even married, she reminded herself. If they couldn't take care of themselves by now, there was nothing she could do about it.

Brad. Roberta tried to feel some sentimentality but couldn't. When had they become so disengaged? She couldn't remember when they had lapsed into a comfortable rhythm of low expectation. She recalled their beginning, when she was giddy in love, happy to give up her last year of college and any thoughts of a career to marry and take care of him. It seemed so easy then, pleasing him. She'd believed men were like linoleum. Lay them right and you can walk all over them for thirty years.

As she washed her face and brushed her teeth, she contemplated her past. She'd willingly stepped out of uncertainty to be plunged into the real world, a life dearly purchased with her future. Roberta was happy enough to take a job while Brad finished his degree and started teaching at Butler University. When the kids came, however, everything spiraled out of her control. Maybe that's what went wrong. She thought she'd read it in Dear Abby: If you want to be happy, don't have children.

And that was when Brad became such a reluctant lover. Once the babies came, he seemed completely oblivious to her desire for excitement and adventure, and offered neither interest nor passion. He made her feel like an ugly stepsister rather than his glamorous queen. Roberta frowned. Her Prince Charming had turned out to be an emotional dwarf.

She peered at herself in the mirror over the sink. Roberta no longer wanted her husband. She had long noted his admiring glances at younger, slimmer women, and perhaps his flagging regard for her created an unbridgeable distance that now, finally, enabled her to act. She owed him nothing. She had discharged her commitment, sacrificing her youth and beauty in the process. Now it was over. And compared to Princezna, what kind of name was Blankenship anyway? Empty and uninspiring. She would scrape off the name like something stuck to the bottom of her shoe.

With her life taking on this new definition, she pulled on the jeans and a slightly too-big T-shirt. She would blend in with the local color, not that she would've stood out particularly in any circumstance. She stared at her feet. Her ballet flats were way out of sync with funky denims. They might as well be glass slippers. She believed this princess should have a pair of running shoes.

*What else do I need?*

It was only at that moment she realized she planned to stay. She didn't know how long, but she wasn't going home soon. It would take time, after all, to familiarize herself with the area and decide what to do with Mother.

A rosy feeling of warmth enveloped her. This was no quick trip to dispose of a family obligation. It was a more spiritual endeavor. Roberta stared at her distorted image in her mother's urn, reflecting her face in several shades of gold. She embraced this effort as a quest, a mystical journey of discovery and transformation, and she was the knight-errant.

The air stirred around her. An unbearable weightlessness swelled in her breast. For an aching moment, she felt her mother's presence. Yes, something was unfinished. A mysterious sadness pervaded Martha May Princezna's life and it would haunt her daughter until she laid old ghosts to rest.

Roberta shook off the flicker of insight and put troubling thoughts aside. Traipsing into the hall with decisive cheer, she stopped short. The door to the room next door—her original room—had been jimmied. The door knob hung on its twisted base and the jamb was splintered as though pried apart with a crowbar. She pushed the door open to look inside. The dresser drawers were all ajar, the mattress was leaning against the wall that adjoined her current room, and the furniture was pulled out of place.

*Has there been a burglary?* She looked up and down the hallway. Only the door to her old room was disturbed. Since there was nothing to take from the vacant room with the soaked carpet, she imagined burglars would have moved on to another. She looked again at the other doors. Pondering this oddity, she took the elevator to the lobby.

"What happened upstairs?" she asked the desk clerk, the same young man who had moved her from the wet room the day before.

"Pardon, ma'am?"

"Upstairs. A room has been broken into."

He blinked.

"Is this a common occurrence? Should I be concerned?" she said.

She could see indecision flit across his friendly face. "No, ma'am. I'll take a look. Thanks for reporting it."

As he took the stairs two at a time, Roberta stepped outside the double doors as if through a looking glass. The day was fine and bright, and a vista swept with radiant color buoyed her spirits. She started walking with a joyous sense of freedom, swinging down the street toward the shopping district. She threaded her way among elderly denizens of the cruise ships who bumped her with bulging plastic bags and walkers as they gawked through windows of the tacky gift shops that pop up like toadstools in proximity to tourist attractions. The smell of bacon wafted from somewhere, and she stopped to sniff the air like a wolf. She crossed the street and pushed through the swinging doors of Bullwinkle's Cafe.

Strictly for the teeming sightseers, the restaurant had a line of people waiting under a kitschy menagerie of stuffed Northwestern woodland creatures staring from above their heads. Repelled by slaughtered animals as a decorative motif, Roberta backed outside and looked to the right and left. She walked another block and took a side street, hunting for the source of greasy breakfast odors. She found herself at an insignificant hole in the wall called Donna's Diner.

Taking a seat at the counter, she ordered scrambled eggs, toast, and coffee. While she waited, she surveyed what looked like a cliché from the 1950s, so like the rest of Juneau: cracked red vinyl upholstery, oft-painted beadboard paneling, and scarred linoleum. Middle-aged men, some with children, none with women, occupied the booths.

The young waitress filled her cup from a freshly brewed pot of coffee.

"Where you from?" she asked.

It took Roberta a moment to realize she was asking her. "Indianapolis."

"You off a cruise ship?"

"No. Flew in yesterday."

"Oh." The waitress leaned on the counter. "Business?" She looked over Roberta's jeans and T-shirt.

Roberta thought about scattering her mother's ashes. "Personal business, yes."

"When you going back to…"

"Indianapolis."

"Yeah. When do you leave?"

"To be honest, I don't know. I was thinking of staying for a while. Maybe." Roberta didn't want to share too much.

"You looking for a job?" The young woman looked hopeful. "I mean, something only for the summer, 'til the snows come?"

The question caused Roberta to sit at attention. Why not? She didn't want to go home. Sitting at a funky diner that seemed a world away, Roberta couldn't imagine returning to the oppressive heat of a Midwest summer, to Indianapolis, where the streets were wide and the minds were narrow. Besides, Brad would expect her to cook, clean, and launder. For a moment, she could hear the hum of the vacuum and thump of the dryer. Brad would also regale her with endless complaints about his fellow faculty members, the frustration of parking on campus, and the meddling university administrations visited upon happily dysfunctional academic departments. He was absorbed with his classes, his angst, and his dreams. She'd had dreams, too, at one time, but she couldn't remember what they were.

She looked directly into the young woman's wide brown eyes. "Yes. Yes, I think I might take a job, if the opportunity presents itself." Not a career, not a stepping stone to responsibility and power, or to personal fulfillment, but a job that paid her way. She thought about the charges on the credit card, costs that would pile up and Brad would resentfully cover. He never complained about money, so she'd never thought about it. She thought about it now.

"Know where I can find one? A job, I mean?"

"We're looking for help. Georgina left almost a month ago. She's living on a glacier outside Anchorage where she trains sled dogs."

Roberta imagined Georgina trading dirty dishes for dog poop.

"I can ask the owner." The young woman gestured to the opening behind the deep fryer and the glass case of donuts where a middle-aged woman cooked up potatoes and onions. "It would be only part-time but tips are good. I'm Fantasy, by the way." She pressed upon Roberta a limp, damp handshake.

Fantasy. Her appearance belied her name. Her dun-colored hair was frizzed and fluffed into a 1980s do, like Meg Ryan or Farrah Fawcett, although neither Farrah nor Meg would have sported the black tattoo of the Harley Davidson logo on her left forearm. Fantasy had taken pains to acquire a number of piercings as well.

"Are you from here, Fantasy?"

"Nope. Boulder, Colorado. It got all commercial, so I left."

"Makes sense that you'd settle in Juneau," Roberta said, thinking that the McDonalds down the street seemed out of place among the old-fashioned storefronts and backdrop of snow-capped mountains.

"I came here because there're nine men for every woman. Thought my chances would improve."

"And have they?" Roberta asked, trying not to look at the healthy growth of leg hair above Fantasy's short boots.

"The odds are good, but the goods are odd." Fantasy glanced at the fortyish man, a thin, graying braid trailing under his cowboy hat, sitting at the other end of the counter.

"I'm simply looking forward to never again pulling on a pair of pantyhose," said Roberta.

"Never wore 'em," said Fantasy. "Must be like wearing someone else's legs. Anyway, too constraining."

"Isn't that what women's fashion is all about? Those six-inch heels and thigh-hugging skirts? Aren't they all just modern-day foot-binding, a crippling affliction we call style?"

Fantasy looked at her as if she'd spoken a foreign tongue.

"Hey, Donna?" Fantasy called to the woman in the kitchen. "Got a minute? Someone's here for a job."

The heavyset woman, wearing an apron decorated with grease stains, barreled through the connecting door from the back. A big smile lit up her face as her gaze settled on Roberta. She stuck out her hand, and Fantasy blinked as though she'd forgotten her lines in a play.

"Roberta Blankenship. Pleased to meet you."

"Likewise. Donna Eliot. So, you looking for work?"

"Yes," Roberta said with conviction.

"We only need you for the summer while it's so busy with the tourists. Nothing permanent. You willing to work a split shift? That would be what we need most."

"Absolutely," Roberta said, not sure what a split shift entailed.

"Breakfast to one, then five to around ten."

Roberta did a quick calculation. It sounded like at least ten hours, maybe twelve. She kept her face a blank. "No problem." For six to eight weeks she figured she could do anything. She was glad not to be asked about experience. But what woman didn't have experience being at everyone's beck and call and dealing out food? She probably wasn't even expected to cook.

The next day, Roberta donned the simple black dress and a checkered apron to stand behind the counter at Donna's Diner. A mere $3.65 an hour plus tips, according to Fantasy, would net her $250 a week if she could manage thirty-six hours.

That first afternoon, she walked back to the Goldrush Hotel with \$18.50 in tips in her pocket. It was exhilarating. Not since her twenties had she earned a penny of her own. Feeling liberated, she took a second look at the Furn Apt For Rent sign in a shop window she'd seen earlier.

Again, why not? As long as I've planned to stay a while.

Roberta turned on her phone and, ignoring the thirty-eight text messages and twenty-two phone calls, dialed the number on the sign, her cell flashing Low Battery. Later that day, she was shown a single room above a shop selling key chains and snow globes encasing either a moose or a bear standing at attention. The knotty pine walls were relieved by faded, framed photographs of Juneau landmarks. The couch and chair were '80s rattan, the bed a narrow metal twin with thin sheets and a pilled blanket. A threadbare rug in a violent shade of orange was tacked by its four corners in the center of the room. She was gratified by the fact there was no kitchen and, therefore, no opportunity to reconstitute her former life of servitude. The room had only a hot plate and an under-the-counter refrigerator, although there was no counter. The place smelled of Pine Sol and dust. Bath down the hall.

She moved in that evening, placing her mother's urn in the center of a beat-up dresser with a scuffed top covered by a scarf decorated with flowers embroidered along the edge. She thought it fitting, as the worn piece of linen looked like something her mother might have made in her youth, an example of the womanly arts that sustained a marriage or an item that was placed in a hope chest. Hope. Most girls probably never imagined the life of mind-numbing grunt work that would follow their dreams of a never-ending story filled with love and excitement. Those wedding bells soon turned into an alarm clock.

Roberta twisted her mouth into a wry grin. Love, like restaurant hash, had to be taken with blind faith or you lose your appetite.

Before she threw her phone next to the urn, she checked her text messages, all from Brad.

**Where are you?**

**Worried.**

**More worried. Pls call.**

**About to call police!!! Need to know where you are!**

Roberta imagined the city's finest showing up and seeing what her house looked like by now. Brad would mow and maybe take the garbage to the curb, but the rest of it—the mail, the dust, and the laundry—would metastasize. Noting the lazy kids and the helpless husband, anyone would understand that no self-respecting wife and mother would remain in such chaos.

Before she turned off her phone once more, she sent Brad a text message.

**Don't worry. Fine. Don't expect me soon.**

Did she plan to return? She doubted it. No real reason existed to return to the bubble, bubble, toil and trouble that was her life in Indianapolis.

She pulled the ill-fitting curtain aside and sat for a long time on the window sill. Golden twilight bathed the street in a somber glow. The sun soon disappeared, dragging the blanket of light after it. The night sky exerted some strange gravitational pull, tugging Roberta from the present into the past. She recalled random images—a college dance, taking her babies home, and her mother sitting on the porch swing. Roberta watched as strangers sauntered below and embraced a sense of loss.

Movement caught her attention. A shadow darkened a doorway in the alley across the way, and Roberta noticed cigarette smoke drift up and away. The fleeting thought that whoever stood there was spying on her as she stared into the darkness crossed her mind. She shook her head, believing she was being fanciful. She had no reason to believe that anyone was interested in a plump, ordinary, middle-aged woman sitting in the window at dusk trying to sort the dark and light of her life into recognizable shapes. She didn't know how long she lingered before she wandered off to bed.

# CHAPTER 3

Roberta awoke early. The darkness was complete. While she waited for dawn, a memory sifted into her consciousness, developing like new blossoms unfurling in the rain. She had wandered into Laura's room, looking for something. Her daughter's stuffed animals, wide-eyed, were lined up along the window seat. A tattered Raggedy Ann shared her daughter's childhood rocking chair with a flawless bride doll, all sparkling white, lovely but unloved. Bradley Jr. stood behind her although she could not see him in the shadows. She could feel them both as though they were touching her now.

Laura and Bradley Jr. The major checkmarks of her life, the gold stars of her soul. She tried to recall their childhood charm, to remember when their laughter was like wind chimes in the peach blossoms. When they were small, she imagined they were seedlings, moist and delicate, growing into sturdy, healthy individuals. What had she hoped for so many years ago? She thought they might be more firmly rooted, clinging to her, thirsting for her time and attention. But that was then. She didn't know anymore. Perhaps she wanted a full life with them, a level of participation filled with contentment if not joy. Now they were largely absent, distant not only in body but mind, and careless of her feelings, oblivious to her needs. That cheerful future seemed impossible. She would have to settle for something else—something less.

She dragged herself out of bed, dressed, and rummaged through her purse. It contained the cash she had earned, credit card, broken bracelet, and the familiar paraphernalia mothers carry: safety pins, hair clips, Band-Aids, and needle and thread wound around a small piece of cardboard. She felt suddenly out of step. How long had it been since her children had required any assistance from the bottom of her bag?

Roberta blinked and submerged her melancholy with a little jolt of anticipation, an eagerness to begin anew. She took off on foot, leaving her dark thoughts behind along with the phone, useless without a charge, on the dresser. She wondered if there was an Apple store nearby, but felt no sense of urgency.

* * *

She easily swung into the life of the diner. Working with Fantasy and Donna was actually fun, the toil lightened by the comfortable camaraderie of women. The only other constant was a wheezing old tabby cat Donna called Snarfblatt. Sporting a crooked tail and missing an ear, he lurked under the dumpster in the alley and kept the rodent population down.

By the end of the week, Roberta learned to open and close, to carry as many as three plates of food while balancing drinks on a tray, and to recognize the regulars and redirect the drunks who wandered in from the main drag. She didn't mind that the hours were long and erratic. Rather than a set schedule, she found herself going in any time they needed her.

She often joined Fantasy in the morning and Donna in the evenings during those days it was busy and obvious she was needed. Her boss was an engaging and cheerful companion.

"Do you own this place, Donna?"

“For sixteen years, next month.”

“And are you a native of Juneau?”

“Nope. Me and my husband came from Fresno. Fresh start. Get away from traffic and all those Mexicans.”

Roberta kept her liberal views about immigration to herself.

“Willy up and died about ten years ago, but I had this place so I keep on truckin’.”

Roberta searched her face for any trace of sadness but found none.

“You know men. The weaker sex? I think the work killed him. Besides,” Donna said, running both hands down her ample hips, “you know how it is. Women who carry a few extra pounds live longer than men who mention it.” They both howled with laughter.

“That man, Willy. He was a trip,” said Donna. “Never knew where he was. He’d just up and disappear when there was any real work to be done. But he never missed a meal.”

Roberta knew she was fortunate, given how responsible Brad was with his job and their funds. She wasn’t sure, however, if the easy life he provided made up for the boredom.

“If Willy was late for dinner, ever, I just knew he was either dead in a ditch or having an affair. Between you and me, I always hoped he was dead.”

“I hear you, Donna,” chuckled Roberta, believing without a doubt it was easier to be a widow than a divorcée.

Fantasy, too, shared her story like a long-lost friend.

“I sometimes miss Boulder.”

“You have any family here in Juneau?” Roberta asked.

“No, nobody. But back home, yeah.” Her mind seemed to wander. “I left my mom and her folks in Colorado.”

Roberta was trying to sort out whether she missed Brad and the kids but didn't feel anything. "So, you still have grandparents?"

"Just my Gramps. Grandma died last year." She fingered a faded band on her left wrist, its beaded braids lost in the elaborate design of her tattoo. "I think of her every day, though. My touchstone." She held her arm closer so Roberta could see. "I made this friendship bracelet for her when I was a kid. She wore it 'til she passed."

Fantasy looked very young. Roberta asked, "Are you still in school?"

"I'm twenty-two, finished with that now." She hesitated. "Actually, I dropped out of college after the first year."

Roberta didn't know whether or not to believe her. "I thought maybe you were younger."

"A lot of people do. I guess I have one of those youthful faces," she said as though she might be fifty. "I look older with make-up."

Roberta's mind flashed to an image of Laura last spring, bending toward the mirror across the bathroom sink, applying a bright and glossy lipstick.

She had asked her, "Does it really stay on for eight hours?"

Laura pulled an exasperated face, communicating to her mother that she was such a dork. "Yeah, along with the hair, lint, and crumbs that get stuck in it."

Why was talking to Laura so difficult for Roberta? She chatted quite easily with Fantasy.

"Did you go?" Fantasy asked.

"Where?" said Roberta, thinking she'd asked about her wandering mind.

"College."

"Oh." Talking to Fantasy was like making popcorn without a lid. "Yes. But only for three years. I dropped out, too."

"To get married?"

"Seemed the most important thing in the world at the time." Having taken a puff of that pipedream, Roberta wanted to lecture Fantasy, tell her what was important and what could wait. She found she was too tired to make the effort.

Roberta nursed her blisters and aching feet after trudging to her room each night, but awoke every day looking forward to hobnobbing with the denizens of the diner, the working-class men—construction workers mostly—who filled their bellies and slaked their thirst for the barest connection with their fellow human beings.

Flannel-shirted truck drivers, carpenters, and plumbers tracked in dust and debris on their heavy work boots and filled the air with their good-natured joking.

"Hey, Donna. What's bakin'?" said the gnarled little man with the long braid each morning when he arrived, giving Roberta a wink. "Heigh ho, heigh ho! It's off to work I go," he called on his way out the door, his shoes speckled with dried paint.

"Bill here calls his john a jim," said a paunchy, middle-aged man, jerking his thumb at his companion.

"Why?" Fantasy fell for it.

"It just sounds better when he says he goes to the jim every morning."

"The wife told me for her birthday she wanted something that went from zero to one-eighty in six seconds," said the man they called Doctor Dish, who installed Direct TV.

"So, whaddaya git her?"

"Bathroom scales."

Shoving and guffaws followed.

Roberta was captivated by their stories. One of the electricians wore old army fatigues with his name stenciled on the pocket. It took a few days, but he eventually opened up.

"I enlisted. Desert Storm."

Having a diviner's talent for discerning deep waters, Roberta hesitated to ask what role he played there. They both looked out the window to the mountains. The sun, as bright as an undashed hope, hovered just above the trees.

He finally had the courage to say, "I was a chaplain."

Roberta was both surprised and saddened. She hadn't expected that. He must have seen so much of the dead and dying close up. "It had to be hard to stay hopeful. Providing comfort."

"No, not really." He took a drag on his cigarette, dismissing her sympathy. "Did you know about half of all people on their death bed see Jesus? I mean, Jesus comes for them. I guess that's not surprising, considering."

"Guess not."

"And not just those dying young in wartime. I worked in a hospice before joining up."

"I see."

"But you know what is a surprise? He's often wearing a plaid shirt."

"Who?"

"Jesus."

"Jesus is wearing plaid?"

"Yeah. I figure it humanizes Him, you know? Like, makes Him accessible?"

Roberta thought about Jesus dressing for accessibility. She was silent for a moment, wanting to know more but hesitating to intrude. "Do most soldiers believe, at the end?" she asked, watching him flick an ash into his plate.

"In Heaven?"

"Well, the afterlife."

"No."

"I heard there were no atheists in foxholes."

"There are no foxholes in Iraq."

"I'm speaking metaphorically."

He grinned, but something closed in his eyes so she moved on with her coffee pot.

Late at night, before locking up, she felt more like a bartender as she poured the last cups of java and working-class men poured out their hearts.

"She didn't even say anything. Can't believe she just up and left, took the kids," said an older man, stooped with grief.

"I'm sorry." Roberta couldn't look him in the eye. She hoped discussing the pain of his loss in some way diminished it.

"Ain't seen or heard from 'em. Nary a one. I work like a dog, pay for everything. You'd think I deserved something. She shouldn't of had no beef with me. I know I'm not perfect, but I did good. I did it all for her. She had no right, leaving that way."

Roberta avoided thinking about her own actions, refusing to pack for that guilt trip. She listened like a friend, wanting to extend comfort, or maybe a warning that she understood well: harboring resentment is like taking poison and expecting someone else to die. A slow, scalding sensation burned deep inside.

The men were natural storytellers, making their grinding work carrying wallboard or bath tubs and hauling crates of vegetables sound more interesting than it possibly could be. With exquisite humor and considerable charm, they recounted accidents, misunderstood conversations, and run-ins with bosses and clients just as they would if they worked in an office shuffling papers.

"The creep cut my hours, cost me a run south," said a trucker.

"Stan, sounds like you should look for other work," Roberta said.

"Nope. What I need is a new boss."

"How can you manage that without changing jobs?"

He grinned. "Maybe a sniper."

"You'd better hope for a benevolent truck to jump the curb. It can't be traced back to you." Roberta was surprised at her own facility with clever repartee.

*Sounds like a job*, thought Roberta. The same ol' same ol' everywhere. These were modern day cowboys, it occurred to her. They did back-breaking work and were highly skilled, yet itinerate. Oddly enough, around them she felt like a mother. Almost daily, she suppressed the urge to minister to their bleeding hands, scraped knees, and bruised egos. Since she'd come here to escape the Ms. Fixit role, she tried hard not to fall into its trap.

And strangely, most of them, at one time or another, mentioned their mother, but only if she had passed on. They had stories of her goodness, self-sacrifice, and thrift. Roberta could have shared many of her own stories. She related only one, early in the evening as she helped Donna prepare for the dinner crowd.

"Mom never bought anything for herself."

"Sounds like my mom," said Donna.

"I always needed something. School clothes, class trip, whatever. Then one year she bought a deeply discounted coat after Christmas, the first new garment she'd had in ages."

"And she wore it forever, right?"

"Actually, she saved it, keeping it for 'good,' you know?" said Roberta. She could still see that heavy black coat with the mink collar wrapped in the plastic dress bag Martha brought it home in and carefully tucked in the back of the closet. She tried it on each time she did her spring cleaning, but she waited for a special occasion to actually wear it, which arrived in the form of a New Year's Eve party years later. By then, the coat was way too big and hopelessly out of style. The memory made Roberta want to cry.

"I do," said Donna. "If she was like my ma, she packed away her nicest stuff and never used it."

"Pretty much," said Roberta. She was resolved, more than ever, to grab everything the world had to offer. Carpe diem. If she'd learned anything from her mother, it was not to wait for any right time or better place to experience life.

Roberta idled for a moment and watched Donna work, her heavy hips swaying with the sweep of her arm as she wiped the counters. Focused on the repetitive motion, Roberta fell into a wistful, trance-like thoughtfulness. Martha May Princezna was a cypher. What shadows had darkened her life? Roberta had but one clue. She recalled with absolute clarity the day she'd met Stella Andromeda.

It was late September, a few months after her mother's death. Awakening to a perfect, balmy autumn morning, the air filled with the scent of dried weeds and the chirp of insects, Roberta had padded downstairs in her stocking feet and poured a cup of coffee. Brad was at the kitchen table reading the newspaper. He didn't speak. She wanted something from him but didn't know what. Perhaps she just needed to share the quiet torment of loss.

It's funny, what she felt then. It wasn't that her life had changed forever or that, having lost both parents, she felt she was next. Dying held no fear for her. The end of her dull life wasn't the problem. She was actually afraid it would go on and on.

"You still going out of town today?" Brad kept his eyes on the paper.

"Yes," she answered.

She wanted him to go with her, and he would if she asked. But she also knew he'd never embrace a psychic or anything one had to say. She'd be better off seeing Mrs. Andromeda alone.

Roberta drove through the Indian summer day, first on the freeway and then on a meandering country road. Fields filled with dusty milkweed blurred by, looking like so much litter. At last, a rusty mailbox tilting at an odd angle bore an address announcing she'd arrived. Turning into a primitive driveway, a fan of weeds flanked by hard-packed dirt and loose gravel, she brought the car to a stop outside a small one-story cinder block building that looked like a converted garage. She emerged from the car to stand in the pale sunshine.

The structure itself was shrouded in shadow. An ancient, looming catalpa tree with its black branches snaking behind and across the roof, provided a sheltering thicket of drying leaves and seed pods. Although a tangle of vegetation obscured the surrounding area, in front of the door a small patch of crabgrass-infested lawn was modestly tended. At the side, an old push mower leaned against a dilapidated fence where autumn flowers, mostly asters and cosmos, bloomed among a liberal growth of purple loosestrife, Queen Anne's lace, and bindweed.

Roberta stood for a moment to acclimate herself to this bizarre place nestled in a hollowed-out spot in the undergrowth. Her peripheral vision caught a forlorn cat slinking behind a metal rain barrel streaked with rust the color of old blood. Chickens clucked and scratched nearby, and a rooster let out a listless crow. Roberta wished she hadn't come.

Then the sagging aluminum storm door opened, its hinges squealing in protest, revealing an old gnome of a woman. With a smile wreathed in wrinkles, she held the door wide.

"Come in, come in, my dear." She sounded not unlike the chickens. "Welcome."

Leaving the warm air, Roberta was enveloped by a cool, gloomy interior that smelled like cat urine and sweeper dust. Two sickly looking felines occupied a large cage placed atop the coffee table while two others lounged confidently on the lumpy couch behind it. The elderly woman motioned for Roberta to sit with them as she settled herself in a large easy chair covered with a dingy comforter. One of the cats took it upon himself to occupy Roberta's lap, and she did not resist his attentions. There was no apology for the cats or the disheveled room, which Roberta found oddly refreshing.

Stella Andromeda must have been at least eighty years old. Skinny and stooped, she was dressed in a faded flowered housedress. Her thin legs were bare, and ill-fitting slippers hung on her feet. Yet her intelligent face, surrounded by a cloud of grizzled hair, inspired confidence.

"You are Roberta," she said in a softened cockney accent.

When making the appointment, Roberta had given only her first name because whatever she learned today, she didn't want to be nagged by doubts that the psychic could have discovered beforehand something about her or her mother on the internet. Roberta was amused by this precaution. This aged woman barely had electricity, let alone access to a computer.

"Yes, of course, Mrs. Andromeda." Roberta leaned forward. "Thank you for taking the time to see me."

"Oh, heavens," she chuckled. "Time is nothing to me. I've nothing but time."

Mrs. Andromeda's smile was as warm as a helping hand. Roberta wondered if she was all alone out there in the countryside or whether she had family around.

As though Roberta had spoken aloud, Mrs. Andromeda said, "My son will be here in about an hour to see to the cats, but other than that, I've the whole day to myself."

Roberta envisioned a middle-aged man with more tattoos than teeth.

"Well, here you are. Tell me, Roberta, why you've come."

Roberta hesitated before she spoke. She liked to think she was a sophisticated audience of the professional spiritualist, someone who knew better than to provide clues and give direction to what she wanted to hear. "I've lost someone dear to me."

"A parent," said the elderly woman. "Your mother?"

A reasonable guess, given my age, thought Roberta.

"Yes. My mother passed away several months ago."

"And you've unfinished business." Mrs. Andromeda stated it as fact rather than a question.

Roberta was surprised until she realized how ordinary that would be. Anyone could identify with that feeling and have the same doubts.

Mrs. Andromeda then rambled a bit, relating stories about her parents and her immigration to the states from Great Britain. Then she returned to the business at hand, making statements that were no doubt true for any woman of her mother's class and generation.

"She loved flowers," she stated with conviction.

*Had she?* thought Roberta. She didn't know.

"She's in the company of a small, blonde woman. Or perhaps her hair is silver?"

*Maybe Aunt Ginnie?* It would make sense they'd be together.

"There's a dog with her. Long-haired and not too large." When Roberta offered no response, she continued. "It might not be hers but a neighbor's or a relative's?"

Her mother had never owned a pet. Roberta felt discouraged, hearing nothing really specific, nothing that wouldn't fit anyone who came for a reading. She concluded Mrs. Andromeda was fishing.

Roberta lost her concentration and her mind wandered as the old woman prattled on, the cat purred in her lap, and the rooster crowed in the weedy garden. Mrs. Andromeda made several pronouncements seeming to have little to do with her mother, but then said something astounding.

"She was the one who didn't belong in the family."

Roberta was stunned for a moment. "What?"

"She was an outsider."

"An outsider? Mother?"

"Yes. Do you understand the significance of this? Does this make sense?"

Roberta looked at her with wonder. The old woman had had a flash of real insight, after all. For the first time, Roberta faced squarely the reality of her mother's past and what being excluded might actually reveal. She'd always known that her mother was considered an intruder. Maybe it was more than rumor, that Martha's birth was, in fact, a dark, painful secret to be hidden from polite society. Or perhaps she was merely unwanted, a disappointment for some reason Roberta couldn't fathom. Was she a change-of-life baby? Had her grandparents desired another boy after having lost their only son at the age of ten? More than likely, sorrow and misfortune soured the marriage by the time Martha came along.

Perhaps 'intruder' was too strong a word. Mrs. Andromeda had it right. She hadn't belonged. Roberta thought of the only photograph she had of Martha with her mother, something she'd recovered the day her father died, the day Martha had destroyed her past. In that faded image, Martha stood apart from her mother, a stern and disapproving presence looming in the background. Martha had the dark, exotic good looks of a distant branch of the Savage family, not the graceful, blonde delicacy of her mother's side, not like the other girls.

But the reality of it might be symbolic rather than factual. She couldn't recall when or if either Mother or Aunt Ginnie had suggested so dark a history. Perhaps it had its genesis in nothing more than a youngster's wish to be something 'other' than she was, a desire to belong elsewhere. What teenage girl doesn't want to disavow her parents? Or just as likely, Martha's rejection by her family had given birth to the scandal, which existed only in Roberta's mind. What could Martha have done to earn such withering reproach? Maybe the most harmful whispers were never true. Her visions of the past were shattered when Donna broke the silence.

"Why don't you take a few minutes, get out of here before the crowd shows up?" Donna said. Startled from her reverie, Roberta shed the troubling thoughts from her mind and felt herself firmly rooted in the present with aching shoulders and tired feet.

She'd been working since six that morning, so Roberta was grateful for the chance to amble around the block and dispel the smell of grease from her nostrils. Moving westward to sit on a park bench outside an antique store, she saw in the distance a rolling lawn filled with gravestones. Despite the presence of the urn in her one-room apartment, Roberta hadn't thought about disposing of her mother's ashes, her reason for being in Alaska, since placing them on the dresser.

Seeing the cemetery beyond encouraged her to do something sooner rather than later. She didn't have to make any snap decisions, but she should at least look into making some arrangements. The graveyard held an odd, almost magical attraction, and she resolved to visit the following day.

# CHAPTER 4

After her evening shift, Roberta boarded the bus at the corner of Whittier and Willoughby. The driver suggested she get off at the Red Dog Saloon and walk the rest of the way to Evergreen Cemetery. The twilight would linger long enough for her to thread her way through the grounds, thinking and considering possibilities. She stood at the entrance. According to the historical marker, Evergreen was established in 1887 to replace the older graveyard on Chicken Ridge, near Main Street, when that location was staked as a gold mine. Money trumped respect for the dead after all.

She turned slowly at the gates to survey the area. Roberta couldn't decide whether Slacker's Funeral Parlor sitting conveniently across the road made for good sense or bad taste. The word 'parlor' seemed musical, associated as it was with ice cream and beauty shops, but the historical connotations were not lost on her. In ages past, the parlor was the room of the dead, where bodies were laid out for family and friends to view before burial. It harkened back to a time when people dealt with the dead and dying on a much more intimate level. Roberta closed her eyes to visualize her mother lying in a quiet room in the dark.

She blinked to dispel the image. Knowing commercial funeral parlors were established at the dawn of the twentieth century, she wondered when exactly they'd become the only acceptable option. It was only then that the 'room of the dead'—the parlor—became what is still considered the 'living' room. Roberta shook off the sadness threatening to overwhelm her before slipping through the gates.

As she meandered among the graves, the sun gathered its soft, warm light and dipped behind the mountains looming in the background. Cool air descended around her and she could smell dew. Should she bury Mother here? Would this be preferable to scattering her ashes in the mountains? In a cool wilderness stream? The ocean? If she were here, Mother could have a headstone that someone might contemplate as they struggled with life's disappointments, as Roberta did now.

Roberta recalled an image from childhood, a tombstone in the garden of the house where she grew up. It was only the top, a broken piece depicting praying hands. She always knew it didn't belong there. As a small child, Roberta was spooked by ghost stories, the ones where a specter roamed the earth to recover its lost head, or lover, or whatever the author conceived; and she had no trouble imagining such a creature searching for the stolen headstone. It never seemed right to use it as decoration. Roberta felt anxious each time her sight settled upon the fragment of bleached and faded marble lying cold and mute among the violets blooming under the lilacs.

Now, in the stillness of the turbid air, she read the epitaphs on the gravestones lined up before her. Beloved daughter, father, wife. Here lies James Harvey, Elizabeth Grand, H.B. Wilson, Purlina Cooksey. Rows of markers, from the simplest flat surfaces eroded into indecipherable cuneiform to the towering monuments topped by angels, stood side by side. After the game, the king and the pawn go into the same box.

Dappled light danced across the graves as shadows deepened and a faint breeze kicked up, causing Roberta to perceive menacing movement from every direction. She shivered, shaking off a sudden sense of confusion. She closed her eyes, allowing the sharp smell of moss, rich soil, and rotting vegetation to overwhelm her consciousness. A sorrowful yearning gripped her heart.

Feeling the sting of unbearable loss, the unease of vanished things, Roberta was drifting into the past when a sound caught her attention. Low, murmuring voices floated on the air and she detected someone, two men she realized, moving in her direction. Alone with her thoughts, Roberta didn't want to encounter strangers on the path, so she angled down a narrow trail off the main walkway and stepped behind some overgrown yews. She caught a glimpse of shadowy figures and heard whispers accompanying the sizzle of footsteps on gravel. The air shifted. Her subtle powers of perception bubbled to the surface with a warning. Her deepest intuition, a preternatural alertness, encouraged her to move farther into the grounds, threading her way among the dark monuments, responding to some reptilian part of her brain insisting on caution. When the men had gone, she relaxed. She was being silly. The idea of harm coming to anyone in a graveyard was the stuff of horror movies and Russian short stories. No danger lurked here where the living came to mourn the dead.

To the west, the sky faded to a pale shade of apricot. It melted into midnight blue as stars appeared like sparkling gems scattered across dark silk. She filled her lungs with the sharp scent of pine and the sugary fragrance of honeysuckle as the perfect silence gave way to the chitter of insects. Bats flitted high overhead, adding a shrill note to the evening song. A corresponding flutter of indecision buried somewhere inside worried at her conscience. Roberta hovered for a moment, as if in that floating place just before waking, and thought about the things she'd had and thrown away.

She didn't dare run her hands over old memories, facing squarely what she'd discarded. Instead, she wandered farther into this lonely place, the cushion of pine needles swallowing her footsteps, to discover the oldest part of the cemetery where neglected marbles were staggered across the landscape, tilting in the gloom.

The place evoked a memory, an experience she'd shared with Brad. They had just started dating, wallowing in those heady days of budding physical desire when both their personalities had a gloss born of mystery. He was confident, and she had begun to succumb to his certainty. During a day trip one damp spring day, they stumbled upon an ancient family burial ground on the outskirts of an abandoned farm. It was romantic to them then, a place forsaken and somehow lost. Wandering among the graves, they made up histories, like tourists in other people's lives.

They spent hours reading the gravestones, brushing the long grasses aside like hair from a face. Holding hands while speculating about those lives, they related wistful stories of their own past, as distant to them now as the time in which those buried once lived. Like lovers, they gathered wildflowers. Roberta fashioned a fragile wreath to place upon Brad's head and plaited a long-stemmed bloodroot into her dark red curls. She had taken a picture of Brad, wearing her scarf, leaning against a tree. And he had taken one of her. She remembered it now: her youthful self sitting on a grave, her arms full of yellow jonquils.

Chastened by her youthful callousness, Roberta returned to the main path. She saw no sign of the intruders, who'd probably visited their site, placed their flowers or said their prayers, and left. Roberta sat on a concrete bench in the shadow of a huge mountain hemlock, not yet feeling the need to go home. Sheltered by low-hanging boughs and surrounded by a thick carpet of marauding euonymus, the spot was as quiet and serene as a chapel. Darkness enveloped her as she closed her eyes and made her mind blank.

A sharp report shattered the silence.

*Was that a gunshot?*

Roberta stiffened, remaining as still as the headstones. Which direction had it come from?

Another shot rang out and she rolled behind the bench into the ground cover and against the tree trunk in one smooth movement, not making a sound. She held her breath.

Pounding feet came directly toward her as another gunshot pierced the air. A shadow ran past, zigzagging through the grounds and vaulting over the markers. Several more shots zinged in her direction, one hitting the trunk of the tree where she huddled with her eyes squeezed shut, others biting into stone or the hard-packed earth.

Somewhere near her, a man cried out. She heard a guttural groan and something heavy crashed to the ground. Swift, stealthy footsteps padded down the path beyond the spot where she cowered. She dared not search the shadows. Seconds passed. She opened her eyes and looked in the direction the gunman had gone. Another shot jolted her as she clung to the tree.

Minutes ticked by as Roberta crouched beneath the hemlock, listening to someone moving in the darkness. The second shadow was a man, judging by his size and gait, moving down the path past her and continuing toward the cemetery gates, disappearing in the gloom. Then all was silent.

Roberta's immediate impulse was to flee. But where was the gunman? Had he had enough time to get away? She didn't want him to see her leaving the scene and realize there was a witness. Maybe she should call the authorities first. Their presence would encourage him to put distance between himself and the crime. She rummaged in her purse until she remembered she'd left her phone in her room. Panicked, she screwed up every shred of courage to step onto the path and race toward the entrance.

The moon had not risen, and the cemetery was black as the ocean floor. The faint dirt path winding through the grounds was barely visible. The tombstones were shadows within shadow on either side. She stopped and stood still for a moment to get her bearings, her heart hammering. Nothing stirred. Moving onward again, Roberta stubbed her toe on a plaque almost buried at the foot of a grave and banged her knee into a headstone. Then she moved forward in a panic, her hands outstretched.

Her foot catching on something, she fell headlong across a large, inert object. The smell of blood made her recoil. She scrambled backward on her butt, whimpering. The body was lying prone, arms flung to the side, between two graves. It was a dark mass barely visible among the weeds and looming markers.

Could he still be alive? It was possible she could save a life by stemming the loss of blood or doing CPR. She leaned forward to touch him but let her hand fall short into the grass. What exactly did she think she was doing? She was no medic and now realized she'd contaminated a crime scene. The idea of touching the body, even to find a pulse, sickened her. Her legs shaking with terror, she pulled herself upright by a headstone, and ran.

# CHAPTER 5

Her lungs burned by the time she sped two blocks to the nearest house. A man in a sleeveless undershirt came to his door and responded reluctantly to her sobbing pleas to call 911. The patrol car that prowled around the corner several minutes later stopped at her frantic waving.

Still gasping for breath, wiping away tears she'd been unaware of, she explained what had happened to an officer who looked no older than Brad, Jr.

"You found a body, ma'am? In the graveyard?"

*Does he think I'm making some kind of sick joke?*

"I was visiting when shots were fired. I—I saw only shadows, heard a scream, and I tripped over someone and, oh, God, I think he's dead." For the first time she noticed she had blood on the knees of her jeans and smeared on the front of her T-shirt. Her right palm was sticky. She sobbed uncontrollably as the officer called for back-up and a medical van.

The next thing Roberta knew she was sitting in an ambulance. She didn't know how long she huddled trembling under a shiny emergency blanket as other people arrived. She remembered being asked a lot of questions.

"Are you bleeding, ma'am? Are you hurt?" The words seemed to swim around her. "What's your name? What did you see?"

Then a tall, good-looking man with a military bearing and a buzz cut filled her vision. "I'm Craven, Chief of Police, Mrs. Blankenship. Is that your blood?"

"No. There's a body … I fell over someone in the cemetery." She hiccoughed. "I mean I tripped over a body." By this time, several uniformed men had lined up behind her.

"Who is it?"

"Who? I don't … I have no idea. I was visiting, sitting on a bench as the sun set. Darkness had fallen. I—I mean eventually, that is, by the time someone came running past. It was a man, I'm sure, followed by another man with a gun." She clasped her hands to keep from shaking. "I heard shots … several shots and someone cried out, I mean the man who has hit cried out. I thought I might be able to help, but I was scared—and I—I just ran." She shivered.

"Do you think you're up to showing us where this body is located, ma'am?"

"Yes, yes, of course." She stood and her knees wobbled.

"Are you okay, ma'am?"

"I think so. I'm just … shaken." For the first time, Roberta looked at the knot of people who had gathered at the disruption. The man who'd called 911 was standing on his porch in his T-shirt adorned with sweat stains. None of the many bystanders looked as if they had recently wielded a gun.

"What can you tell us about this altercation, ma'am?"

"Nothing, really. I didn't hear them say anything. There was no arguing. I heard the shots and a scream."

Roberta discarded the blanket and staggered with the Chief and three uniformed cops toward the front gates of the cemetery. Several officers had gone before them, their torches sweeping across the graveyard causing the stones to flash and leap forward with reflected light. She took the path at the entrance and then got confused. It branched in three directions. Which had she taken to the bench beside the hemlock tree?

She closed her eyes and willed herself to be calm. She took a long, slow breath. “I think it was this path.” Most people bear to the right, so it stood to reason she had taken that route, as she was not a woman who defied convention. Cones of light bounced about her, back and forth, up and down. The police followed Roberta as she trudged forward toward a slight incline, the path curving around monuments and between stones. It didn’t look the same. The bench and the tree didn’t appear as she thought they should. It didn’t seem she’d gone this far.

As she was wishing she’d left a trail of something like breadcrumbs, a flashlight beam caught the bench ahead of them and she yelped, “There! I was sitting there when it happened.”

All the cops converged and focused their lights on the bench and tree.

“Here,” Roberta said, pointing. “A bullet hit this tree as I hid behind it,” she indicated the trampled euonymus where she’d cowered for the duration of the gunplay.

One of the cops examined the bullet hole and set an orange marker on the ground beside it.

“A man came running down the path after the first shot and went that way.” All the beams swung toward the path simultaneously, like a ravenous beast in search of prey. She headed in the direction she believed the body lay, a lump of apprehension growing in her dry throat.

It seemed so different now. She searched for a familiar landmark. Surely some monument or bush would jog her memory. Now that several cops with their lanterns swarmed the area, nothing looked the same.

"After the gunman ran toward the gates, I went this way, off to the left. I'm not sure exactly where." The cops followed her, stopped when she stopped, and waited expectantly as she looked through the rows of headstones. Roberta searched for a clue, something that suggested a direction, but saw only the staggered graves and the thick groundcover with the gregarious habit. Everything looked foreign, as if no earthly inhabitant had visited for ages.

Her armpits prickled with sweat, and she felt the pressure of expectation as clearly as the throbbing pulse in her temple. She walked forward despite being unsure of the direction, and the officers fanned out behind her, their flashlights probing the ground. The stars had been joined now by a sliver of moon. A slight breeze had dusted any clouds from the sky.

After what seemed like hours, and walking over the same ground again and again, she started to cry.

"I don't know why we can't find him. I fell over the body. It has to be here."

Her declaration was met with silence. Or was it hostility?

Chief Craven, who had stuck close behind her, said, "My men will continue searching through here. The sun will be up in a couple of hours. And we can get the dogs." His voice was flat, but she detected an undertone of exasperation. Maybe she was projecting her own frustration.

"We need to get your statement," he said. "Would you be willing to come back to the station, Mrs. Blankenship?"

It wasn't a request. "Of course. Yes."

It was a much greater distance to the waiting ambulance and idling patrol cars than she thought it should be had they been in the vicinity of the body. They had walked too far into the cemetery. Why couldn't they find it, dammit? But then again, maybe her mind was playing tricks on her. She was partly relieved. It was bad enough to be aware of the blood that dried on her jeans and shirt. She blanched at the thought of encountering the corpse again.

At the station, they ushered her into an interview room. It was vintage, with its tired linoleum floor and concrete block walls painted a Crayola flesh color. The eye of a camera stared from a corner near the ceiling and a small window with glass she couldn't see through suggested watchers on the other side. It was also hot and humid. And they had taken her purse as she passed through security and into the bowels of the facility, making her feel disoriented, unable to shake the feeling that something was off-kilter.

She sat alone for a long time. What can they be doing? What keeps them so busy before dawn? She imagined them checking her driver's license, making phone calls, and running a search on her credit rating or some other useless activity.

The door suddenly banged open. Snapping to attention, Roberta realized she'd dozed for a moment.

Chief Craven threw a tablet of paper on the table, its slap like a gunshot. A bolt of adrenaline zinged through her body.

"You need to write down everything," he said, not at all friendly. "Okay, Roberta?"

Uh oh. First names. They've dispensed with the niceties, she noticed. She'd gone from concerned citizen doing her duty to suspect. Suspected of what?

"Gladly," she responded, all cheerful cooperation despite her weariness.

Craven removed his heavy horn rims and aimed his gunmetal grey eyes at her. "You want coffee? A soda?" He handed her a pen from the pocket of his fitted, flawlessly pressed shirt.

"I need a drink."

"Not one of the amenities we offer," he said with a humorless smile. His eyes were fanned with wrinkles no more revealing than ripples on a pond.

"Then water, please."

He left the room without another word, closing the door behind him. Roberta wiped the sweat from her forehead and took up the pen. She started her story with the bus ride to the Red Dog Saloon. She scribbled for almost an hour, wondering whether her request for water would be fulfilled. After another hour, the door opened to admit Craven and another man in uniform, one she didn't recognize, who stood against the wall.

Craven sat and looked at her with those steely eyes, never taking them from hers. She was equally steady. This was a game. Good cop, bad cop. Craven would take the bad role. The other officer was young and cute. Bastards. They were treating her like a criminal. She should be offended. She played along instead.

Chief Craven slid a bottle of water toward her as he reached for the written statement. Not until she picked up the bottle and drank did he take his eyes off her to read what she had written.

After several minutes he said, "You can be prosecuted for making a false report, you know."

This is not what she expected, and her surprise must have shown on her face.

"Is this some kind of gag, Roberta? You playing a game of some sort?"

"No! Of course not!"

"There is no body, Roberta. Of course, you know that."

"I know no such thing." She plucked her T-shirt with thumb and forefinger and directed his attention to the blood smeared across it. "Explain this if there was no body."

"I don't know where that blood came from, but I know where it didn't come from. There's no body."

"There is! There must be."

He glanced once more at her written statement, staring for a long time. Those eyes studied her again. "What were you doing in the cemetery after dark?"

"It wasn't dark when I got there."

She couldn't think of anything to say. She couldn't admit she was scouting places to bury her mother. Not this far from Indianapolis. A place neither she nor her mother had ever been. It all sounded suspicious. "I find cemeteries interesting. Historically, I mean. I'm a newcomer to the area. I was curious."

"You're from Indianapolis?"

They had her purse full of ID: driver's license, credit cards, library membership. "Yes."

"Why Juneau?"

She couldn't tell him she'd run away from home. That she wanted to get as far away as possible from her husband and children. It made her sound like a degenerate. Men don't understand these things.

"Why not Juneau?"

"No particular reason?"

"Only that it's as far as I could get from Indianapolis without a passport."

"You don't have a passport?"

"I forgot to renew it. And I've decided to stay here. Anywhere I needed a passport would require a work visa, immigration status, whatever. Is it a crime to move to Alaska?" It made her feel giddy to say it, that she had actually relocated here. *Have I really done that?*

"You running away from something, Roberta?"

"No." She didn't want to elaborate about Brad and the kids. It wasn't a crime.

It went on for over an hour, Craven asking her to repeat the facts she had already written down, asking what she had witnessed, and why Juneau, why the cemetery, why, why, why.

"And there's no one to corroborate your story?"

"No one, no." Then she perked up. "What about the bullet hole in the tree?"

Craven's face showed no emotion, giving her no consideration. "That could've happened yesterday, or a week ago, that gunshot."

She was annoyed. "So, how did I find it among the acres of trees?" She snorted. "I must have amazing powers of observation." As he remained silent, Roberta stared into his attractive face with its square jaw and high cheekbones. Then she remembered.

"No! Wait! There was someone else there, earlier."

Craven arched an eyebrow.

"Maybe they left before the gun started blazing, but maybe not. I saw two people, two men. They were behind me on the path."

"What did they look like?"

"I had taken a side trail and they never got that close. I have only a vague sense. But they might be able to tell you something, if they hadn't left the cemetery before nightfall."

Craven nodded to Cute Cop, who scribbled something in his notebook. "See, Roberta? How you've remembered something?" That only started another round of questions. Roberta went over her story yet again, with the strangers trailing behind her at Evergreen included in the narrative.

At last, she raked her fingers through her hair and squeezed her eyes shut. She'd told her story a dozen times and her answers did not vary.

Craven let out an exasperated sigh. "Okay, Roberta. That's it for now." He stood, looking disappointed and ominous at the same time. "I'll be in touch." He turned to the uniformed officer. "Process her. See that she gets home."

Now came the cream and sugar. Cute Cop sat down after making a sour face at Craven's retreating back.

"Sorry about that. He's such a hard-ass. You feeling okay?"

She decided to give in a bit. "No. How could I be? I find a body," she indicated the blood stiffening on her clothing again, "and no one believes me."

"Yeah. Funny, that. What do you suppose happened?"

For the first time, Roberta contemplated other possibilities. "Maybe the guy wasn't really dead? Got up and wandered off?"

"No evidence of that, Mrs. Blankenship. No trail. No blood. Well," he patted her hand, "let's get you processed out of here."

They took her clothing to test the blood in case it was needed as evidence of a crime. They tested her hands for gunshot residue, just routine. They took her fingerprints, which she was too tired to protest. They dropped her at her place in a patrol car, wearing a prison jumpsuit, which made her feel like a criminal. At least it was before six a.m. when few people were up and about. She had to open the diner in less than an hour.

* * *

She walked through the day like a zombie, operating on pure adrenaline. The busiest day she'd yet encountered, it kept her hopping. After working the lunch crowd with Fantasy, she walked to her room and collapsed upon the bed without even counting her tips. She slept like the dead, oblivious to traffic, laughter in the streets, and the clatter and clank of men working in the alley across the way.

She was awakened by pounding on her door.

"Police. Open up."

She sat up, smoothed the wrinkles from her clothes and her face, and opened the door.

Craven filled the doorway with his crisp uniform and the smile of a snake. "Well, you got your wish, Roberta."

"What?"

"We found your body."

She blinked, trying to focus her eyes.

"It's not my body. You found it?"

"Yep. You need to come with us."

"Why?"

He squinted at her. "Why do you think?"

"No clue."

"Identification."

"Chief Craven, it was dark. I saw a shadow run past me. I fell over a body in a spooky, deserted cemetery and ran away as fast as I could. Beyond assuming it was a man, I know absolutely nothing else. I didn't see his face, clothing or any other details. Are you even sure it's the body

I saw?" She thought for a moment. "The body I think I saw? Last night you didn't even believe me." She had begun to like the idea of the man she tripped over actually getting up and going on his way.

"Oh, yes, Roberta. It's your body."

"You're sure?"

"Sure as shootin', it is."

She thought the figure of speech in bad taste, considering.

"His blood matches that on your clothing," he said, his eyes riveted on hers. "Now you've got some explaining to do."

"I've already explained. I was visiting the cemetery. The shooting started, and I was an innocent bystander. I don't know anyone in Juneau. I can't possibly tell you anything."

While she protested, she was escorted into the back of a patrol car again. This felt like an unfortunate habit. This time Cute Cop, who made sure she got home yesterday (or was that this morning?), was driving again, and Craven got in on the passenger side.

"The morgue," said Craven, and the car pulled away from the curb.

Roberta's stomach lurched. The bodies she usually saw were dressed for a funeral, scrupulously scoured and carefully made up. She didn't like this at all.

They drove to the other side of town, parking near a nondescript square stucco building off a small side street. Entering through a steel door, they took steep metal stairs to the basement. Roberta's anxiety increased as she was enveloped by flickering fluorescent light and a dank, chemical smell. The cold made her flesh crawl.

"I don't know what you expect me to tell you. Surely you can't force me to view a corpse." She trotted reluctantly along, Craven holding onto her elbow.

Before she knew it, Roberta was standing before a steel gurney shoved against the wall in the hallway outside an autopsy room. The attendant hesitated a moment and then drew back a white plastic sheet. As the odor of damp things that grow in the dark swam up to her, she squeezed her lids shut. She clenched her teeth as she opened her eyes.

The first thing Roberta recognized was the striped shirt. The sharp features under the limp brown hair and two-day stubble caused her to gasp. "William!"

Craven caught her before she fell, and she collapsed against him. He hustled her to an empty room at the end of the corridor, sat her on a wooden chair, and produced from somewhere a glass of tepid water. She drank it in three gulps and took a shuddering lungful of air.

"See there," Craven said, his face split by a grin. "You do know this guy. What'd I tell you?"

"No," Roberta said, shaking her head. "No. I don't. It's all so impossible. I can't believe it."

"I think, Roberta, you haven't played it straight with me. You didn't start at the beginning, did you?"

"I thought I had," she said realizing that the story began not in the cemetery but the Seattle International Airport.

The words gushed in a torrent, bearing a simple sincerity. She told Craven, as Cute Cop took notes, about meeting William and Carrie in the airport, buying them lunch, finding herself boarding the plane alone, and leaving them behind in the waiting area.

"Now that I think about it, I should have realized something was odd. Was I being followed?" She entertained an uneasy thought about the men behind her on the path in the graveyard.

"You tell me."

"Oh, for Heaven's sake," she barked. "Stop acting like a psychiatrist. I met them in the airport, by happenstance. How or why William ended up here, I have no idea. Surely it's a coincidence." She waved her hands around to indicate the entire episode of odd events. "None of this has anything to do with me."

"Let me get this straight. You meet a man and his girlfriend at the airport in Seattle, you buy them lunch, arrive in Juneau, and two weeks later visit a cemetery where the man ends up dead." Craven shook his head. "I got to admit, Roberta, this does not make sense. I do not believe in coincidences."

"I can't help it. What I'm telling you is the truth."

"The truth? We'll see about that. Let's go."

Roberta was back in the police station, amending her original statement to include meeting William and Carrie. She remembered their backpacks, the clothing they both wore, and the limited words they spoke.

For hours they questioned her. She went over her statement again and again. Her head swam and her voice became hoarse. Eventually, there were things she wanted to know.

"Chief Craven," she asked, "where did you find him? In the cemetery? How did we miss him?"

"I wondered when you were going to ask that, Roberta. People usually don't ask questions when they already know the answers."

"Don't be ridiculous." It was all so absurd she couldn't help but rant. "Please tell me what you think this is! Do you imagine I'm an international jewel thief here to meet Russian spies that steal across the border, that William was a government agent, and I killed him rather than be caught? Is that kind of drivel what you want to hear?"

"All right," Craven said. "This doesn't help your situation."

“Please tell me what would.”

“The truth.”

“I’ve told you what I know. You’re the one with no answers.”

Craven didn’t respond. He narrowed his eyes and stood, indicating the end of the interview at last. When she exited the building, Roberta was surprised to find it was once again evening. The last of the lingering twilight bleached the sky to a pearl grey, and darker bands of cloud curled around the moon like a claw.

The Cute Cop drove her home again. “Sorry you have to go through this.”

Roberta had no patience for his routine. “Yeah, right.”

“You should really tell Craven what he wants to know. He’ll get it eventually. He always does. Son of a bitch, that’s Craven.”

Ignoring his sympathetic grin, she got out of the car without saying good-night. She paid no attention to the patrol car pulling away, as her awareness was drawn to a darting shadow across the street. She stood in the vestibule in the dark for a moment before going upstairs, her eyes riveted on a doorway where someone had scurried out of sight. Apprehension broke over her like an ocean wave. Craven was right. None of this made any sense.

She decided her mind was playing tricks. Or, more likely, the shadow across the way was a policeman sent to keep an eye on her. Great. Exactly what she’d hoped for when she fled to Alaska. Suspicion. And menace, intrigue, and murder.

## CHAPTER 6

A creaking floorboard outside Roberta's room jolted her awake. Every nerve ending sparked with fear. Someone was there. Her eyes wide and staring, she looked at the buzzing clock radio. Two twenty-five. She sensed a presence, as palpable as if she'd been touched, standing in the hallway. Sitting up and swinging her legs out of bed, Roberta crept to the farthest corner and cowered.

Huddling against the wall, she blinked to focus her eyes, and tried to steady her trembling legs. The sliver of pale light beneath the door was broken by a dark shadow. The doorknob, burnished by a gleam of moonlight, moved first right, then left. Feeling trapped, she sidled to the window. Maybe she could escape through it. She looked past the sharply pitched porch roof dividing the second story from the first and peered into the street. It was only the second floor, but still quite a drop. She'd surely break several bones. Shaking, she slid the window open all the way and looked out. No ledge or handhold offered refuge. Her chest felt hollow, and her heart pounded.

A thundering crash split the silence as the door banged into the wall. A huge shadowy figure pounded across the room. The intruder was upon her before she could scream, overwhelming her in the darkness. His hands around her neck, he shook her like a ragdoll.

Roberta felt herself floating, then falling through the night before bright stars flashed in her head. Sharp noises, something metallic, ricocheted around her. A jarring impact consumed her. Her lungs ached as she struggled with a panicked urgency to breathe. She lost consciousness, only to awaken with a gasp, sucking in air like a drowning victim. A blur of flashing lights pierced her awareness and loud voices called to her.

"Lady? Lady? Are you okay?"

"Can you wake up, ma'am?"

Hands touched, prodded, and lifted her limbs. The wailing siren faded as it all went dark, Roberta slipping away from the conscious world like a seal dipping underwater.

* * *

A familiar voice broke through to her, faint and muffled, as if it came from a great distance.

"Roberta? Mrs. Blankenship?" Craven leaned over her, blocking the light.

"Uuummffff…" She had trouble getting her mouth to work.

"Roberta? Can you hear me?"

She came to like a diver coming up for air. After Roberta opened her eyes, it took a moment for the image of Chief Craven to stop wavering.

"How do you feel?"

*How do I feel? I'll have to figure that out.*

She shifted her gaze from Craven to white walls, white bedding, and an IV attached to her bandaged wrist. The last thing she recalled was flying through the air, a scream caught in her throat, hitting the roof and rolling, and finally landing with a sickening thud in the street below her window. There was a burst of light as the air was knocked out of her.

What seemed like ages later, she awoke bound to a backboard, unable to move, wires and tubing attached everywhere. The sky was black, the lights were blue, and she'd felt like one big bruise.

The emergency room had been a blur, with the rattle of the narrow gurney and the swift trip past white lights overhead. She wasn't sure at the time whether it was a hospital corridor or the tunnel leading to the afterlife.

Now, Roberta blinked, trying to clear her head. A machine behind her beeped and gurgled. Her head, elbow, and wrist sported thick bandages.

"Roberta?" Craven said again.

She couldn't focus. She didn't want to focus. Roberta succumbed to her confusion and slipped away again.

* * *

Vaguely aware that the sun rose and set once more while she lay physically immobilized and emotionally withdrawn, Roberta floated through a dreamy half-sleep. The next day, feeling smothered, panicking over a wisp of memory from a feverish nightmare, she awakened with a sharp jolt.

Opening her eyes, she saw Craven sitting beside her hospital bed. Everything fell into place—flying out her window, the ambulance, the emergency room, and days of drugged stupor. "Are you moonlighting, Chief?" she croaked, her voice rusty from disuse.

"What?" He stood and leaned over her.

"Second job? Ambulance chasing?"

He smiled. Perhaps he was relieved. "Should be a bodyguard."

Her mind clearing somewhat, she remembered the shadow across the street. "Did you have someone keeping an eye on me? I mean that night, when I was attacked?"

"No. Why?"

"It's just—when I got home after the delightful evening with you and your colleagues, someone was hiding in the dark across the way." For the first time, fear rippled down her spine.

"Hiding?"

"In the doorway across the street. I told myself it was the Juneau PD lovingly watching over me." She struggled to sit up.

"What did you see?" He helped her to right herself and put another pillow behind her.

"Shadows. Subtle movement in the darkness. If I hadn't believed it was the police keeping an eye out, I wouldn't have thought it had anything to do with me."

"Like the body of William Enders has nothing to do with you?"

There it was again, suspicion. "Is that his name?"

"We found his place. Camp at the edge of town. Recovered his backpack. William Enders, Los Angeles. Last address known at 47 Louden Street, West Hollywood. Anything ring a bell?"

"No."

He nodded. "You feel up to telling us about the other night, Roberta?"

Since he seemed to genuinely want to know, she gave the information without exasperation or resentment. "Got dropped off by your buddy at nine-thirty or so. Washed up, went to bed. I was awakened at about two-thirty when I realized someone was outside my door, trying to unlock it."

"Did he knock first?"

"He did not."

"Were you expecting anyone?"

She declined to be offended. “Not a soul. I happen to be sleeping alone these days.”

“Had to ask.” He didn’t even look sheepish. “So, he tried the door?”

“Yes. Then it flew open as I contemplated jumping out the window. He grabbed me by the neck and threw me out without asking if that was my preference. Otherwise, I’d have gladly exited under my own steam.” She noticed for the first time that her neck hurt, and she was wearing one of those whiplash braces.

“What’d he look like?”

“I didn’t see a thing. It was dark. He seemed tall and very big. And he was strong enough to grab me and throw me out a window like I was weightless, which you can clearly see I am not.”

“Anything else?”

She thought for a moment. “Cigarettes. I smelled stale cigarette smoke on him.” She recalled that the shadow across the way was also accompanied by wisps of smoke. “Like I said, he was nothing but a black shape.”

“You seem to be in the shadows a lot. Don’t you ever see anyone you encounter in odd places?”

“My room is not an odd place.”

“You know what I mean. How it is you can never tell us anything?”

“I tell you everything I know. Now, you tell me something. How bad is it?”

For the first time, Craven showed a human emotion. He took her hand and leaned forward with genuine concern etched on his face. “You’re going to be fine. You’ve got bumps, sprains and bruises. Nothing broken. You’ll be out of here in a couple of days.” He released her hand and stood. “The other guy got the worst of it. Busted leg.”

She was confused. “What other guy? My attacker?”

"No. The bicyclist you fell on."

"I fell on a bicyclist?"

"Yep. Just minding his own business, peddling home from a bar." He grinned. "Who knew it wasn't safe to drink and cycle?"

The scene came back to Roberta with minimal clarity: hurling through the air and encountering flesh and metal rather than the hard ground.

"Lucky for you, if you ask me. He broke your fall along with his tibia. You might have come out a lot worse if not for him."

Roberta tried to conjure feelings of gratitude but was too tired.

Craven rose from his seat and took a step back. "I'll see you later today. Buzz me right away if you remember anything. But you rest up now."

"I will, Chief," said Roberta, overwhelmed by exhaustion despite her modest exertions.

"We have security right outside the door, in case."

Despite her pain and disorientation, she noticed once more how attractive Chief Craven was. Slim, broad-shouldered, and wearing a crisp uniform with a sharp crease in the trousers, he looked like a man who could take care of himself. It appeared he not only managed a gun, and maybe his fists, but also his laundry.

He strode toward the door, which opened silently, and disappeared. Well, at least she wasn't completely addled if she could still appreciate a handsome man.

* * *

She slept for hours. Eventually she showered and ate for the first time since her collision with the unfortunate bicycle rider. Having taken pain meds, she was feeling comfortable and pampered. When Chief Craven appeared again, she was delighted to see him. Roberta considered the possibility of a growing connection between them. His attentions might just go beyond his interest in the crime committed against her. Roberta felt herself surrendering to his charm.

The spell was broken when he asked, "What's going on at home, Roberta? Your husband didn't even know you were in Alaska."

"Brad? You've talked to Brad?" For some reason it annoyed her to have her husband brought into a situation that was absolutely none of his business. The last thing she wanted was Brad riding to the rescue to fix everything like she couldn't manage her own life.

"Naturally. First off, to check on you after the incident in the cemetery. He corroborated your story. He was shocked at the thought you could be involved in a murder, reassured us you were what you seem to be."

"Really? His word was more important than mine?" She felt like a fool. Of course, they would talk to Brad. Naturally, there were things they hadn't told her.

He smiled his lazy smile.

Roberta was peeved. She wasn't a child needing parental permission. It annoyed her that anyone thought she couldn't be involved in anything violent or criminal because Brad said so. She had trouble sorting her feelings on this one, feeling conflicted. A husband should be a helpmate and a supporter in such a situation, so she couldn't really be angry.

"And, of course, we told him about you being attacked, apprised him of your injuries." Craven pinned her with his shark's eyes.

She imagined Brad walking through the door any minute, both angry and relieved. She was annoyed at the thought of his interference, telling her what to do, and taking over.

Craven stood and moved across the room toward the corridor. "I talked to him myself. He informed me he was on his way to an important meeting but would be available by phone this afternoon. I imagine he's anxious to hear from you."

Roberta was stunned. "What? It's business as usual?" Brad wasn't coming? His wife had been injured, could have been killed, someone actually tried to kill her, and he had a meeting to attend. Now Roberta was furious because he wasn't rushing to her bedside. She tried to remember what blasted academic silliness he had to attend to, what might be more important than she was.

Chief Craven appeared to be oblivious to her inner turmoil. "Well, he's a doctor, right? Can't just up and leave any time. And he'd know more than most you were okay from talking to your docs here."

Roberta sighed, having to explain it once more. "He's not a medical doctor. He has a PhD, Doctor of Philosophy. His doctorate is in astronomy."

Craven looked puzzled. "He said something about PT? I thought it was physical therapy."

"That's P and T. Promotion and Tenure." Roberta gritted her teeth. Brad had been appointed head of the Astronomy Department's promotion and tenure committee this year, a real honor for a newly minted full professor. So that's what kept him at home. She frowned.

Swell. Her physical well-being was second to his career. She started a slow burn but, out of habit, tried to see it from Brad's perspective. The committee's deliberations were of great importance in academic life. Tenure was the portal providing access to the next level of power.

Roberta knew that, once having accomplished this feat, some faculty members became all-powerful—they donned the cloak of invisibility and were never again seen on campus; others could leap tall buildings in a single bound, from the classroom to the chair's office, or even the dean's. Worse yet, you lived with your tenured colleagues for a lifetime. A mistake could be disastrous.

So what? Roberta seethed. They couldn't reschedule?

Was she being unfair? She struggled to weigh her personal crisis against Brad's professional responsibilities. To academics, bestowing tenure was a mind-boggling task worthy of a mythological hero. Brad wouldn't miss the opportunity to endow such privilege. He declined to be at her side to play dragon at the gates instead. She was a damsel in distress who could wait.

As Craven eased through the door again, Roberta sank into her pillows. How do you like that? Some husband. After fuming for a few minutes, wondering what she really wanted, Roberta allowed the painkillers to take over and fell once more into a now-familiar dreamless sleep.

# CHAPTER 7

At high noon, Roberta waited to be discharged from Bartlett Regional Hospital. After two more days of complete rest, seven bland institutional meals, and four phone conversations with Brad, the first expressing concern about her health and safety and the others about himself, she was ready to return to her one-room apartment.

His whine came across the telephone lines perfectly. "Why did you suddenly leave home?"

"Call it a compulsion." Roberta didn't mention sticky floors, piles of soiled clothing, and a stench from the cat pan in the basement. She hoped someone thought to feed Tinkerbelle more or less regularly. Otherwise, she might follow Roberta, starved for attention and appreciation, and move on to greener pastures.

"Why didn't you say anything to anyone? If you'd waited a few weeks, I could have come with you."

He didn't get it. "It was better that I came alone."

"For what possible reason?"

She didn't know how to explain it to him. Or even to herself. She was tired of forever compromising, always conforming to someone else's schedule, considering another's convenience, never doing exactly what she wanted whenever she wanted. Wait for this, consider that, weigh the options.

"Brad, please, call it a spur-of-the-moment decision, an emotional crisis, a fit of anger, however you want it. But I'm here and I'm committed."

"Well, I can't leave right now. Things at the university—"

"I don't want you to come."

"Roberta, you're being unreasonable. You—,"

Perfect. He couldn't come to help but he wanted her to want him there.

"Brad, you need to get over it. Your opinion, or your presence, won't change anything."

Silence.

"I will heal up perfectly fine wherever you are." It pained her to say it, actually. A husband should soften the discomforts and misery of life, and take her side. She had never felt so alone.

After taking a few minutes to calm down once she'd hung up on Brad, she'd called Fantasy to tell her why she'd missed her shift.

"We know. The cops have been here. You okay?" Her voice sounded like a child's over the phone.

"I feel fine for a woman who's been thrown through a window." What was the word? Defenestration.

"I'd have come by," Fantasy said, "but I'm working your hours."

Roberta detected a hint of resentment. "Listen, Fantasy. I've got a sprained wrist and elbow. I have to ask Donna about taking a few days. Sorry."

Afterward she turned the phone off again, freeing herself from its insistence. Her women friends would be shocked. Severing the lone remaining family tether was the moral equivalent of locking a baby in a closet.

Roberta put on the black dress a policewoman had retrieved from her room, gingerly pulling it over bandages and the neck brace, as she prepared to leave. She was not surprised to see Chief Craven appear when she was ready.

He checked his smart phone, scrolling through notes. “You remember anything more about your attacker?”

“No. It’s all a blur.”

“Any thoughts?”

“Only that it must be connected to William. But I don’t see how.”

“His belongings. William’s. I’d like you to take a look, see if there’s anything you recognize. If you’re up to it.”

“Sure. Whatever floats your boat, Chief.” She didn’t bother to insist it was a waste of time. She’d concluded that she didn’t really know what was going on.

She followed him to the parking lot, noting the graceful roll of his shoulders. She stood straighter, lifting her rib cage, wondering if she’d made the best decision, choosing a bra that fit like a sock.

She was at the station again, seated before items strewn across a long table, presumably things from William’s backpack. Craven handed her a pair of plastic gloves, which she pulled on with care given her sprained wrist.

“The bag itself is the only thing that looks familiar.” She touched it because she thought she should, somehow, to suggest she was taking this seriously. The bag was gray, dirty at all the seams, and extravagantly worn. The pull tab on the main compartment zipper was gone, and the mesh at the side was coming unraveled.

“These other things,” she frowned at the comb and razor, a scuffed cell phone, a paperback missing its cover, several T-shirts, a pair of khaki shorts, underwear and socks, “don’t look familiar.”

Craven picked up the tattered copy of A Hitchhiker's Guide to the Galaxy and flipped through it. A small piece of paper fluttered out from among the pages and settled on the floor. He bent to retrieve it, and then studied it, his face impassive.

"So, what was the name of the girl he was with?"

Roberta wasn't fooled. She knew he remembered. "Carrie. She never mentioned her last name."

"Ever hear of a Martha May Princezna?" he said, staring at the slip of paper.

"What?" She reached for it with her uninjured hand and he let her look.

Seeing the expression on her face, he said, "Do you know her?"

For a moment she was speechless. "Chief Craven," she said at last. "Martha May Princezna was my mother."

## CHAPTER 8

"Then you're saying William Enders knows your mother?"

"No, of course not. She died in 2009."

"Why would he have written down her name?"

"I don't know."

"How would he even know her name?"

Roberta recalled the conversation at the Seattle airport. "When we met, Chief, I was carrying my mother's ashes. The urn was engraved with her name and date of death." Now she was genuinely puzzled.

"You were toting an urn?"

"Yes."

"Okay. Where's it now?"

"In my room."

"No. No, Roberta, think again. Your room was searched after you were attacked, since it's a crime scene. There was no urn." His look was one of pure suspicion.

"Of course, there's an urn. Do you think I'm crazy? That's all I was carrying from Indianapolis, my mother's ashes. It was my reason for being here, to scatter or maybe bury the cremains. Potentially."

"And why didn't you tell us about the ashes, Roberta?"

"Why would I?" She shook her head, which caused her to wince with pain. "What has that got to do with anything?"

"Evidently, quite a lot. It appears to me the attacker who threw you out your window took the urn."

"No!" Roberta's jaw dropped. "I don't believe it."

"Trust me, you can believe it. Unless you're not telling us everything."

"But I am."

"No, not by a long shot. If I look at your statement, both the original and the revised, does it mention anything about an urn?"

"No."

"So, what else haven't you told us, Roberta?" He leaned forward, towering over her.

"Oh, for heaven's sake. I haven't told you my life story. Clearly, I've told you only what seems to be pertinent."

"Appears to me you're not the best judge of what might be pertinent."

Roberta said, "Well, you got me there, Chief."

"So, I'm going to ask you again, Roberta, what were you doing in Evergreen Cemetery Friday night?"

* * *

They went over it all again, with Cute Cop taking notes, and Chief Craven sitting unnervingly still and emotionless. But this time, Roberta could see a bigger picture than she had before. Carrie and William were not only linked to the cemetery shooting, but also to the attack in her room. Her mother's urn was the connecting thread.

After a few moments of silence, Craven said, "You're saying, suddenly, several years after your mother's death, you had to up and fly here to Alaska, a place where neither you nor your mother had ever set foot, to scatter her ashes? That right?"

"As odd as that sounds, yes."

“Are you prone to capricious or erratic behavior?”

“Several years, Chief, does not denote capricious to me.”

“It’s the Alaska part, where you get on a plane with no luggage and without telling a soul where you’re going.”

“Are you married, Chief Craven? Or ever been?”

“No.”

“A wife could explain it to you.” Roberta let out an exasperated snort. “Don’t you see? For whatever reason, I was on my way to the farthest point I could get in the continental United States with my mother’s urn. My reason for disposing of her ashes in Alaska was immaterial. I met Carrie and William in Seattle where I changed planes, and I felt sorry for them and treated them to a meal. In the restroom, Carrie distracted me for a moment while William must have put something in the urn.”

“And the TSA didn’t inspect it?”

“We were already through security. I don’t know why they didn’t carry the stuff, whatever it was, themselves.”

Craven looked thoughtful. “Maybe someone was waiting in Juneau and they couldn’t take the chance. The Feds have stepped up surveillance on smuggling and other criminal activities at the border. Or, maybe they were operating a shadowy scam of their own that their cohorts didn’t know about.”

Roberta wondered who might’ve been waiting for them. Not until that very moment did she realize William and the gunman were the men behind her in Evergreen Cemetery, and if they weren’t following her, they were at the very least in her wake, there only to find the urn William assumed she’d already buried. She suppressed a brief shiver of fear. “Whoever these people are, Chief Craven, they are after the urn, trying to recover whatever is in it. I don’t know how or why the gunplay started or why William was killed. The theft of the urn is understandable if you look at it this way." These revelations made her injured head ache, and she searched through her purse for a Tylenol.

Chief Craven offered a noncommittal grunt.

"This also explains why my original room at the Goldrush was trashed. They hoped to grab the urn before I had a chance to do anything with the ashes. There must be a police report. I'm sure you can look it up." Roberta recalled an image of William standing beside a table upon which her mother's urn sat, a table wiped completely clean. Of course, he had tidied up at Tim Hortons. Opening the urn must have left a fine residue of dust behind.

"Doesn't it make sense?" Roberta said. "They were anxious to get whatever they'd hidden. They couldn't allow me to open the urn and find whatever was in it."

Craven looked at her thoughtfully as he let a few seconds tick by. "I think, Roberta, I'm going to have to hold you as a material witness."

"What? You mean, put me in jail?"

"Place you in protective custody."

"In other words, jail."

He leaned forward, an earnest look on his face. It had been a long time since a man had been so focused upon her, had been concerned for her well-being. But being locked up?

"No! You can't. I won't be stuck in a cell waiting for you to figure out what's going on."

"May I remind you, Roberta, that someone threw you out a window?"

"Yes, and now they have what they wanted, the urn that holds my mother's ashes, for reasons we already suspect. Why would they want to bother with me again?"

"Well, Roberta. I'm not sure. I'm not certain where you fit into all of this." Those steely eyes focused like search lights on hers once more.

Everything else she might have imagined was overshadowed by the prospect of being thrown in a cell, for whatever reason they chose to justify it. This turn of events was insane. She didn't believe for a minute she was a pawn in a dangerous game. She was nothing! She hadn't anything to do with this. She was being battered by some absurd force unrelated to her.

As Roberta sat in the police station fighting to strike the appropriate combative attitude, she imagined herself in a large gumball machine. As one gumball was removed from the total configuration, the others shifted slightly, realigning within the confines of the bowl. That was how male-dominated bureaucracies operated, after all, with minuscule decisions stirring minor changes resulting in inconsequential effects. She had to get out of there.

Roberta, feeling like she'd stayed too long at the ball, slouched in her chair with a stubborn jut to her chin. "I want a lawyer."

## CHAPTER 9

Hours later, Roberta returned to her dark, still room for the first time in almost five days. After cleaning up the fingerprint dust, she stood longer than necessary in the shower, trying to relieve her painful shoulder, elbow, and wrist. To add insult to injury, she had now racked up $500 on her credit card for fees to a local lawyer.

Bastards! This is how innocent victims, the ones that play by the rules, are treated in this country.

She could see a public defender in Carrie's future if they ever caught up with her. And as long as the police were focused on Roberta as someone who had all the answers, she decided, the real culprits were getting away with murder.

Roberta wondered if they were even looking for her mother's urn. She felt an aching sense of loss. It was a desecration that William would hide something with her mother's cremains. That someone had stolen them made her heartsick. A wave of pity and sadness mixed with indignation swamped her. Her mother didn't deserve to end up a victim in some dangerous intrigue. She merited care and protection, even at this stage of her existence. Roberta closed her eyes and suppressed tears, wondering at her obsession with her mother's ashes. Was she trying to earn her love even now?

Roberta stepped out of the tub and stood at the bathroom sink. Mirror, mirror on the wall, she thought, searching her face as though answers might be found there. A transformation was taking place before her eyes. Maybe she'd been thrown from a window, or maybe she'd fallen down a rabbit hole.

The cops were incompetent. If the best they could do was focus on her, they were a sorry excuse for protect and serve. Chief Craven, with his confident swagger and sharp eyes, was no more capable than Cute Cop with his sympathetic simper. She spent a sleepless night wrestling with the injustice.

Roberta started the next day with a renewed sense of purpose. She was not going to let the cops push her around. She hadn't done anything wrong. She wasn't going to let Brad intimidate her either. She was an adult and could go where she liked for any reason she pleased. Men. She'd had quite enough of their bullying.

Pulling on her underwear, she realized the elastic was looser and the bottom bagged a bit. Had she lost weight? She ran her hands over her midsection. Her waistline hadn't been so defined in years. She squared her shoulders. She didn't have access to a scale, but she was certain she'd dropped a few pounds. Well, who wouldn't, running around at the diner, then spending all that time at the police station or hospital, so wrapped up in the murder she couldn't eat. She'd have to abandon thoughts of an underactive thyroid and confess to an overactive knife and fork.

She removed her neck brace and struggled into her second-hand dress. One thing was certain, she had to buy some additional clothing. Stuffing credit card and cash in her pocket, she left her purse and phone on the bed. The bag held nothing of value and the phone was dead. She wanted to feel fully unencumbered.

Tired of diner food, she stopped at McDonalds. After purchasing an Egg McMuffin and coffee, she sat at a table to watch people stream in and out. Across the room sat a black-clad man in a pair of elaborate cowboy boots, nursing a Coke. She stared at him so long he must have felt her gaze, and he turned to look at her. They exchanged shy smiles for a few seconds until she felt sheepish. The last thing on her mind should be a man, even one as handsome as he was. She shifted her attention to the street as a noisy truck rumbled by. When Roberta looked again, the man in black was gone.

After discarding her trash, she swung down the street with the tourists, looking in shop windows. She was sure she didn't want the overpriced sweatshirts and cheap prairie skirts offered to the cruise ship transients and decided to go back to the Volunteers of America. She was exiting The Wandering Wardrobe when she saw Carrie enter a trendy shop up ahead. Roberta stopped, her eyes wide.

Is it really her?

She snaked her way inside the store Carrie had disappeared into and ducked behind a middle-aged woman wearing a Pepto-Bismol-pink cowboy hat. Carrie stood at a glass case with her back to Roberta. She was contemplating some jewelry, mostly beaded and feathered items, no doubt Native American-inspired but made in China, where the sacred succumbed to profit. She was wearing a very expensive-looking blue silk shirt over a pair of white denim jeans. Her high-heeled sandals made her look taller than she had in Seattle, and the clothing revealed her as svelte rather than just skinny.

Darting behind a rotary postcard display, Roberta watched Carrie as she paid cash for a pair of gleaming silver earrings, which she wore out of the store. She looked nothing like the poor, pitiful waif who had bummed a sandwich at the airport.

Roberta followed as Carrie sauntered down the boardwalk, looking aimless, as though she needed to waste time. Keeping her face averted, Roberta stepped in and out of doorways watching Carrie meander ahead of her. When not looking at Carrie, Roberta glanced left and right, up and down the street to see if she was also being observed. Someone had murdered William and she was darn sure it wasn't Carrie.

Carrie crossed the street and entered a coffee shop. Roberta lingered outside an antique store window. As she stared past her reflection in the glass at Fiestaware and a Bakelite-adorned tea service, she kept the coffee shop entrance in her peripheral vision. She didn't know what to do next. Should she call the cops? She had no confidence that calling Chief Craven would result in anything positive.

On a whim, Roberta crossed the street and walked straight into the café. Spotting Carrie seated in the back, her head bent over her cell phone, Roberta strode forward and slid into the booth opposite her.

Carrie looked up, her face puzzled. The silver earrings, pieces of hammered metal shaped like arrowheads, dangled barely above her shoulders.

Roberta said, "Hi, Carrie. I wondered if I'd run into you."

Recognition dawned and Carrie's mouth dropped open. "It's you. From the airport."

"Roberta Blankenship."

Carrie blinked, rearranged her face, and tried on an unconvincing smile. "How are you? Enjoying Juneau?" She put her fingertips together, her elbows resting on the table, and her hands reminded Roberta of the carving on the wayward tombstone in her childhood garden.

"It's been a bit more exciting than I'd imagined, Carrie. While I thought I'd be," she hesitated, thinking of her mother, "otherwise engaged, I've actually spent most of my time in the police station, the hospital, and the morgue."

"The morgue?" repeated Carrie, looking at Roberta as if she'd sprouted horns.

"Why are you here, Carrie?"

Carrie glanced at the time on her phone, then out the shop window. "I'm waiting for William."

Roberta's face heated and her chest swelled with anxiety. "William?" Didn't Carrie know?

"Yeah. He said he'd be here by now." Carrie stood. "Maybe I'd better wait outside." Her nervous smile trembled almost as much as her hands. "The coffee's great. Try the hazelnut dark roast."

She practically ran for the door and Roberta followed, grabbing at Carrie's arm but catching only her shirt. "Stop, Carrie. Listen to me. Just listen."

"I have to go. William—"

"William isn't coming."

At this, Carrie stopped and stood rigid on the sidewalk in front of the café. Her eyes wide, she opened her mouth, but nothing came out. She stared at Roberta, her expression anxious.

"William is dead, Carrie."

The color drained from Carrie's face. "I don't believe you," she whispered.

"I was asked to identify his body."

Carrie's knees buckled, and Roberta steadied her, helping her to a nearby bench where she collapsed. Tears came with gasping sobs.

"Oh, God. Shit, shit, shit, shit," Carrie muttered, her teeth clenched.

Roberta put her arm around her shoulders and held her tight. "I'm sorry."

As Carrie cried, Roberta struggled with what to do. "Can I call someone for you? Is there anyone who can help?"

"Shit, shit, shit, shit, shit." Carrie was louder now. She turned to Roberta with hot, angry tears streaking her red face. "Tell me what happened."

Roberta tried to collect her thoughts. "I don't know, Carrie, but I was actually there."

Carrie grabbed her hands and pulled her closer. "What do you know? How did it happen? Who did it?"

Roberta winced at the pressure Carrie put on her sprained wrist but told her story, including Evergreen Cemetery, the morgue, being tossed out a window, and the hospital. Carrie was so distressed, and obviously grief-stricken, that Roberta felt she should know everything. She avoided, however, saying anything about the possible charges against her, the suspicions of the cops.

"The son of a bitch!"

"Carrie, you have to come with me, to tell what you know to the police."

"I'll kill the bastard who did this!"

"If you know who did it, you have to clear things up," Roberta hesitated, thinking an appeal on her own behalf would be ineffective, "for William."

"Where is he?"

"I assume his body is still at the morgue."

Carrie jumped up, shoving Roberta away. Staggering backward, Roberta caught Carrie's elbow.

"Carrie, please."

Carrie turned and pushed hard. Roberta tripped over the bench, falling to the ground. She scraped both palms on the concrete, inflicting wounds on a heretofore uninjured portion of her anatomy. Her bandaged wrist throbbed. Dazed, she looked up to see Carrie, her earrings catching the sunlight, running across the street and down an alley. Shaking off dizziness, Roberta managed to get on her hands and knees. She had to get to Chief Craven. Carrie could help solve the mystery of William's murder.

A dark car screeched to a stop beside her and the door flew open. A pair of polished boots blocked her view of Carrie's retreat.

Roberta heard a concerned voice through the ringing in her ears. "Are you all right, ma'am?"

She recognized the handsome stranger from McDonalds and clasped the helping hand he extended. "She's getting away! Catch her!" Roberta said, struggling to stand and pointing toward the alley. "Hurry! Go after her!"

"I'll get her!" the man shouted. "We won't let her escape."

Roberta shoved her way into the front seat, banging her temple on the door frame as she did so. She'd barely closed the door before the car lurched ahead with a roar and careened down the street where Carrie had disappeared. As Roberta's head swam, the driver circled the block at breakneck speed, weaving past trucks and pedestrians, and shot down one side-street, then another.

The car jerked to a sudden stop. Carrie was nowhere to be found. Roberta listened to the tick of the engine before she turned to the man and tried to focus her eyes. Although she had commandeered the car, a reckless thing to do she realized, it seemed to her the driver was already familiar with the object of the chase.

"Almost got her this time," he said.

Roberta stared at the forty-something, rugged type in black jeans and fitted T-shirt. It appeared to her that the men in this neck of the woods were surprisingly buff. She noted pale blond hair threaded with silver and a mustache anchoring a tanned face before she thought about whether or not she was in peril. Her hand probed her temple where a large lump was forming.

"You know Carrie?" she asked, now wary. She had to stop being so impetuous.

The man whipped out his wallet, which opened to reveal a badge on one side, an ID card on the other. "Tim Westlake, U. S. Treasury Department." He looked like the hero of a '50s western, all strong jaw and piercing eyes, but without the white hat.

Roberta expelled a breathy sigh and relaxed her shoulders. Surely, no harm could come from being in the hands of the U.S. government.

"That young lady is an object of interest in our investigation of an international smuggling ring."

"Really?" Roberta was shocked, but it seemed to fit the circumstances.

"Mrs. Blankenship, it is a pleasure to meet you at last."

Confusion clouded her face. "You know me?"

"In a manner of speaking. I know what your involvement in this affair has been."

"Through Chief Craven?"

"No," he said, his mysterious, dark eyes wreathed in lines as intricate as a spider's web. "I'm afraid the local authorities are not aware of my participation. We're keeping a low profile. Locals are often inept. You know, anxious to demonstrate their superiority, too eager to take credit. They get territorial and want to show off."

"Tell me about it," she muttered. She tried to focus her eyes once more. "So, you're undercover?" It was not lost on her that he'd materialized out of thin air, like a genie out of a bottle.

"I can't confirm that, but I ask that you keep my presence to yourself. It's impossible to explain, but it's crucial to our investigation."

"I'm not on such good terms with the police, actually, Detective...Agent?"

"Call me Tim, Mrs. Blankenship. No formalities."

"Okay. Then it's Roberta." She wished she had a classier name. It was a mystery where Roberta came from anyway, since no Roberts were in evidence anywhere in the family.

"Roberta it is." His grin created long parentheses about his mouth. "Are you okay?" He searched her face. "You ought to have that looked at." He reached toward the swelling on her head, thought better of it, and put his hand back on the wheel.

"It's nothing," said Roberta with a wan smile, dropping her hand into her lap. "Only a bump. I've actually had enough of hospitals."

He glanced in the rearview mirror. "Can I drop you somewhere? We should talk, but not now."

"I guess so. Just get me back to the main commercial strip. I can get along from there." She was reluctant to reveal where she lived even though it was likely he already knew. His presence at McDonalds and knowledge of her activities in Juneau suggested she was being watched.

The car glided onto the road and headed in the direction they'd come from. Roberta didn't stare but watched Tim Westlake from the corner of her eye. His strong hands gripped the wheel with confidence, his shoulders were relaxed, his profile composed. He must be with 'the Feds' that Craven had mentioned, the people providing greater surveillance against smuggling and other border violations.

He pulled the car in front of the coffee shop where she'd confronted Carrie. "Can we meet here tomorrow morning?" he said, indicating the shop with a nod of his head. "About eight?"

"Sure." But Roberta wasn't sure at all. "I don't know what I can do to help."

"Roberta, you know more than anyone. You are the key. Nothing will be resolved without your help, I'm afraid."

She felt suddenly more engaged. Really? A suburban wife and mother didn't typically get to feel so important. Especially with such high stakes. Murder, assault, theft, and the United States Treasury Department. Maybe they would give her a clever code name.

As she opened the door and stepped out into the late morning sun, Tim leaned his broad shoulders toward her and said, "Remember. Tell no one we have met. See you tomorrow."

He sped away in a burst of gravel and dust.

## CHAPTER 10

It was two-thirty before she made it to the Volunteers of America. She sang along to Bruce Spingsteen's "Born in the USA," switching the lyrics to "made in the USA," as she searched the racks of castaways, noting only Chinese-made garments. She selected two pairs of jeans, this time choosing a size smaller and without an elastic waist, three shirts, and a simple dark dress. She passed up a matronly frock, longish and shirred under the bosom, for something more tailored. She had a flashback to her closet at home, Laura zipping through items of clothing declaring, "Yenta, yenta, yenta," expressing her low opinion of her wardrobe.

Once confronted with the funhouse mirror in the make-shift dressing room, Roberta's newfound swell of confidence burst. Her cheekbone below the knot at her temple sported a blossoming bruise and the bandages on her wrist and elbow were filthy. In the morning's excitement, she'd dismissed her injuries, but now they ached.

Her sinking spirits were buoyed when she pulled on a pair of size eight jeans and they hugged her slimmer figure like a glove. The fitted shirts emphasized her trimmer waistline. She actually looked toned, even without an armor-like carapace of undergarments.

With the newly acquired items draped across her arm, Roberta roamed the aisles of the store looking at shoes, bags and jackets, none of which she needed, she decided. There was something freeing, even energizing, about reducing her stuff to the bare necessities: cheap shampoo that doubled as body wash, only nine items of clothing neatly lined up on hooks along the wall. She reflected once more on her closet at home, where summer things wrestled with winter clothing that languished in the warmer weather. A woman's closet was like a time capsule. It reflected ages past and informed the unfortunate future. Roberta hadn't given much thought to it, but her spring cleaning earlier this year had signaled a sea change in her life.

That day, the fresh April air had encouraged her diligence. She'd knelt in the closet doorway, pulling shoes and empty boxes from dusty recesses. Untidy heaps of footwear were strewn across the floor. At her age, there was no point in trying to cram aching feet into four-inch heels, she'd decided. She had the sneaking suspicion that stilettos and thick platforms no longer enhanced her best qualities.

She'd spent a wistful moment of silence over the scarlet snakeskin, the green satin, the yellow suede, and midnight blue faille shoes that would soon find their place in a local resale shop, where, she hoped, some youngster with an abiding appreciation for retro styles would discover them.

She paused, recalling the purchase of the peach-colored leather sandals she'd held in her hands, her favorites for so many summers. She remembered when she first wore them, the day she'd met Brad's family. It seemed like yesterday, the time Brad took her home to meet his folks. Suddenly pensive, she sank into the past to relive that sunny day. The Blankenships lived in impoverished gentility in a great, rambling house filled with shabby furniture. Brad's younger siblings felt like fourteen kids rather than four, with television, radio, and the stereo blaring at the same time, mixing with the street noise of their urban setting. The raucous din of rattling pans, jazz or symphonic music, and shouting voices were all more or less joyful, a cheerful, unselfconscious cacophony.

Frank Blankenship was an outgoing man who never met a stranger. "How are you, my dear?" he'd greeted her at the door, his shirt unbuttoned and his sizable belly hanging over a pair of pink Bermuda shorts.

He engaged her without hesitation. "Do you play contract bridge? We'd have a fourth with the missus." He was sipping a warm Pepsi, worn flip-flops on his feet.

"Or Scrabble. The girls will play." He then quizzed her about any interests in philosophy, science, and music.

In the colder months, Frank exchanged the Bermudas for plaid pajamas, the seat of which was always worn thin. His hair awry and a track of cigarette burns down his flannelled front, Frank expressed himself with elegance on any number of issues from architecture to Shakespeare.

"You familiar with Wordsworth?" He held up a thick book of poetry.

"You play an instrument, Bertie? I'm a piano man, myself."

Or, opening to a random page, he'd read from a history book or biography, holding the rapt attention of the room. He was like everyone's favorite teacher or that beloved uncle whose visits were the highlight of the year. He was the only person who ever called her anything but Roberta. Not even Brad had a pet name for her. She smiled, thinking of him, but shook herself back to the present.

She'd focused once more upon her task, the burgeoning closet. She tossed the shoes. It was time to discard clothing from the late '90s, too. Even if she managed to lose weight, they were hopelessly out of style. She pressed a little black dress to her body, its dark crepe against the paler crepe of her skin. Even had it been still fashionable, it was now too young for her. She would never again expose that much leg, so much bosom.

And the vintage stuff would have to go. Now that she was in her forties, it'd just look like she was wearing her old clothes. Roberta was ruthless. She retrieved two empty boxes from the hallway and folded the black dress and other evening wear into one of them for the resale shop. The second box received items for Goodwill. She knew that for each destination, she'd have several boxes, some containing delicate chiffons, beaded velvets, and gowns with whalebones and sequins; others confining sturdy wools, sober corduroys, and print blouses with missing buttons. Each would find uses with someone else.

Standing still for the moment in the middle of the Volunteers of America—a world away from her past and the mind-numbing, relentless requirements of life in Indianapolis—Roberta thought again of Brad. Her mind flashed upon their bathrobes, their wrinkled, homely shapes, sagging side by side on the back of the bathroom door. She blinked to dispel the mundane domestic image from her head.

Roberta quashed a swell of loneliness as she continued to cruise the store. Having taken such pains to shed the anxieties presented by her family, she'd be damned if she would miss home. That she felt a sense of loss surprised her. What was it? No longer being depended upon, no longer being the center of everyone's needs and demands, she decided. The routine of drudgery had defined who she was. She grimaced. Now was the time to establish a new persona, different expectations of the world and herself in it. She lifted her chin at a jaunty angle.

Catching glimpses of her thinner self in the narrow mirrors hung intermittently between racks of clothing, she saw her hair had grown too long, weighing unbecomingly on her small face. Because it was easier to catch her hair at the crown of her head rather than go to the trouble of getting a haircut and maintaining a style, Roberta added an unopened 3-pack of elastic scrunchies to her armload of clothing. She'd rather look like a kid than sport some old-lady bubble-head hairdo.

She also inquired of the girl at the checkout counter about an Apple store. There wasn't one close by in downtown Juneau, she learned, but she was able to buy a charger for her phone at Herb's Appliance Mart, which was located not far from her room. She managed to make it there just before closing, then sauntered home in the twilight. When Roberta plugged her phone in, she was once again at the beck and call of the outside world, consisting entirely of family in her case.

"When are you coming home?" Brad was petulant when he finally picked up.

Roberta clamped her jaws to keep from snapping.

"And what are you doing in Alaska anyway?" He voiced no concern at all for her physical well-being.

"They need me here," she said with a bit of hubris.

"Why?"

"I'm a material witness," she said. "Actually, I had to hire a lawyer to stay out of jail." She was exaggerating, but it suited her purposes. She felt smug during the moment of stunned silence that followed.

"A lawyer? What did that cost?"

Wrong! "I'm involved in a murder, Brad. Got it? It ain't cheap."

"You? Murder?"

Wrong again.

"I have to go. We'll talk later." She ended the call before Brad could sputter another word emphasizing his limited expectations of her.

When she deleted the thirty-four unanswered calls on her phone, she noticed the last three were from Chief Craven. She was tired and couldn't think of any reason to submit herself to additional harassment. Having gotten into the habit of unavailability, she shut off her phone again, showered, took her pain meds, and went to bed.

Despite easing into unconsciousness, Roberta slept fitfully through the night. Dark images inhabited her dreams. Carrie was pulling her deep into the cemetery, where William waited, blood all over his shirt. They insisted she follow them. After shifting through the scattered headstones, they came to the edge of a dark and humid forest. As Roberta moved toward the trees, she was pushed to the ground and fell headlong onto an old grave. She sat up and drew the weeds away from the stone with a trembling hand. It read, in elaborate script,

*Here Lies Martha May Princezna*
*Beloved daughter, sister, wife and mother*
*1942 – 2009*

She dug into the earth like a dog, flinging dirt behind her into a pile. Two feet down she encountered her mother's urn, the engraving caked with soil. She wrestled it from the earth and handed it to Tim Westlake, who was suddenly standing behind her. He snatched it and ran away. Roberta scurried after him but lost him in the dark. She awoke with a start.

It was a bit past six, the light just beginning to break. She rolled over and nestled into her pillow, favoring her injuries. Once remembering her upcoming rendezvous with Westlake, she felt a cheery jolt of anticipation, popped up, and scooted down the hall to the bathroom. The bruise on her cheek had the look of rotting fruit, but her elbow and wrist felt better. She decided to dispense with the elastic bandages, which reminded her of Grandma Princezna, who wore them wrapped about her feet and ankles like socks. In her room again, Roberta took particular care with her hair, which required a bit of coaxing, and slid on her second-hand jeans. She chose the shirt most flattering to her coloring, a yellow and blue paisley.

By seven-thirty, Roberta was on her way to the coffee shop, striding through the brisk morning air. No tourists milled about this time of the morning, so it was easy to keep an eye out for Carrie. Roberta, unable to think of any reason Carrie should stay, imagined she was long gone by now. She wondered why Carrie was in Juneau in the first place. She hoped Tim Westlake could fill in the blanks.

She took the same booth she'd shared with Carrie yesterday, almost expecting to see her sitting there. Roberta was early, so she ordered coffee and a carrot muffin. She didn't want to be stuffing her face in front of the Treasury Department.

Tim arrived before her food did. She saw his tall, muscular body in silhouette as he stood in the café doorway. With the alertness of a bird of prey, that attitude of menace and expectancy, he searched the dim interior. Finding her, he strode forward and eased his lanky frame into the seat opposite her. More so than yesterday, she was attracted to his pale hair and full mustache. What kind of man was he? When he curled up in front of the fireplace at night, was it with a good book or a bad girl? Her heart did a little flip.

"Good morning," he said, signaling to the waitress. "What're you having?"

"I've already ordered."

Her pastry arrived with his coffee. Now that she had rested her eyes on his lean arms and muscular chest, she didn't want it any more. He ordered a fruit and yogurt smoothie.

*Figures.*

She offered him her muffin, but he resisted.

Tim tapped his cheekbone, indicating hers. "What happened?"

"You must have seen it. Yesterday," she said, "Carrie pushed me, and I tripped on the bench outside. Isn't that why you stopped?" Roberta was loath to admit that, like a klutz, she'd hit her head on the door frame while leaping into his car.

"Yes, of course. We were watching. I didn't realize you'd been hurt."

"It wasn't as painful as being hurled headfirst out a window."

"We heard about that," he said. "Then you do realize you're in danger?"

"Me?" A tiny zip of anxiety shot through her body as she realized it was true. "But why?" She thought of William. "I don't know anything." She struggled with the truth, not wanting to accept reality.

"It's hard to explain without putting you in jeopardy even more."

"That doesn't make sense. None of this has anything to do with me."

"It has everything to do with you."

"Then tell me why."

"That knowledge might put you deeper into harm's way."

Roberta pondered his mysterious position. "But shouldn't I know something? So that I'm aware when I'm in some kind of danger? I mean, why the Treasury Department?" She could think only of counterfeiters.

"It's complicated. But I can tell you I'm with the Financial Crimes Enforcement Network."

"Never heard of it."

"We regulate dealers in precious metals, valuable stones, and jewels. We try to prevent money laundering."

It struck Roberta that the joke she made yesterday in Craven's interview room about smuggling jewels to Russian spies might actually have some validity. Swell. If Craven and his cohorts got wind of this, they might think she knew more than she did. Craven was a clever man. He would know that some people always tell the truth because nobody ever believed them. Her uncanny ability to see more than the obvious might actually get her into trouble.

"The characteristics of jewels and precious metals that make them valuable also make them vulnerable to those seeking to launder money. Counterfeit or marked dollars can easily be converted. The money supports the drug trade, human trafficking, and other serious criminal activity."

Roberta thought about what might fit in her mother's urn. "So, William and Carrie, they were involved in smuggling jewels? That's why William was killed?"

"I shouldn't reveal any more. But generally, it does you no harm to know the Treasury Department regulates those who deal in easily transported valuable commodities to ensure the Bank Secrecy Act is followed, to protect our financial institutions. The Patriot Act requires a certain level of oversight of all banking entities for BSA purposes. Money laundering is serious business. The next attack on the home front might involve banks rather than bombs."

"Are you saying NSA is involved?"

"Yes. And the FBI, the CIA, the whole alphabet."

"I'm not sure I understand."

"For your protection, Roberta, I can't reveal the details."

She resisted the implications. How was she a part of any of this? When Tim reached for his coffee cup, she saw the outline of a gun in a shoulder holster under his denim jacket. An overwhelming apprehension silenced her. She thought of William and her growing belief that he had put something in her mother's urn in the airport after they'd gone through security. Jewels made perfect sense. She could see now how they probably figured in some bigger crime, like drug smuggling, the sex trade, or even terrorism. Still, it was hard to wrap her head around the fact that all this was happening to her.

"So, William must have put jewels or something in my mother's urn and now he's dead."

"Yes, it appears that way. You can see how serious this is. Roberta, where is the urn now? It is dangerous for you to have it in your possession."

"Don't you know? It was stolen."

He stopped cold, halting his cup halfway to his lips. "Stolen? When?"

"Last week. That's why I was tossed out a window. Some guy broke into my room, pushed me out of the way, and took Mother's urn."

He looked dumbstruck, his mouth slack. "This was what, five days ago?"

"Yes. Tuesday."

"Who did it?" His face turned red, and he had difficulty speaking.

"I don't know. The police don't know. I was so scared, I didn't see much."

"Can you remember anything at all about your assailant?"

She stared at the remnants of her muffin, concentrating.

"Think, Roberta. You don't realize how important this is."

*Is he angry or frightened?*

"I was awakened in the middle of the night. He burst into my room. I didn't see his face, but he was large and extremely strong, and he shook me like an empty shirt and threw me into the street. He was quite broad through the shoulders. It was dark, and I was scared, and that's all I can remember."

"And you don't know what became of the urn?" He snapped at her.

Roberta was defensive. "The man took it, obviously. It was on the dresser when I went to bed, but when the police searched my place after the attack, it wasn't there."

"Our contact here in Juneau was unaware of this development." He searched her face with troubled eyes. "This is unexpected. It sets everything back."

"I'm sorry," she said. "I wish I could be more helpful." She felt like it was somehow her fault for not being more careful.

"Roberta, you're in danger. As long as they want the urn and think you have it, you'll be a target."

"Why? I don't have a clue where it is now. And didn't 'they' take it?"

"That isn't clear, but it appears to me the bad guys we're watching don't know about the theft. You need to trust me. I can't explain without revealing details about our investigation."

She imagined being tortured in a dank basement by thugs with strange accents and scars or tattoos on their faces, goons wielding fiendish devices for inflicting pain. Obviously, Tim couldn't trust her. That must be why he wouldn't reveal what he knew.

"What should I do? I'll help in any way I can." Roberta covered her fears with a touch of bravado.

He relaxed and took her hand. His dark eyes probed hers. "Go about your daily routine and act like nothing's wrong. We'll have a detail near you, keeping you safe. Say nothing to the police or anyone else about this meeting."

"Of course, if that's necessary." She felt a gentle flutter in her breast as his fingers pressed into her palm.

"We'll talk again. You'll hear from me."

"When?" She hoped he hadn't detected the eagerness in her voice.

"I'm not sure," he said. "The phone is too dangerous. We can't trust anything electronic. Our people will know where you are at all times. I'll be in touch."

He stood and looked about the almost empty café. "Keep an eye out for Carrie or other suspicious persons. I have to get this information back to my team."

With a nod, he picked up the check and left it with a twenty-dollar bill on the service counter. Roberta watched as he crossed the dusty road, disappeared into a large dark car, and drove away.

## CHAPTER 11

Roberta's injuries now presented only minor twinges of discomfort, but she bandaged them again before going to the diner. It was time to get back to work, where she would be kept hopping, and she didn't want to have to baby her wrist and elbow. On the way to Donna's, she didn't notice anyone tailing her. The Treasury Department must be very good at surveillance.

"How are you feeling?" Fantasy asked when Roberta appeared. Everything seemed to stop. Fantasy looked at her wide-eyed, and Donna came from the kitchen. The three people at the counter halted their forks halfway to their mouths.

"Good, considering." Roberta tied on an apron and pitched right in, bussing dirty dishes and mopping up the counter. "I'm sorry about all this," Roberta said, nodding to her elastic bandages as Fantasy and Donna stood by expecting more.

"Who'd you piss off?" asked Donna. "You got a boyfriend already?"

Only then did she realize that neither Fantasy nor Donna was aware that the altercation at her place involved a theft. And no one would know that it figured in something larger, possibly drug smuggling, sex slavery, jewel heists and, most certainly, murder.

"And the cops showed us pictures of some dead guy," Fantasy said. "Asked if we'd seen him hereabouts. They wanted to know if he'd been here looking for you."

Roberta was shocked into silence for a moment but then adopted an innocent expression and shrugged her shoulders. "They showed him to me, too. Didn't know the man." She was certain Tim and company would expect her to disavow all knowledge. The less her coworkers knew about her and recent events, the better.

She shifted her glance to the men seated with their coffee and greasy breakfasts. They were all regulars, but could one of them be a cohort of Tim's? She thought she played the innocent quite well as she imagined herself being watched for signs of bad faith.

"Hey, fellas." She tossed them a friendly grin as she filled coffee cups.

It felt good to be at work again, doing something familiar, participating in easy banter with the customers and pocketing tips. To make up for her absence, she told Fantasy she'd cover her evening hours. As a result, she worked a split shift and spent the afternoon catching up on her sleep. She returned to the diner in the early evening as the light began to fade. Her shift went by quickly.

Walking home after ten, she had the uneasy feeling she was being watched. The long twilight had yet to be swallowed by darkness when she let herself in by the street door, quickly locking it behind her.

The hall light was out. Every nerve in her body was taut. Before taking the stairs, she stopped and listened, peering upstairs into the gloom. The stairs creaked under her weight, reminding her of the intruder who'd attacked her several days ago.

With shaking fingers, she fumbled with her door key. A ripple of fear crawled up her back as she felt another presence in the hallway.

Once she had unlocked the door, someone hustled her inside and closed it with a swift, deft movement while holding onto her. Terrified, she gasped in an effort to scream.

"Shhhh. It's me," said Tim. He'd placed a firm hand across her mouth, his other arm around her shoulders, pulling her close.

Lit by blue neon pulsating from across the street, he motioned for her to stay silent. He moved quickly to both windows and pulled the blinds and curtains. He snapped on the small lamp next to the bed, the weak light pooling on the bedside table.

"What…" she said, holding a hand against her throat.

Tim shook his head and touched a finger to his lips once more. Then he proceeded to open each of her dresser drawers. He felt around gingerly, moving his hands inside them, then around the perimeter of the furniture. He ran his fingers around the edge of the windows and doors and looked thoroughly at the walls and woodwork in the closet. On all fours, he studied every inch of the floor and baseboards. He lifted the mattress and inspected the springs and the bedding.

Roberta watched his graceful movements while calming her racing pulse. The fist of fear in her breast softened into an exquisite excitement at his nearness. The aura of danger surrounding him, his commanding presence, caused every cell in her body to respond, warming her, and quickening her pulse.

After five minutes of searching every inch of her three hundred and thirty square feet, he turned to her with a smile. "Sorry about that," he said. "We can't be too careful."

"Are you looking for a bug?"

"Keep your voice down. They could still have equipment that picks up sound trained on us." He glanced across the space until he spied the hot plate. "Put on some water, okay?"

She filled the teakettle and turned the burner on high as he stood, tense and wary, behind her. They both remained silent, their eyes locked, until the kettle sang softly. She felt the heat from his body and wondered if he could smell desire.

"What's going on?" Roberta asked as steam whistled in the background.

Tim spoke in a whisper. "There's nowhere we can talk and not be monitored. Your room is actually the safest place because they expect you to be alone."

"Who? Who expects me to be anything at all?"

"In this case, the cops."

"Why? What do they want?"

"You're all they have, Roberta. There's nowhere else to focus their investigation."

"Are you talking about William's murder? For God's sake, I can't believe they think I had anything to do with that."

"They're spying on you, nevertheless. Meanwhile, it's gumming up the works for us."

"The Feds, you mean?"

"As long as the cops are interfering, running surveillance, interviewing you, the guys we're after won't make a move. They must feel free to act. We need for them to make a mistake."

"What does that mean, Tim? Are they going to do something to me?"

"It means we've laid a trap."

"Am I the bait?"

"No," he said. "Of course not. We wouldn't put you in danger that way. But they think you have something they want, the local cops aren't clued in, and, well, let's just say things are in a delicate balance."

"They still think I have the urn?"

"Yes, and whatever they put in it. It's best you don't know anything in case…"

"In case what?" Roberta blanched. "Tim, you're frightening me." A shiver ran up her spine. Any thoughts of a romantic encounter dissipated as dread welled in her stomach.

"Look, Roberta. We're taking care to keep you safe. We've got your back. But I'm here to tell you to be on the lookout."

"If it's all the same to you, Tim, I'd rather you passed me a note at the diner than jump me in the hallway. I nearly had a heart attack."

"Sorry. I had to speak to you. Tell you what's at stake." He leaned close and probed her face with his gaze.

She could smell his warm skin, scented with something musky. She again felt the strong pull of attraction, a sensation not unlike centripetal force. Was Tim drawn to her as well? She wasn't sure an interest in her would be appropriate. He might be crossing a line, Federal agent-wise. It wasn't easy for Roberta to succumb to a belief in her desirability, but she didn't know everything. People got lonely, despite their professionalism and their training, in spite of a commitment to someone else. Roberta glanced at his left hand, looking for a wedding ring.

She lowered her gaze and regained her composure.

Tim took a cleansing breath and relaxed. "I've got to get going before someone discovers we've talked. We can't be seen together, but all the same, I'm nearby, watching."

He peeked behind the blind. "I'll shoot out the back." He crossed the room, opened the door a crack, and searched the hall. "Lock your doors and don't answer unless it's me."

Then he was gone. Roberta flipped the now ill-fitting lock and stared at the broken chain she had yet to repair. She pulled up the blind and scanned the shadows out front, but Tim didn't reappear. He must have taken the alley out back to the next street over.

* * *

She slept surprisingly well considering the cloak-and-dagger mystery that swirled around her, not to mention the promise of a clandestine romance she entertained. Tim's presence last night was unsettling, but not the way she might have thought. She couldn't get him out of her mind, remembering his lean body and rugged face. A sexual relationship was the last thing she expected to find in Alaska.

She bounced out of bed despite her stiff limbs and peeked into the hall to see if the toilet was occupied. She tiptoed to the bathroom in her nightgown and took a quick hot shower. Standing before the sink in her room, she dried her hair with a towel and fingered her natural curls into a pile atop her head, held with one of her new scrunchies. She was going in at eight to work with Fantasy through the lunch hour.

"Donna says you'll do dinner tonight?" Fantasy asked as Roberta tied on her apron.

"Yes, indeedy," Roberta said with carefree cheer. Breakfast, lunch, and dinner, just like home.

"Should be slow. Wednesdays usually are. That okay with you?"

Then Roberta remembered. Fantasy had rearranged her workweek so she could attend a square dance at the high school. She had a date with the teacher who was chaperoning. Roberta was essential to the plan, the only one working that night.

"Sure, no problem," said Roberta. Donna was on call in case there were too many hamburgers or bowls of chili to sling. Roberta didn't expect any difficulty. She imagined demand would be steady tonight but not heavy.

Roberta strolled home to nap before her evening shift. She walked along the dusty, weed-choked sidewalk, kicking a bottle top toward the gutter and keeping a lookout for anything strange. She saw only the usual collection of rabble: construction workers replacing the concrete curb, painters working on the hotel shutters across the way, and a woman delivering plastic sacks of advertising flyers. She glanced above and wondered if someone lurked behind the curtains on an upper floor, watching her.

A cat slinking across the street attracted her attention. He looked just like Chuckie, her children's old tomcat. She hadn't thought of him in years. He was Laura's first pet, and they were heartbroken when he didn't come home one day. A year later, Roberta discovered he'd moved in with a family down the street, apparently having found a new, more interesting place. She'd caught sight of him lounging, serene and self-possessed, in their picture window, his enigmatic eyes registering no recognition when she happened by. She felt a sudden, uneasy kinship with Chuckie.

She reached the sanctuary of her room and locked the door. Roberta was relaxed enough to fall asleep as she read, propped up in her single bed against the thin cushion from the only chair and her one pillow. The thumps and bumps made by those who shared the building were comfortingly familiar. Music wafted from somewhere. She awoke as the sun faded into the long twilight.

Her first thought was of Brad. What must he be doing tonight? She frowned and banished him by recalling his amusing family instead. She'd loved his mother. While her father-in-law was all southern charm and classical education, Brad's mother, Evie, was the workhorse. If Frank was the flower garden, Evie was the soil. She was a small wren of a woman, plain and physically unremarkable, flitting about tirelessly to manage the demands of living.

She'd call from another room in her sing-song voice, "There're clothes in the dryer," or "It's garbage eve. Who's taking out the trash?"

Of course, she was talking to the girls. The males were content to loll about, do-less, while the hum of activity was decidedly feminine. This explained, of course, why Brad was always content to allow Roberta to respond to the requirements of house and yard. Annoyed with him once more, she rolled over.

Evie knew how to fill a home with warmth and to create a sense of belonging. Her walls were festooned with faded, sepia-toned photographs going back four generations. Images of women wearing great feathered hats and standing next to fancy cars, boats, and even airplanes hung beside those of farm folks holding a hoe or a rake, wearing tattered, ill-fitting work clothes. Great Aunt Claudia was draped in veils and dangling earrings as she cradled a crystal ball. A professional photograph of Brad's grandmother Shirley in elegant, full-male drag hung beside another of her wearing a shapeless house dress, leaning against a dilapidated farm building, the furiously scratching dog in the foreground captured as a black blur with teeth. Those charming images swam before her, then disappeared.

Unable to relax any longer, she rose and worked the kinks out of her limbs.

She arrived at work twenty minutes early. Fantasy, relief written all over her face, glanced at her watch.

"Go," said Roberta. "Have fun. I owe you this."

Fantasy grinned and skipped out the back to her ancient blue Honda. Roberta cleaned up tables near the two booths occupied by teenaged boys as an older couple came through the screen door, looking expectant, blinking in the fluorescent light.

“Sit anywhere you like,” sang Roberta. “Be with you in a minute.”

Roberta bustled through the evening, feeling efficient and empowered, managing the business by herself. She served up fries, jerked sodas from the old-fashioned fountain, and dealt out slices of pie. By a quarter ’til ten, she had locked the front door and turned out the lights in the dining room.

Roberta was swinging a heavy, smelly plastic bag into the trash bin when she saw a police car ease to the curb in front. Snarfblatt sat under a bush at the corner of the building, his yellow eyes glowing in the headlights. Almost by reflex, she stepped behind the dumpster. Car doors slammed as she melted further into the shadows. She stifled a scream as strong hands grasped her shoulders.

“Don’t make a sound! It’s me,” Tim hissed.

Roberta’s voice quivered. “Stop doing that.”

“Come on,” he said, taking her by the elbow.

They crept down the dark alley behind the diner to the cross street where Tim had parked. He unlocked the car with a beep and a flash of the lights and they scurried into it. Roberta’s mouth was dry and her eyes wide. She was running from the cops. What they could possibly want was a mystery.

Tim started the engine and the car rolled from the curb like a rodent slinking through the gutter.

“Did you know the police were coming?” Roberta asked as the street lights overhead slid past them.

Tim hesitated for a second. “Yes, I did.”

“What is it? What’s wrong?”

“They’re going to arrest you for murder, Roberta.”

"What? Oh, my God. How could they? Why?"

"You're the common denominator for everything that's happened."

"Coincidence. It's just a coincidence." She went over in her head meeting Carrie and William, the cemetery, the theft of the urn, everything. She was, indeed, the point person. The center of all activity. She'd be excited if she didn't feel so threatened. Surely, they couldn't put her in jail. "What evidence do they have?"

"A body. And you're the only one who knew him." He shifted his gaze to her. "A mysterious woman who seems to have no past and no real purpose here."

"That's absurd!" she said. Was that how she seemed to them? It was all so innocent, so perfectly understandable, how she came to be in Juneau. She felt a sinking sensation in the pit of her stomach.

She turned to Tim. "Where're we going?"

"Out of here. We can't let those idiots put you behind bars. It would ruin everything."

"But why?"

"If you're out of commission, all activity stops. If they know you're locked up, they won't make a move, thinking you're the only one who knows where to find the urn."

Roberta had the uneasy feeling she was being used as a pawn or, worse yet, a sacrificial lamb. "Really," she said with a frown. "Why do they think so?"

"You're the last one to have it, as far as they know. They obviously are unaware of or don't believe your story about the theft. They have to have that urn."

"But if they don't they have it, who does? I have no clue."

"Right now, we don't know who has it, Roberta. But the thugs we're after think it's you. And so do the cops."

Fear seized her body like a muscle cramp. She was being hunted down by the people who killed William. Or, perhaps, the people who killed William already had the urn, and the people hunting her were another group of creeps entirely. If what Tim said was true, the cops didn't believe her tale about the assailant in her room taking the urn either. Her head swam. "Tim, I'm frightened. I don't know how to deal with this."

He looked at her, shadows slipping across his face in the moonlight. "I do. I'm taking you someplace safe."

She pressed her hands against her breast to calm her pounding heart. Then she realized she had not only left her purse behind, but also was still wearing her diner apron. Roberta peeled it off and threw it into the back seat as though she were shedding her ordinary life.

# CHAPTER 12

They drove for hours, up into the dense black forest surrounding the coastal cities of Alaska, on roads leading nowhere except abandoned mines or defunct logging camps. Roberta was excited for the first couple of hours, but finally succumbed to sleep, awakening achy and disoriented. She stared into the black night, one darker than she'd ever seen. Although stars punched through the heavens, only the headlights offered illumination, scrambling through the brush along the side of the road like a living thing.

Roberta nodded off again, jerking awake when they left the smooth paved road to bounce along a rutted track. She opened her scratchy eyes to a lavender sky. After what seemed like ages, they pulled in and stopped at a small hunting lodge along the dirt road. As she stepped out of the car, the chill in the air made her shiver.

The place was sadly decrepit, sagging and weather-beaten, as if a good huff and puff would blow the shack down. Tim used his shoulder to force open the door, which had swollen shut. Inside, the air was musty and dank. Dust and the stale odor of disuse told her this place had been empty for a long time.

Tim ushered her inside with a grin. "Step into my parlor."

*Said the spider to the fly*. The verse popped into her head unbidden and made her skin crawl.

"Where are we?"

"A spot where you won't be found."

She didn't like the sound of that either.

"It's very remote, way up here," he said.

Roberta accepted that it would be difficult to discover this place, hidden so deep in the woods. But something didn't seem right. Roberta's mind was teased by some vague, niggling doubt, like a pea under a mattress. With effort, she shoved her misgivings aside. She rested her tired eyes on Tim. "You must be exhausted, driving all night."

"Yeah, you're right about that." He heaved a big sigh and scrubbed his hands across his face. "Let me build a fire and make some coffee. Then I'll get some shut-eye. Afterwards, we'll talk."

The muscles in his back rippled as he put kindling and small logs into the blackened fireplace and lit it with a match. He opened the flue and fanned the flames into a roaring fire in no time. After removing an old, moldy-smelling quilt from the seat, she sat in a handmade rocking chair near the window. Roberta was too weary to make conversation but looked about at the bare floors and rough-hewn furniture hugging the walls of the single large room.

Roberta followed when Tim went to the makeshift kitchen, turned on a propane-powered stove, filled a teakettle from a water pump in the rusted sink, and found a jar of instant coffee. Other provisions on the shelves looked recently acquired: crackers, tins of tuna, powdered milk.

"Sleeping quarters are upstairs," he motioned to a set of open steps along the wall. "Come on, I'll show you around."

Roberta trailed behind him to the two small rooms off a tiny balcony on the second floor. He opened the first door, where a brand-new sleeping bag still in plastic sat on a narrow cot, its mattress covered in dirty ticking. Tim nodded toward the one grimy window. "Restroom facilities are back there," he said, pointing to an outhouse a short distance from the house. "Sorry. It's a bit rustic."

"It's fine," said Roberta, thinking about a joke her grandmother used to make, that she grew up in a house with three bedrooms and a path.

"I'm next door," Tim said, jerking his thumb to the left. He then disappeared into the second room. She could hear the springs squeak as he flopped with a groan of exhaustion onto the bed.

Wondering how long they'd be here or even if they were staying for more than a few hours, she crept downstairs, poured water from the steaming kettle into a cracked mug, and added powdered coffee. It appeared the only hot water would be what was heated on the stove. A large, chipped enamel pan hung by a nail on the wall.

She felt uneasy. Why she was about to be arrested, and what Tim and the Treasury Department knew about it, she had no idea. And why he was so willing to be her knight in shining armor was a mystery as well. She'd been so caught up in intrigue and frightened that she'd thoughtlessly gone along on this adventure. But now she had so many questions, not the least of which was why they were at this particular place in the middle of nowhere. This didn't look like any safe house the government might use. Then again, maybe Alaska offered few options. She was too tired to think it through.

After poking around and discovering a stack of threadbare linens on a table near the fireplace, a wooden box full of rusty tools under the sink, and gardening implements in a corroded metal cabinet on the porch, she realized no one had been there for years other than to drop off the food and sleeping bags. Although the spade and pick ax in the cabinet looked almost new, an ancient canteen hung on a sagging hook, and the linens were smelly and spotted with mildew.

Before the sun cleared the mountains in the distance, Roberta returned to the bare room with the cot and lay down on the unfurled sleeping bag, which smelled like chemical sizing. She did not nap but mulled over the events of the past weeks and wondered at her current circumstances. And about Tim. She felt like Sleeping Beauty, who had dozed and awakened with the man of her dreams. She'd have to be careful. Fantasies were deceptive. Fairy tales stripped away the illusions about the permanence of life and revealed the truth: you died a short-term death and awoke transformed. And like any change, transformations were painful.

Not for the world could she figure out how she'd arrived here. Was it fate? She imagined she'd been careless or had made a series of bad decisions, if not in this life, then in one that had preceded it. Roberta knew she wasn't perfect, but she believed her faults were minor ones. She stared at them often, turning them over in her head, and had begun to think of them as mild, harmless, rather charming little things, not like the glaring defects in other people's character. She watched dust moats dance in a shaft of light knifing through the gloom.

When hours later she heard Tim go downstairs, she ran her fingers through her hair and followed him.

"Hey," she said. "Feeling better?"

Tim's presence, along with his muscled arms, broad shoulders, and engaging smile, was reassuring. "Much." He looked at her with concern. "We didn't expect this, Roberta. Things are happening more quickly than we thought."

"What do you mean? I don't understand."

"It's best that you don't."

"But why?" she asked. This sounded a bit too much like 'don't worry your pretty little head about it,' and she bristled. "And how did you know I was going to be arrested?"

"We have someone on the inside," Tim said, then frowned with distaste. "I shouldn't have told you. How you interact with the police, what you say, should be natural. You shouldn't be second-guessing or wondering who you're dealing with. The more you know, the less chance we have of a successful outcome."

This seemed more reasonable to her. "You expect the police to catch up with us? Here?"

"No, of course not. This place is hours from Juneau. It's not on any map and no one has lived here for years. But it's not the police we're worried about. We're hiding you from terrorists who will stop at nothing. Right now, they don't know where you are. They'll continue to look and make stupid mistakes. Just one misstep will make them vulnerable and then we've got them." He stared off into the distance, a look of hardened determination on his face.

"Terrorists?" Roberta swallowed a lump rising in her throat. Jail suddenly didn't look like such a bad idea. "How long do we stay?" Roberta was beginning to regret fleeing. She glanced at the enamel pan that looked disturbingly like a substitute bathtub and the tins and boxes on the shelves. Canned ravioli, for God's sake. A cell might be a bit better than this, after all. It seemed to Roberta her freedom came at the price of indoor plumbing and edible food.

"You need to hunker down here, out of sight for a few days. Not long. Depends upon what happens in Juneau."

"And this is all about my mother's urn?"

"Of course not, Roberta. It's about what was placed in the urn at the Seattle airport, priceless gems that are part of a huge money laundering scheme funding the destruction of our country."

"Are you serious?"

"It's not only this one incident, not just those stones and this particular smuggling operation. It's been happening for a long time. This kind of activity funded September 11, the Boston Marathon, Benghazi, and a dozen other terrorist attacks across the globe. We've been tracking the thugs behind it for years, and now we're so close."

"That's why you're chasing down Carrie?" It was hard for her to believe that Carrie was an international terrorist.

"Carrie, William, and people like them are small cogs in a big machine. They're not that important, but those behind them calling the shots are."

"Why did they use my mother's urn? They were already through security. Why didn't they carry the stuff themselves?"

"Too dangerous. They knew both sides were looking for them, I guess. The Feds were on to them, that's certain. Obviously, the bad guys caught up with William first."

"Who's responsible for his murder?" Roberta asked, doubtful that she wanted to know.

"We're not sure. He might have been a double agent, although we have no evidence. He was probably killed because he was a threat. Or it was a message. We're still trying to figure that one out. We don't want anyone else to be hurt," he said, leaning close to her. "We'll give our lives to keep you safe."

Roberta's dry mouth watered. The sacrifices she would have to make paled in comparison to the efforts Tim and his associates made every day. She took his hand in hers. "Tim, I'm with you all the way.

Anything you need, anything I can do. If we have to sit tight here for a while, I understand."

For a moment, their eyes locked. Roberta's face heated and a blush crawled up her neck. Her heart gave an unsettling lurch as Tim moved his hand to her shoulder. Roberta's hold on her emotions was tenuous, like a raindrop on a twig. Almost as if in a trance, she leaned forward and parted her lips. The moment she felt the prickle of his mustache, his mouth on hers, she hesitated. She was unsure how far she was willing to go. She immediately regretted her discount store granny panties and white cotton bra. And there was Brad.

Tim's brief caress led to a quivering embrace. "We mustn't lose ourselves, Roberta." He sighed and held her close. "We have to keep our focus. It's enough to know you're on our side."

Warmth spread through her with a tingling sensation. "I am, Tim. You know I am." She was reminded of Snow White, awakened by a kiss.

They drew apart and Tim looked flustered. "I hate this part, Roberta, but I have to leave you here."

"Alone? Why?"

"I'm heading the operation in Juneau. They need me there."

"For how long?" Her eyes were drawn once again to the canned goods in the cupboard.

"I'm not sure. Three days at most." The muscles in his arms flexed as he grasped her arms and sat her in the rocking chair. "You'll be safe here. You have everything you need, and I'll be back before you know it. Stay inside and don't worry about anything."

He picked up a Coleman lantern from the mantle and showed her how to fill the reservoir from the can of kerosene next to the fireplace.

"I'll be back with more provisions and, hopefully, good news," he said. "All you have to do is hang tough." He smiled. "I know we can depend upon you, Roberta. You are the key to everything."

A frown lined her face as she stood and looked about the cabin.

"It's okay. You'll be fine hidden away in this place. Don't go roaming around, and nothing can harm you."

She mustered a wan smile.

"Good," he draped an arm around her shoulders and patted her. "I'll wrap that smile up and take it with me. And when I return, I promise you the best plate of spaghetti ever."

After another longing look that snapped with sexual tension, he swung through the screen door, ducked into his car, and sped away.

Roberta was at once overwhelmed. Forget Sleeping Beauty or Snow White. She was Rapunzel, the princess abandoned in a tower, trapped alone in a wilderness with no way out. She felt light-headed and suppressed a spreading anxiety. Maybe she was hungry. The last time she'd eaten was an omelet at the diner mid-shift yesterday. Now it was early evening, a day later. She looked around for a clock, but of course there wasn't one. No books, radio, or TV either. No electricity for that matter. What was she to do with herself here all alone?

The first requirement was to eat something. She opened a package of saltines and used a rusty can opener to rip the lid halfway off a tin of tuna. She ate the entire can, without even draining the oil, and almost the whole box of crackers. Then she folded the rest away, accepting that she'd have to pace herself.

Evaluating the foodstuffs, she decided they would last for three days or more. Besides the tinned ravioli and tuna, she discovered chickpeas, beans, and several kinds of soup. At least she wouldn't be tempted to overeat out of boredom.

Roberta stepped onto the porch to survey the surrounding terrain. She was enveloped by tall trees that blocked her view except to the west, where a glorious sunset lit the sky like a forest fire. Deciding to explore while it was still light, she took several long strides to the dirt road where the car had stood an hour earlier. It appeared to be an old logging route, a ten-foot-wide swath of hard-packed yellow earth, deeply rutted and dusty. She looked right, then left. In both directions the road disappeared into the trees.

Roberta walked along the abandoned track in the direction they'd come from. She looked for the highway and its location relative to the spot where she stood. It might be minutes away by car, or hours. She regretted having fallen asleep on the way here because now she had no clue how far they'd come or from which direction. Even if all there was to see were trees and rocks, she wouldn't feel so disoriented had she been paying attention, picking out landmarks like a geographic trail of bread crumbs.

She blanched at the thought of how isolated she was. Her eyes searched the growing gloom as she listened to the night insects and the light breeze in the treetops. When she left the road to enter the forest, she was embraced by huge, bough-draped firs, the ground spongy with pine needles.

A twig snapped. Fear surged through her like a wave, seizing her lungs. She stood for a moment, rooted to the ground. Bears, big cats, or wolves might be hidden in the shadows. Or even other night creatures, those that hunted warm flesh.

A tremor of terror shook her and she sped to the cabin, hoping she didn't look like prey. Hurtling through the screened door, she shoved the solid one shut and leaned her weight against it. Only then did she realize why Tim hadn't used a key: it had no lock. Accustomed to city living,

Roberta couldn't imagine that a building could not be secured. Well, locks would secure what? With nothing to steal and, miles from anywhere, no one to menace her, she had no need to worry. She relaxed. Her nerves were getting the best of her. Nerves and exhaustion. Her limited and uneasy sleep last night was the problem. She had nothing to fear in this forgotten, desolate place. As long as Tim came back for her when he said he would, she'd manage just fine. In spite of her efforts at reassurance, she tasted something like dread in the back of her mouth.

Readying herself for bed consisted of a spit bath in the large enamel pan and cleaning her teeth with baking soda and a washcloth. She resolved to boil the musty linens in the pan on the stove in the morning. The privy, filled with spiders and mouse droppings, was much more intimidating in the dark, the Coleman lantern throwing creepy shadows. On the way back inside, Roberta felt the cool dampness settling around the cabin. Upstairs, she spread her sleeping bag over the dirty mattress again, then retrieved Tim's from the other room and unzipped it to use like a blanket. The flannel lining smelled like him, carrying his masculine odor, reminding her of cedar chests or sandalwood incense.

She crawled into bed in her underwear. As she tried to get comfortable, she wondered at the poor accommodations. The Federal government, known for extravagant, wasteful spending, wasn't squandering anything on her. An out-of-the-way motel would have been better. But maybe the bad guys would have looked for her in someplace like that. She let it go, deciding to trust Tim. He must know what he was doing. She nestled with the memory of his kiss until her face flushed with embarrassment, thinking of home.

It was surprisingly easy to discard Brad. Roberta felt like a shape-shifter, an altogether different animal than the woman he'd married twenty-two years ago. Brad was still the same person he was then. Only she had transformed. People are born to change, so she didn't know why he hadn't. She wanted suddenly to embrace the transience of life, something she'd fought against until now, mistrusting the unknown. Now she was ready to plunge into the mysterious future.

## CHAPTER 13

The night was short, and Roberta awoke to weak light filtering through the dirty window, silence enveloping her like an exhaled breath. She had struggled to sleep, her head burdened with worry over what she'd left behind in Indianapolis. She justified herself with reminders of the mind-numbing requirements of living—harvesting soiled laundry, retrieving dirty dishes she'd stacked, gleaming, in the cupboard only a day before, and cooking endlessly, preparing the same old dishes until she had no appetite. Dusty window blinds and cobwebs demanded more emotional investment than her children.

She wondered what Laura and Brad Jr. were doing now. If they missed her at all, it would be because the pot roast didn't materialize on the table or their clean clothes appear like magic in the wardrobe. Roberta imagined if she were home, she'd be crabbing about nail polish spilled on the furniture or trying to hear herself think over Brad Jr.'s ear-shattering music. Somehow, she had managed to raise both her children to be supremely self-absorbed. She declined to think about it any longer and rolled out of bed.

She stretched and faced the daunting task of entertaining herself in this lonely, barren spot. Pulling on her shirt and jeans against the dawn chill, she shuffled downstairs in untied Keds.

Boiling water for coffee and munching a few soda crackers, she put the large pan filled with water on the stove. She seasoned it with soda and a sliver from the one bar of soap, sliced off with the sole sharp implement she found, a pocketknife with a two-inch blade. Roberta simmered the towels and wash cloths for what she believed was an appropriate amount of time, rinsed them in the sink, and draped them on the porch railing. She then bathed in the warm soapy water. Feeling like a pioneer, she was buoyed by her ingenuity and independence. Now dwelling off the grid, she was quite resourceful. So far.

Before the sun rose above the trees, Roberta struck out on the dirt road, this time going up the slight incline. She climbed the gentle rise to see the tops of trees below her, clear-cut spots in the distance, but no sign of human habitation. No trailing smoke from factories or light glinting off metal met her eyes, nor did traffic sounds or voices reach her ears. Beyond the valley below, a shimmering stream unfurled like a ribbon in the sunshine.

The space was vast and empty, and her heart sank. Although Roberta had no idea where she was, her foreboding was tempered by the realization that she could always follow the dirt road to the highway and the highway would lead somewhere. Then she gritted her teeth, wondering after how many miles, how many days. She turned full circle to take in her surroundings. What if something should happen to Tim? She hoped someone else knew she was here. She had no illusions about how long she could live off the land if no one came back.

This is absurd, she thought. She was, after all, involved in some preposterous way in an important crime-fighting program. If nothing else, Chief Craven and the Juneau police, who still sought her in connection with William's murder, would look for her. She would not be forgotten. No good reason existed for all the drama, or for speculating about the worst possibilities or direst circumstances. But Tim might at least have left a phone so she could reach him. This whole thing didn't seem to be very well thought out.

Roberta ventured off the road into the cool shadow of ancient trees. The canopy overhead smothered any vegetation that might have struggled up around the cedar, spruce, and pine. Across the road she saw aspen and birch. Birds twittered above, but she would have to wait for nighttime for the healthy chatter of insects. She heard the wind but could not see evidence of it. The air was still where she stood on the stony ground.

Wandering a good distance from the cabin, she was careful to keep the dirt road in sight. It would be disastrous if she got lost. And with the clothes on her back her only armor (offering not even protective coloration), she would be unable to defend herself against the smallest assailant, such as a raccoon or a fox. Did foxes attack people? She thought not but considered carrying the pocketknife, or maybe the pick ax, the next time she walked this far. Tim had not told her what to expect out there, but maybe he didn't know either.

She sat on an outcropping of rock in a small clearing deeper in the woods and leaned against a mountain hemlock in the dappled light, her skin warmed by the sun. Perhaps she was destined to take refuge against its reddish-brown bark as she had in Evergreen Cemetery. She shrugged off memories of the shooting that night.

Roberta closed her eyes. A profound stillness unspooled around her. Something about the scent on the breeze caused a flood of sensation. After things we can see and touch are worn and discarded, smell alone lingers, enduring, faithful, poised like a ghost. She was transported to the past by the fragrant air—that warm, clean, sun-on-the-grass perfume. She saw him again in her mind's eye, Professor Anders Becker, her first sexual conquest. Well, not hers, really. She came to understand afterwards her name was one on a long list of vanquished undergraduates.

"Note my office hours, Miss Princezna."

Roberta went at his suggestion, but she felt completely powered by her own initiative.

"The finer points of 'The Love Song of J. Alfred Prufrock' are worth exploring." He appeared to address the entire class, but she knew the message was for her, particularly. She was an innocent at the time, a fresh and uninitiated coed with all the pleasures of the world lying ahead for her to embrace.

That spring, the campus was awash in shades of green and gold when Roberta wound her way across the quad to the oldest structure at the university. She climbed the stairs and turned right at the top to approach a set of double doors marking the transition from Sealy Hall to the connecting building that housed the Department of English and its faculty. Below the sign that read You are now entering Drake Hall someone had scribbled Abandon hope, all ye who enter here. She'd smiled at the anomaly of the literate graffiti artist. And she had taken care to wear her shortest skirt and to show up at the end of the day.

"Please, come in." Professor Becker's cultured, heavily accented voice floated through the door in response to her bold knock.

She angled into his cramped office, every wall filled to the rafters with a clutter of books. The one large window was shrouded in ivy, giving an odd under-sea quality to the light bathing the room. She felt transported, as if entering another realm, one where the pattern in the carpet danced, and the sun's alchemy turned everything it touched into something precious. There, in the presence of a besotted older man, so worldly and so wise, she was not a girl but a woman—powerful, beautiful, and adventurous.

That bubble burst soon enough. Reality arrived weeks later in the form of his middle-aged wife. Roberta fled the dumpy office, barefooted, shoes in hand, and with her bra stuffed into her pocket, pursued by a shrieking bundle of brightly colored scarves and graying hair.

"Whore! Little whore!"

Somewhere between that unfortunate indiscretion and her junior year, everything changed. Brad arrived, if not exactly on a white steed, at least in a getaway car. She traded the classroom for a tiny two-bedroom bungalow and began to keep house rather than make time. Taking pleasure in experimenting with a stew pot and tidying a yard, she left the daddy issues behind for motherhood.

Roberta settled deeper into the recesses of her past. She remembered that tiny house, her first home, and the feeling of purpose she had in managing it, the control she'd exercised over the kitchen garden and the manicured lawn. It was fun then, the noon heat on her skin and the wind in her hair. Under cerulean skies, she'd yanked at weeds rioting along the fencerows and skeins of vegetation tangling up the posts. She ripped English ivy from tree trunks and garage walls. She pulled at masses of Virginia creeper, the vine letting go of the soil in small bursts of dirt like silent machine-gun fire. Stabbing at the moist earth with a trowel, she turned up turgid worms above an ancient layer of paving stone from someone else's lifetime. Surrounded by the smell of the earth and fresh air, she left the emerging shoots of spring bulbs and volunteer larkspur undisturbed. Wild morning glories bloomed in the bright sun—today's blossoms damp with dew, yesterday's puckered like a kiss.

She was happy there, in that small house, until it was filled with playpens and cribs and smelled of dirty diapers. But she was disciplined, thanks to her mother, and knuckled under, hoping for the drudgery to pass. It really didn't get better when they traded up for more space and better schools. There was simply more of the menial work she hated most. Still, she believed that joy was attainable, and expected it at any moment, the way the poor expect prosperity or the lonely expect love.

Roberta pushed off against the tree and meandered toward the road, surveying the broad vistas before her. Why did humans feel the need to tame the land with mowers and weed whackers? Why spend time with scouring pads and dish soap (which, actually, she was kind of missing right now) when you could luxuriate in natural splendor? She could imagine herself living there in serene quiet, far from Burger Kings, Krispy Kremes, and Dollar Stores selling magnets saying ***Thou shalt not weigh more than thy refrigerator***. Brad should see her now, she thought sourly. Roberta shifted her loose jeans upon her leaner hips. Ducking through heavy boughs, she questioned the direction she and Brad had taken. Marriage was an assembly-required affair, and Brad seemed to have handed her all his tools.

Sauntering back to the cabin, she pulled up some long, dried grass that grew along the dirt track. She wrapped a bunch around her hand, marveling at its supple strength and variegated colors, blending from green to a purplish brown. She didn't know what they called it in Alaska, but it looked much like the switchgrass that grew in profusion near the roadside in Indiana. The tall weeds reminded her of home, with the rusting fence sagging across the backyard, the gate hanging by one hinge like a loose tooth.

Roberta sat on the porch and separated strands of grass by hue.

What would Brad be doing now?

Fixing chili for the kids, probably. Or macaroni and cheese, since those were his only culinary accomplishments. More than likely all of them, including her adolescence-delayed son-in-law, were polluting their bodies with Big Macs.

She retrieved the pocketknife to trim the ends of the grass, making their lengths uniform. Maybe Brad would suggest that Laura or Bradley take responsibility for meals since neither of them worked full-time. She selected several strands and wove them together, recalling a project from childhood at Vacation Bible School.

Roberta set aside resentments about her family while braiding the supple grasses into a figure eight, connecting the loose ends with knots. The design reminded her of a Victorian mourning pin her grandmother sometimes wore. Under a protective center crystal and decorated with black onyx, several colors of human hair had been tortured into an intricate floral design.

*Whatever became of it?*

Roberta had seen those kinds of pieces many times since, of course, in antique or jewelry stores selling estate items. During the Civil War such macabre craftwork was popular as either a talisman for the living or a memorial for the dead. Although it struck her as rather ghoulish, she knew they were made with loving hands: a grieving widow, a mother weaving the strands of hair retrieved from her lost children, or perhaps a hopeful fiancée awaiting the return of her lover. What kind of patience and skill did it require to make something so intricate and detailed? Some great depth of devotion must have driven such dedication.

The repetitive work calmed her, but she wondered what to do with this piece of woven art. Thinking of hair, Roberta searched the roadside for a small twig. She used the knife to cut a six-inch length and strip off the bark. Whittling one end to a dull point, she used the stick to fasten the braided grass piece in her curls, which she'd knotted atop her head. She reveled in a small thrill of pleasure. In an hour's time she had made an attractive and useful object, a barrette to pin her hair. Similar ornaments were available in gift stores and Roberta imagined using it to catch Laura's tresses in a classy up-do.

Roberta had had so much to offer, so many talents. She was good with her hands, artistic and clever. No one at home seemed to remember. Majoring in clothing design when she was in college, she knew she was good. Laura was always dressed more artfully than other children thanks to her mother's eye for color and skill with a needle. She appliquéd flowers or sewed ruffles or beads on all those simple denim dresses the young girls wore. And that prom dress fashioned from an old satin bedspread made Laura stand out like a Paris model. If Roberta hadn't dropped out of school, she could have had a career of her own in a creative field. At such a distance, and having had no test of her abilities, she could speculate about what heights she might have achieved.

Tears gathered in Roberta's eyes. Things hadn't turned out as she'd planned. She'd married too young, on the rebound from an unfortunate love affair. At twenty-one, she didn't know anything about life. Only what she'd gleaned from House Beautiful and Ladies' Home Journal. Home-making seemed to be about decorating each room in coordinating colors and fresh flowers. And sex. All those happy activities faded into the background when the children came along.

And neither Laura nor Bradley was sentimental about her gifts, whether material or spiritual, that spoke of the love she felt for them. She searched her memory for the special times they'd shared.

*I was an attentive parent. I loved them as much as any mother could.*

She'd been a faithful archivist. She'd kept locks of hair, baby teeth, scribbled pre-school papers, and handprints in plaster. Roberta harbored worn toddler's slippers, although she couldn't remember to which child they'd belonged, albums stuffed with photographs, videotape of every holiday, and artwork made of crepe paper and pipe cleaners cluttered the basement. The sporting events, theatre programs, and science projects were all carefully chronicled. Even their childhood illnesses were dutifully recorded in their immunization records. The preservation of their history was dismissed without due appreciation. Whenever Roberta brought out the camera, Laura greeted her with a groaning, "God, Mom," and Bradley Jr. paid no attention, always glued to the television or listening to heavy metal, the musical equivalent of a leaf blower.

Even her husband didn't seem to realize all she did for them. She'd asked her pastor about feeling excluded, even discarded, and he told her, "God moves in mysterious ways, Roberta." She thought that was a stupid thing to say, a trope suggesting people needed to believe in a purpose behind their sacrifices and meaning underlying their suffering. She wasn't so certain, having begun to think her religion was a scam, something to keep her in line.

Somewhere it had all gone wrong. She'd lost faith in everything. She wasn't even sure she was really where she was meant to be. Roberta imagined that Brad had never crossed her life's trajectory, that she'd met some other young man and connected with him through chemistry, admiration, desire, or need. She contemplated having been present in someone else's right place and at someone else's right time.

Roberta leaned against a porch post and closed her eyes, recalling the day she and Brad first met. Their paths intersected during a fall mixer at one of the fraternities, where girls hoped to get pinned and the boys hoped to get laid. Brad, shy and awkward, asked her to dance. She was the distant one, cold and uninterested, having already been burnt. He was wearing a pale blue sweater with a little 'M' sticker still stuck to the front and a bad haircut. But he was persistent, calling upon her almost daily, dropping by with Gibran's The Prophet or Morrison's Beloved. Brad intended to be provocative with those books but, science major that he was, remained unfamiliar with their contents.

It wasn't always tedious. She'd married him, after all. And she had no difficulty tapping into the bittersweet memory of their beginning. Their college service organization—the one Brad had joined because she belonged—had planned a trip to a state park, a retreat intended as a trust-building exercise. She knew in advance what would happen. Catching her unmistakable signals, Brad knocked tentatively, then opened the door to her cabin on that last day. She stood in the darkness wearing silk the color of candlelight.

They embraced without speaking, shared kisses as deep as coitus. Roberta pulled him toward the bed and they lay across it under the open window. The cool air, swollen with damp, and the endless dark of the forest poured in with the chirp of crickets. Powdery moths flickered against the rusted screen. Wafting on the night breeze was also the unmistakable odor of skunk.

"Is that skunk?" he said, his insistent mouth on hers.

"Indeed. Skunk," she responded between staccato kisses in the dark. "You're mighty smart for a city boy." They both laughed as he fumbled with her bra straps.

When his body sank into hers, she kept a hold on her emotions, refusing to be carried away by any sense of magic. Still, they slid their hands over one another, exploring every crease and hollow, each touch having both tenderness and urgency. The pleasures they experienced were so intense as to be almost unbearable. Hours later, they drew apart, sated. Brad lay on his back, his eyes closed. She rolled over, turning away from him.

"Well," she said after a lengthy silence, pulling the tangled sheet across her breasts.

"Well?" He caressed the hair curling on the nape of her neck.

Roberta wondered what she really wanted.

After a while, he said, "You're very quiet. What're you thinking?"

Turning to lay on her back, she looked thoughtfully at the beams overhead. "It's important that I tell you something."

"Yes?" He raised himself on one elbow.

"Promise you won't forget?"

"I promise." He seemed to hold his breath.

She tore her gaze from his before speaking. "I just want you to know," she hesitated only a second, "whenever I smell skunk, I'll think of you."

He laughed in that way she would become accustomed to and, digging his fingers into her ribs, they wrestled playfully.

That summer, they took endless walks in the moonlight. A budding astronomer, Brad loved the moon in all its phases, and he'd taught her its science and mythology.

"The line dividing the lit part of moon's surface from the dark side is called the terminator." She'd just watched one of the old Schwarzenegger movies and felt enlightened.

"To the Greeks, it represented the goddess Artemis, the huntress, protector of wild things," he said, laughing, "including virgins."

She thought him so provocative then. He seemed to know everything as they stood in the spidery shadow of a redbud tree.

"Harvest Moon, keep a shinin', Harvest moon I'm a pinin', for the one I love," they sang that first autumn they were together. She couldn't carry a tune and he'd teased her about it.

She seemed to have thoughtlessly, and quite unintentionally, made him a central part of her life until there was nothing left to do but marry; it appeared they fell effortlessly into a life together. Either she was afraid it was her last chance at marriage and children, or she finally discovered his finer points. It was hard to remember after all this time. She couldn't remember now why she fell in love, or even if she really had. It might have been only sex, getting even, or, she had to admit, boredom.

And now it had all passed her by. As if by the sweep of a magic wand, time fled like sands through an hourglass. Roberta suddenly regretted how often she'd parked her children in front of the TV while she cleaned house, prepared meals, or volunteered at the school or library. She realized she'd squandered all her time and talent on things that didn't matter and people who didn't care. Her dull Midwestern life stood in sharp contrast to the vast Alaskan sky. She made a conscious effort to keep the Toaster Strudel jingle from running through her head in an infinite loop.

Returning to the even more troublesome present, Roberta watched fog gather among the trees. She picked up a small stone and launched it into the weeds nearest the cabin. When it landed, something hidden in the bushes jumped and bolted through the underbrush. Fear shot through Roberta's body, and she held her breath.

# CHAPTER 14

Feeling vulnerable, exposed, and defenseless all at once, Roberta remained motionless rather than dare to run inside. Terrified, she scrutinized the spot where she'd detected movement and sat as still as the blood thrumming in her veins permitted. Her eyes riveted on the shadows, Roberta blanched. Seconds passed. She heard a footfall. A tall milkweed trembled. Roberta watched the wall of leaves part as a slender leg emerged, followed, slowly, by a small black-tailed deer. Her large ears twitched and her dark, moist eyes held Roberta's as they stared, immobile, at one another.

Roberta didn't know how long she sat mesmerized by the tiny creature. She felt a kind of kinship along with a sense of wonder. The little doe stood at the edge of the woods, her flanks quivering, ready to take flight. Roberta shivered as if to shake off her needless distress. Then the deer flinched and hurtled into the weeds. Roberta watched as she bounded off, strained her ears for the last sound of swishing grass, and caught a flip of the doe's tail before she disappeared.

Dispelling the tightness deep inside with a healthy breath, Roberta jumped up and entered the cabin. She dismissed the sudden swell of anger she felt toward Tim, not wanting to blame him for something he couldn't control. He was doing the best he could, keeping her safe, resolving the dangerous activities swirling around her.

She wondered what was going on in Juneau, imagining Tim in peril. The bad guys might still be searching for her, and possibly, they had identified him as her champion. They might be on their way to the cabin regardless of its remote location. Maybe they'd found out, through some secret communication intercepted or, she felt a twinge of anguish, they'd tortured Tim or one of his associates to reveal what they knew. The criminals might be creeping through the forest even now, scouring the woods for her hiding place.

Not knowing was the worst. Roberta plastered herself against the lockless door and peeked out the window. Goose bumps danced up her arms. It wasn't just fear. The cabin was freezing. She wondered if she dared start a fire. Light spilling through the forest or the smell of smoke could beckon the enemy. She searched the trees and leafy vegetation surrounding the cabin in the dim twilight. Shadows danced in the faint breeze. The tiny black-tailed deer was out there somewhere. Perhaps she was also frantic and lonely, concerned about the means of survival.

Deer traveled in herds. They weren't solitary creatures. Why this little one was alone in the wilderness was a mystery. She must have a mate nearby, or maybe even a fawn or two hidden in the brush. Roberta had learned one thing, at least, from her stay in the shack. She, too, was a herd animal. Or, she guessed, tribal would be the better word. She pined for human contact.

She also pined for a sweater. Not wanting to drag around the musty quilt or her voluminous sleeping bag, she rummaged for the largest towel and draped it over her shoulders.

Swear to God, how men could be so clueless was beyond her, she thought, huddling near the lantern to keep warm. Perhaps she should be grateful she wasn't stuck in a tent or burrowed in the undergrowth like the poor little deer.

The poor little creature must be lost. She was probably desperate to find where she belonged. Maybe she'd wandered off, as Roberta herself had done, in search of adventure or just to see what was beyond the horizon. Roberta shook her head. She was being fanciful. Animals operated on instinct. Humans made choices and changed their minds. And lost their minds.

Roberta certainly felt she'd lost hers. If not, she wouldn't be stuck out here in the Alaskan wilderness. Leaving home was only one of many unfortunate choices she'd made. Was her husband another one? She began to wonder why she'd chosen Brad.

Looking back, she realized Brad had come as a package deal. It wasn't just that he had captured her imagination so long ago, but his entire family—his "tribe," if she wanted to think of it that way—had enchanted her. They reveled in the kind of happy life she'd never even dreamed of. An only child growing up in hushed quiet, Roberta recalled somber holidays, her mother wearing the same clothes she had the day before and her father often absent. Visits with Grandfather or extended relatives required silence and obedience. Brad's large, rambunctious family provided a stark counterpoint to her dreary, small clan, which appeared withdrawn and secretive by comparison.

Roberta came to recognize in Frank, her father-in-law, whose family came from Mississippi, the vestiges of the Southern gentleman, that breed of male who replaced financially remunerative labor with intellectual interests such as mathematics, literature, and art.

Brad's mom, Evie, was industrious and energetic. Roberta often gravitated to her kitchen while dinner was being prepared, feeling privileged to be helpful to her. She wanted to be part of that productive busyness, wanted the feeling of inclusiveness and belonging.

At mealtimes, the Blankenships passed bowls of food around the Formica-topped table set with mismatched dinnerware and paper towels while embarking upon word play, spelling contests, or trivia games. No one kept score. Brad and his brothers seemed to have mastered the state capitals, the U.S. presidents in order of appearance, and, oddly, the distances in miles between major cities. The girls' strengths were in math and language. There were discussions of political events or artistic movements, and Frank good-naturedly corrected everyone's English, which was just as good-naturedly received.

The silence during dinner at Roberta's home was broken only by the loud ticking of a clock. The first time Brad cheerfully ensconced himself in Roberta's parents' kitchen, her mother regarded him with the same disquiet had she encountered an elephant in her bathtub.

The Blankenships seemed to have an innate talent for happiness. This was evident in so many ways. Frank would play the piano and everyone broke into song, warbling with gusto, nonsense words filling in for forgotten lyrics. For the first time in her life, Roberta belted out show tunes and rock songs. Sometimes they sang hymns, or even a mysterious ditty of their own composition, a melody and words that hearkened back to some shared experience or private understanding.

They were also full of family lore revealing a charming unconventionality. Haunting stories of the Great Depression, the war years, and life on a dairy farm accented the holidays. The family included hobos and teachers, carneys and Bible salesmen. Frank's Uncle Mike was a famous vaudeville comic and Roberta smiled, recalling the naïve question she'd asked: "Where exactly was vaudeville?"

In response, Frank had beamed his beatific grin, the same one she used to get from Brad, and said, "You are the best thing since sliced bread."

An endless cast of colorful characters populated the Blankenships' lives, and upon hearing about them, Roberta understood how little she knew of her own family and their past. There were no sepia-toned photographs or picturesque stories connecting her to a larger sense of herself.

Roberta suddenly felt lonely, missing Brad's family. Everyone was so confident and comfortable in their own skin. She recalled so much unspoken affection and affirmation, the mark of happy people accepted by their own kind. That was, of course, where Brad got his accepting nature, his ease with everyone. She had forgotten, after so many years, what she'd admired in him.

She was wistful as she unpacked her memories. Brad's childhood home now seemed like a dream. The dark Alaskan forest provided a blank canvas where images flickered like candle flame.

Roberta thought about opening a can of soup but settled into the rocking chair next to the window instead. The quarter moon hung in the evening fog like a lantern lighting her way to the past. It shimmered before her. Brad's family was so—unexpected. She was drawn to the excitement of the unexpected. Maybe that's why she was out here in the middle of nowhere with nothing but the clothes on her back. Brad didn't seem as interesting without them. It was as if Roberta had fallen for the whole family rather than for Brad himself. He never read poetry aloud or initiated impromptu musical performances.

Somehow, they hadn't created the colorful lives that his parents and grandparents had fashioned for themselves. Was it her fault? She imagined she'd brought the dreariness with her when they married. Or was Brad too conventional, too self-centered, or just plain lackluster to compete with eccentric kin? Her head swam with uncertainty. She found she didn't care to figure it out. It was, perhaps, time to walk away from what used to be.

For heaven's sake, she thought, frustrated, she didn't want to be thinking so much of home, having finally escaped its confines. Going over all of that was useless. Safely tucking her past in the back of her mind, Roberta contemplated another life: a future with Tim. She imagined being part of his world, being the woman he came home to after successfully eliminating international criminals and terrorists. He wouldn't be around often, just a few days here and there between assignments. Because they never had enough time together, the relationship would remain fresh with anticipation and excitement, characterized by the way lovers talk only about themselves. He would for the most part be present at the holidays, and she fantasized about him joyfully cooking for her all the typical seasonal meals, and about eating the usual foods prepared in unfamiliar ways.

She ignored the more likely scenario, refusing to dwell on the mundane routines of marriage, the toothpaste on the bathroom mirror, snoring in front of the TV, and the smell of his feet. Someday, whatever charming defects he possessed would be a source of irritation. The practical part of her knew she would put up with untidy truths while in love, the same truths she would complain about once the bloom had faded.

As darkness fell, the chill in the air encouraged her to try laying a fire despite her earlier misgivings. She filled the fireplace with wood from the stack at the side of the house, suppressing a shudder as the spiders she disturbed scurried into shadowy recesses. Roberta struck several matches, many of them too damp to catch. She was surprised the flaming warmth she planned was so elusive, her efforts resulting in nothing but smolder and smoke. How Tim managed it was lost on her.

Kindling was no doubt the missing ingredient. Glancing out the window, she decided not to go looking then for small dry sticks or aged bark. She pulled the towel closer around her and again huddled next to the lantern cradling a cup of hot coffee instead.

The wind kicked up. She smelled rain in the air, which blew through the ill-fitting door. Roberta rose and stood at the window as large fat drops fell, snapping against the glass like teeth. Deep shadows filled the forest as the trees danced, tossing their heavy boughs in the squall. For a moment, she fancied they were menacing giants, moving toward her in the gloom. She blinked and swallowed, dispelling the frightening image.

Before her imagination conjured additional phantoms, Roberta washed and, despite the lingering twilight, took the steep stairs to bed.

# CHAPTER 15

The morning sky was a dull, unpolished pewter. Roberta wondered whether last night's storms would linger or be chased away by the sun. The sun prevailed. Once again, she embarked upon an endless walk in the wilderness, where now the dust was settled, dampness released the vegetation's fragrance, and spider webs sparkled with raindrops. She detected a hint of the winter to come.

She climbed high on a bluff overlooking a rolling meadow and imagined this place when the snows came, a blanket of pristine white upon the landscape, the trees bowed under the ice. Roberta fancied herself lost in these woods, never to find her way out. She would make her home in a snow drift, and just as in the story of the Snow Queen, her tears would form windows and doors. She hadn't thought of that fairy tale for years. It focused on the struggle between good and evil, where a magic mirror failed to reflect the good and beautiful and exaggerated the bad and ugly. Splinters of the broken mirror lodged in people's hearts, spoiling everything.

"Maybe I've done that," she said aloud to herself. "Let some distorted disappointment lodge in my heart, feeding my dissatisfaction."

Roberta didn't realize how important mirrors were to her until she didn't have one. She had to admit she was a vain woman. In her bedroom at home, she harbored a large antique vanity topped with what could only be called a looking glass. Reflected in it was a glittering arsenal of lotions and creams lined up like troops on a battlefield. Sitting before it, Roberta made the effort each day to defeat age, to slow advancing time. Too often of late, she'd taken a hard look at the aging face staring back at her and felt the full force of reality, admitting the many unpleasant possibilities that were likely, or even inevitable, as time passed. She would grow old. She would face illness. Brad would grow old and face illness, as well, and they would nurse a growing, silent anger between them. They had already replaced goodwill with resentment. Had they stayed together, they'd struggle to weather the inescapable disappointments and unavoidable misfortunes along with any accomplishments or happiness they would admit to.

The sudden sting of tears clouded her vision. She stepped as close to the edge of the precipice as she dared. In that moment, Roberta felt smaller, lighter, less dense—and alone.

"I don't know where I belong. I'm unsure of who is on my side," she whispered, choking back sadness. She could feel no other way after all these years of marriage to a man who devoted himself to only himself. She looked off into the distance as though answers might be written on the wind.

Soon the sun would disappear once more, taking the world outside with it. Maybe the night would be black and moonless, or it could sparkle with stars. There was no way to know in the bright light of day. The nightfall was the only thing she could count on.

She had a sudden flashback to the interview room at the police station, to her face reflected in the two-way mirror. At the time, reality seemed to shift. Someone was no doubt looking in although she could not look out. She didn't know which was real, the woman or the reflection. She felt she had no substance, that she was no more than a sum of her experiences, the sum of her desires.

Roberta felt a vague discomfort, as though she had her underwear on backwards. But it wasn't some nagging irritation keeping her on edge. She wasn't sure what was coming next. And she was so bored she believed she might die of it. She had the sudden urge to fling herself off the cliff, but the fall wouldn't be enough to kill her.

Roberta took in the vast wilderness, contemplating the foreign world before her. High above her, a silver plane glinting in the sun left a silent trail of vapor. She shut her eyes against the sharp glare and opened them to the earth beneath her feet.

Then she saw it. In front of a large rock that provided a comfortable spot for sitting, grasses and weeds were crushed as if someone had stood and waited there, and several cigarette butts had been ground into the dirt. She swung her head toward the cabin. From that spot, high on the cliff, she could see the shack, the outhouse, and the yellow, rutted road that wound past them standing out, stark and clear, against the trees. Someone had been spying on her. There appeared to be a watcher in the woods. She suppressed a shiver and tamped down the bile that rose in her throat.

She bit her bottom lip and wrinkled her brow in concentration.

"Who would be spying on me? And why?" She spoke to herself in disbelief. Not the Treasury Department. They would approach her, making their presence known. They knew where she was and she knew they knew.

It couldn't be the terrorists.

If so, they would have come for her at once if they were searching for her and wanted something important from her.

She thought about the Juneau PD, Chief Craven and company.

They would capture her as soon as possible as well. It made no sense that she was being spied upon.

Roberta knelt to pick up one of the cigarette butts. It was wet with last night's rain and fell apart in her hand. For all she knew, the butts had been there for weeks, left behind by some careless hiker. She looked for other signs of human presence like trash or a camp fire. She found nothing. She relaxed. Like a dog might slip its collar, Roberta shook off her sense of unease and decided it had nothing to do with her.

She returned to the cabin and hunkered down for the rest of the day, only vaguely unsettled. For some unaccountable reason, she was exhausted and again went to bed before the light faded to black. She lay staring at the threads crisscrossing in the fabric of her sleeping bag, trying to clear her mind of needless worry and aching boredom.

Hours later, not much past midnight it seemed, she snapped awake. The nylon sleeping bag had slid to the floor. Now alert, she wandered below to the kitchen, feeling her way in the dark.

With a cup of steaming coffee to warm her hands, she stood in the window looking out at the night sky, black velvet aglitter with stars. The pale slab of moon cast the terrain into shadow, tipped the trees and brush with silver, and threw everything in the foreground into stark relief. She stood in the deep silence, entranced by the eerie stillness, a study in dark and light.

She froze. Something had moved. Something looming in the dim recesses of the forest altered shape and darkened.

*The watcher in the woods.*

Roberta felt a prickling on the back of her neck. She willed herself to stare without blinking, certain she'd become vulnerable in that split second. Every cell in her body screamed, told her to take flight, to hide. Her mouth was dry, her breathing ragged.

In a heartbeat, her body seized with terror. Her breath caught as the gloom deepened to an unnatural black. It separated itself from the trees and gave the impression of slowly rolling toward her along the ground, of shape-shifting and vibrating in the dark. Inching forward, it appeared to expand and deflate. Then it flattened and lay upon the rocky soil, not like a shadow but like a living, pulsating thing.

With some effort, Roberta looked away. Lifting her eyes to the night sky, she saw a cloud scuttle across the moon. When she looked again toward the woods, she saw nothing but trees. She released a shaking sigh.

That's all it was, a cloud throwing a shadow on the ground.

Her mind was playing tricks on her, she decided. Her seclusion, her uncertainty, and finding evidence of someone else in the forest played upon her nerves. Her horror subsided to hollowness. She hated this, being alone and feeling threatened.

She drank another cup of coffee and wolfed down saltines as dim light appeared in the distance. The morning was flooded with soft light, the high banks of cloud masking the hot sun as it crept above the mountains. She languished inside the cabin, having nothing to look forward to except another long day of lonesome wandering, hiking through limitless trees, stumbling across the rocky terrain into the wilderness. She thought she might go out of her mind without another human being to talk to.

Instead of taking another trek in the woods, she napped. It was hotter than it had been the last few days and all her energy was drained. She moved her heavy limbs through muggy air as she dressed and ate again. She waited until the sunlight slanted against the earth before she left the cabin.

Roberta walked west this time, going farther into the forest than she'd gone the day before. Following a lazy stream toward the lowering sun, she came upon a still ponding of water. She picked her way along the boggy edge, where stones both large and small made the ground muddied by the rains easier to traverse. Approaching a large flat rock, half in and half out of the water, she took one careful step across to it and sat. It had been warmed by the afternoon sunshine. She drew her knees to her chest, draped her arms across them, and relaxed. As she settled her body, she at last quieted her mind.

At the far end of the smooth expanse of deep water, as still as the sky above, trees hid the mountains beyond. The encompassing woods harbored an uneasy silence. Two drab ducks glided and bobbed nearby. Sparrows wheeled overhead. She closed her eyes against the sunlight, the underside of her lids red, and listened for insects, for that constant, steady hum so common in the Midwest but less evident here. Nothing but the sharp call of a crow could be heard above the gentle sound of lapping water. She felt a shadow fall.

Opening her eyes, Roberta saw nothing but sunshine glistening on the water. Then there it was. A large dragonfly darted silently past her line of sight. It hovered for a moment before settling close by on a blade of grass slanting out of the muddy ground at the edge of the pond. She watched it quivering there, its body iridescent green, its finely veined wings transparent.

She lifted her eyes to the spotless sky.

*How have I gotten here, my life burdened with such inconsolable sorrow?*

It wasn't Brad. And not the kids. She plumbed her psyche. Roberta at last admitted to herself that she'd never come to terms with her mother's death. Nothing else explained her scent in the air or her voice in the trees. Buried in the wilderness, so far away from everything familiar, Roberta perceived her mother with such clarity, so distinct and unmistakable. At home, given the clutter of everyday life, she wasn't able to distinguish the spirits lurking in the corners from distant echoes. Here, in this vast space, there was no room for avoidance, no place to hide.

A vision of her mother seared her memory. Roberta was fourteen. She was home on a school day because her father had died without any warning on the first day of spring. They had opened all the windows, and warm spring breezes banished the chill of winter from the corners. Both she and her mother were seated on the floor in the dining room in front of a waning fire. A large album was open across her mother's lap, and her fingers dug at the photographs. One by one, she loosened the edges, then ripped them off, leaving parts of the back stuck to the page. Her mother pitched the pictures, one after another, into the fire. She took her time. The two of them focused upon the yellow flame licking at the edges until it turned blue, and each snapshot curled, blackened, and floated like a delicate leaf away from the flames.

"Mother?"

Martha did not respond.

Roberta watched her mother in profile, willing her to turn and look at her. "Mom?" She had so many questions, but Martha remained silent.

Roberta witnessed Martha May Princezna destroy her past, watched her stare as it disappeared like the narrow ribbons of smoke spiraling upward and away. Without a glance at several loose candid shots stuck at the back, Martha tossed the album into the flames. The fire flashed as the paper lit up in a burst of sparks. After her mother rose and went upstairs, Roberta spied a photo that had floated unblemished to the fireplace floor and settled in the ashes away from the heat. She was arrested by the image.

Reaching in to catch the edge with one finger, she pulled it out. It was an old Polaroid, faded with age. Roberta felt the weight of irrevocable distance between past and present, the fundamental pathos of the photograph. Shaking it off and angling the picture toward the light, Roberta held it as delicately as a memory. It swept her to a time she knew nothing about. Her mother, about the age Roberta was then, stood with her own mother, Roberta's Grandmother Savage, in front of the house where Martha grew up. Her grandmother looked quite ill, although she lived well into her eighties. She had the appearance of a painted skeleton, her thin skin hanging upon her bones like a shroud. The two stood apart, communicating a lack of affection. Roberta knew, even then, what was whispered about her mother.

After rescuing the photograph, Roberta kept it hidden away, the sole depiction of her mother as a girl that she possessed. She couldn't understand why Martha had done it, burned every picture. Perhaps she was ready to let go, ready to move forward—or maybe it was backward—to that authentic person she used to be before she was a wife. Before dedicating her life to making her husband's tea and organizing his paperclips. Roberta would never know whether her mother destroyed her wedding album in anger or in sadness.

Or maybe she was rejecting her childhood. How little she understood. Martha communicated nothing to Roberta about her deepest feelings. Despite all their intense emotional tangles, Roberta never knew her. Their fights were never resolved, never resulted in comprehension, acceptance, or closeness. What Roberta wanted from her, she wasn't sure, but whatever her mother failed to give made her angry. And she held onto it. The dead were always with her in a way that even the living were not. Past regrets, like pentimento, bled into the present. Roberta continued to make her arguments and take her positions and fight the same battles. Missing her mother ached like a phantom limb.

She looked deep into the pond, to the muddy bottom where weeds, still and colorless, hovered. Her vision telescoped, and her face swam up from below like an image from the bottom of a well.

A hawk launched a high-pitched call, startling her to attention. The hollowness dispelled, she felt the empty unease of loss again, the pain settling over her like a heavy blanket. In losing her mother, she'd fallen into a place where there were no tears and, therefore, no relief. A sharp pang pierced her breast. Roberta missed her mother every day that she'd been gone. And someday Roberta knew she would lose everything dear to her until she, herself, was lost.

Roberta struggled with the sudden and complete destruction of her faith in the inevitability of happy endings. All life seemed to tremble on a thread as fine as spider's silk. Any memory of her would fade like a warm breath on a cold window pane.

Roberta searched once more for the dragonfly. For the Japanese, it was a symbol for something. Transformation? Change? She couldn't remember.

Her eyes traced the bright green algae, lacy with bubbles, rimming the edge of the pond, caught in the weeds. The dragonfly was momentarily lost in the intricate, shifting patterns created by water, sunlight, and vegetation. Then she saw it. Still there. Silent. Waiting.

She stared at it for what seemed a long time. Without warning, it rose from its profound stillness, swept off soundlessly to the left, then darted to the right. Coming to within a foot of her, the dragonfly went straight out over the water and, just as swiftly as it had come, disappeared as if into another dimension.

## CHAPTER 16

Roberta flinched at a bird's piercing cry as she stared at the patch of sky visible through the grimy bedroom window. The third day. If someone had told her a week ago she'd be spending three days in the woods, Roberta would've imagined she'd been dead for two.

She had to get out of here or go crazy. For the moment, with both grief and love sublimated, her husband, her children, her suburban home, and her past were left in the cluttered background. Tim Westlake was foremost in her mind. He would be back tonight. Or maybe it would be tomorrow. Any thought of Indianapolis was overshadowed by the adventurous excitement embodied by this sterling example of the Treasury Department. She couldn't help but smile, a spark of anticipation shooting through her limbs. She admitted to no fears or scruples. She knew by now if you obey all the rules you miss all the fun.

She shifted off of the cot, her body awkward, sandwiched as it was between two polyester sleeping bags. The backs of her knees were sweaty. She'd love to have some sheets, or a cotton blanket. For the first time, she wanted to be sitting at a keyboard, one of the amenities of home, ordering something from Amazon.

Even "You've got mail," announced in that ever-present, robotic voice would be welcome.

Truth be told, she missed her computer more than anything else. It was definitely friendlier than the cat. Always responsive and attentive, the computer was sometimes her sole source of humor and kindness. It anticipated her every need, thoughtfully reminding her of recipes, weight-loss opportunities, miracle wrinkle cures, and every website she had ever visited in the form of advertisements, pulsating from the screen in pestilent reds and virulent greens.

She sat on the edge of her sagging cot and blinked. For a moment she contemplated the blossoming pink as it attenuated the dark sky. Then she popped up as if she had things to do.

After washing her face and hands with cold water as the teakettle heated on the stove, Roberta ate beans out of the can and sipped instant coffee from her cracked mug. Her limbs thrummed with energy until she bolted out the door to take a brisk walk through the trees. The cool air made her shiver. She must have walked for miles until she angled back toward the cabin, taking a shaded route through the woods and ending up at the dry gully behind the outhouse. She stooped at its edge and contemplated the thin weeds and the stony ground, wondering when the rains carved out this narrow fissure in the earth. It might have been just last month, or ages ago. Dirt trickling down the sides sounded like tiny, scurrying feet.

Plucking a broad blade of crabgrass, she stretched it taut across the hollow between her aligned thumbs, put her mouth against them and blew. It made a high, piercing squeak then buzzed like an insect or quacked like a duck. An image of her mother sitting cross-legged on the warm grass came back to her with a crystalline clarity. Her face the delicate oval of a medieval Madonna, her mother had her dark hair caught with a red scarf at the nape of her neck and her jeans rolled above her calves. A breeze ruffled her collar as she held Roberta's tiny hands, positioning them just so with the blade of grass.

"Roberta," she'd said in her musical voice, "this is a grass harmonica."

Roberta remembered squinting in the bright sunshine. "I wanna do it myself, Mommy."

They laughed when Roberta managed to bring forth a resounding, unexpected *blaahhht.* The hot sun beat down on their arms and white clouds drifted overhead as the earth spun, relentless and unceasing, on its axis.

Feeling a prick of torment, Roberta wondered if she would recover her mother's ashes. If possible, should they somehow be returned to her, Roberta would scatter the cremains here in Alaska's wooded wilderness, a world of pristine vistas and endless skies. Her mother deserved, even if only in this symbolic way, to 'slip the surly bonds of earth.'

Roberta picked up a smooth stone and weighed it in her hand. She gathered other stones of varying sizes and shapes, rubbed them clean with her fingers, and began to stack them into what the native people called an inukshuk. She used two small stones on the bottom to look like legs or feet, then two larger ones on top for the body, one broader stone to depict arms, and a small, round one for the head.

A poster depicting these stone structures hung at the diner and had piqued her interest.

Fantasy had enlightened her. "To the Inuits, inukshuk means 'it looks like a human,' and native people treat them as objects of respect. They mark places of power or a spot where spirits hang out or something," she'd said.

Roberta later read that these small structures were common throughout the circumpolar world, stones used as landmarks, for communication and survival. Given what she was feeling herself, Roberta imagined they were a welcome sight to a traveler on a featureless and forbidding landscape. She imagined pre-historic messages written on the land, unrecognized and violated, in the place where she'd lived all her life.

She built one inukshuk and then three more, digging small stones out of the yellow dirt, positioning one atop another until they balanced. "Laura," she said out loud at the first one, craving the sound of a human voice, even if it was merely her own. "Bradley," she also said, to remain impartial, like a good mother, after building the second. The figures represented the four of them. She stared at the piles of stones as though, magically, she could will them to life.

Bibbedy bobbidy boo. She focused upon them, as if she could will them to become animated. Perhaps she could also will a different set of circumstances, a variant of what was—by all standards—a charmed but exhausting existence.

I'm just bored. First world problems. The bane of the pampered housewife.

Maybe that was the only thing wrong with her life. A shiver rippled through her as the sun warmed her skin.

Roberta stood and looked into the vast heavens. All at once she was transported. She felt a visceral tug, some kind of deep kinship with those ancient mystics who embraced life as all encompassing, who believed we pass through all forms, being reborn time and again, first as rocks or sea water or plant life, then as animals, and finally as humans, until the highest spiritual understanding was achieved. She was flooded with a sense of connection, a kind of cosmic knowing.

She frowned in concentration, trying to remember an uncomfortable conversation she'd had with Bradley Jr. not long ago.

"Some scientist named Grof did research into the effects of LSD," he'd said, trying to convince her she was wrong about drug experimentation. "He discovered something he wasn't even looking for, like, a glimpse into reincarnation."

"Sounds like hooey to me," she'd dismissed him.

"Listen, Mom. This Grof guy's subjects accessed former lives, telling of impossible things given their education and background. Like, they talked about living in other centuries and foreign places, reporting experiences as animals, plants, and even minerals, you know?"

"Every kid your age thinks they've discovered something new in mind-altering drugs." Having become fearful as a parent, Roberta avoided mentioning her own earnest explorations while in college.

"But his test subjects related all this accurate information about the nature of other creatures and other structures, things nobody knew at the time. Like, stuff about mating dances, courtship rituals, and complex reproductive cycles," Bradley said, smug in his superior knowledge.

"You learned this in biology class?" She figured he'd found that crap surfing the net.

But at this moment, Roberta was more open. She stared into the distance, feeling herself a part of the wind, the earth, and the sky.

Shifting her sight above the trees to the impenetrable mountains, Roberta felt exposed, as if her life was turned inside out. For years she had compensated for the unvarying limitations of her horizon with the finely polished finish of her foreground. The husband, the kids, and the Pottery Barn home were just a distraction. Maybe she, too, could conjure up evolutionary memories, including those of animals, of their physical characteristics, behaviors, and habits. Perhaps she might discover crystalline shapes or a foreign cellular structure within herself. She wanted to reach down inside and discover awareness exceeding her human knowledge.

Roberta looked at her dirty hands as if wondering where the stone in her palm had come from. She drew back her arm and pitched the rock as far as she could, feeling the ligaments of her elbow and shoulder strain with the effort.

*If a tree falls in the woods and nobody hears...if a stone launched into the air is lost to sight...*

She massaged away a pain near her clavicle.

Be careful, she felt the weight of anxiety. If she injured herself or fell ill, there was no one to turn to for help.

She wondered who she really was. Did she, or anyone, even know the true nature of mankind? Perhaps consciousness was a basic cosmic phenomenon existing throughout the universe, and the human variety was only one of many. This spoke to a larger spiritual world, a more complicated world, than Roberta had been taught to believe in. She wanted to embrace this larger vision of herself. If she believed in reincarnation, her individual life really meant something; it was part of a broader whole, a thread in a vast fabric. If this was the case, then the only thing that mattered was the here and now. Sliding into the tortured past was meaningless.

Roberta felt herself floating. She was diminished, less individual, more like the dust she stood upon. Closing her eyes, she embraced an absence of all sensation, erasing the boundaries of time and space. No sound, smell, or touch registered. She banished the past and future to enter the endless present. For how long, she didn't know.

Suddenly, she heard as clear and distinct as the closing of a door, the words 'It's Mom' spoken aloud. The spell was broken.

She opened her eyes, squinting in the sunshine. She wasn't really sure she'd heard someone. It could have been a figment of her imagination, or a dream. Roberta shook herself awake and sat on the hard-packed earth. She stared at the inukshuk that represented her. The life choices she'd made seemed not to matter in the grand scheme of things. Had she chosen another path, perhaps the outcome would have been the same. Perhaps everything was preordained. Maybe she'd have made the same bad choices, perpetuating the same unfortunate patterns, no matter what. She couldn't imagine now what metamorphoses awaited her.

Transformations are a given. She'd gone through many in the last twenty years. And she knew she could never have been dissuaded from her own sorry decisions. She saw the kids in this way, too. Laura had married after her second year of college. Someday she might learn to regret that choice, having repeated the same mistake Roberta had made. Hardly more than a child, Laura had changed her name from Blankenship to Barrett, just as uninspiring and 'bare' a name, suggesting an empty page, something devoid of interest and free of content.

It appeared that Bradley Jr. would follow in his father's scientific footsteps. The same ol' same ol'. She felt like everyone had stagnated. Well, Brad had, anyway. After all, she was in Alaska running from the cops. Or terrorists. She wasn't sure anymore.

Anger welled from the depths of her soul. Roberta swallowed air and sighed. She stood and dusted off her backside after knocking over the largest inukshuk with a flick of her finger. The stones representing Brad scattered across the ground like Humpty Dumpty. She might have been happy once upon a time. She couldn't remember. Forever after never seemed to last.

She turned slowly, a full three-hundred and sixty degrees. She scanned the trees, miles and miles of unending forest against the relentless blue sky. Fear suddenly overwhelmed her, making her knees quake. She'd been abandoned out here. She was lost and alone. It was crazy, what she'd done, slipped into Tim's car and allowed him to spirit her away to nowhere. She should never have allowed him to leave the cabin without her. Roberta willed herself out of her panic. After all, that didn't make sense, that someone would dump her out here with no plans to return. It defied common sense, why anyone would do that. She had too much time on her hands and was thinking too hard, that's all.

Get a grip! After all, her only choice at this juncture was to trust the Treasury Department. If Tim didn't return, she'd figure it out. She relaxed her tight shoulders.

It was getting late. The sun was high, the air heavy with heat. She was hungry and thirsty. Tim hadn't even thought to leave her bottled water, only that smelly old canteen she refused to carry. She was beginning to think the Treasury Department was a raggedy stepchild of the bloated U.S. government. One thing was certain: men were running this show. Otherwise she'd have a change of underwear.

Stumbling down the hill to the cabin, she opened a can of soup for lunch, then another for dinner. The time separating the two meals was spent in continued quiet contemplation. This would be a good time to learn to meditate. She also reminded herself of the past twenty years and her ardent prayers requesting peace and quiet, time alone for herself.

"Be careful what you wish for," she muttered, a wry smile twisting her lips.

Roberta watched the sun melt away, smearing its brilliance across the horizon. The glowing orange and reds faded into pale lavender and sapphire blue. The twilight seemed to go on and on, but at some point, the night fell softly, as black as deep space. She stared into it as stars blossomed, one by one, and filled the heavens with icy sparkle. No ambient light from cities, streets, cars, or any man-made object interfered with her view.

She'd read once that much of the light we see came from stars that died eons ago. The concept was unsettling. What lasting mark would she leave upon the world? Nothing, she feared. After her death, absolutely nothing of her would remain behind.

# CHAPTER 17

Roberta jerked awake to total darkness. She'd heard a creak upon the stairs. Her heart hammered, her eyes open wide. Another creaking sound was accompanied by a low moan. Her gaze shot upward as something slid across the roof. A wave of anguish washed over her, and fear ran like ice water down her spine.

It was the wind, nothing more. The bough of a large blue spruce, croaking with resistance and dragging across the mossy shingles, swung wildly outside her window in the gusts that blew down the hill toward the valley. Roberta sat up and leaned forward for a better view of the night sky. She had no idea what time it was. Dark clouds obscured the moon. Not that it mattered, since she couldn't tell by its position how long she'd slept or whether it was morning.

Taking inventory of muscle and bone, she decided she was no longer tired. Rising, she put on her bra and panties, which she'd boiled on the stove and hung on the bedrail before retiring. They were only slightly damp around the seams, so she figured several hours had passed. She pulled on her jeans and shirt, both smelling sweaty and soiled.

She heated water for coffee and opened the can of chickpeas, which she smashed and ate on saltines, a real treat compared to the soup she'd been forcing down for several days. Tim had said he'd return in three days, but she didn't know what he meant exactly. She thought this was the fourth day, unless she'd lost track. A week ago, she might have imagined that spending her life with someone like Tim in the Alaskan wilderness would be romantic and exotic. The last few days had disabused her of that notion. Living so far from civilization would only be lonely. And full of drudgery, the like of which hadn't been seen since the 1930s, she thought, as a whiff of the outdoor privy assaulted her nose.

At dawn, she took another endless walk, ambling for hours, exploring the surrounding woods. Ever more confident of her ability to get back to the cabin, she climbed farther into the trees, meandering downhill in the tangled weeds. She always kept the small creek in sight, just in case. She stopped suddenly.

*What was that?*

A thumping sound broke the solid wall of silence.

*Wump. Wump. Wump.* It repeated over and over, emphatically manmade.

Roberta stepped behind a screen of bushes and cocked her head. She searched the landscape as far as she could see in every direction. The noise was coming from up ahead. Once she was certain she could not be seen, she moved from tree to tree, always behind cover, crouching to make her body smaller, toward the pounding that filled the air.

She moved forward with stealthy steps toward additional sounds of muttering and grunting. Then she saw him. A very large man, whose most distinguishing feature was a head of thick, curly blond hair, was driving a tent stake into the ground. Although there was something oddly familiar about him, she was sure she didn't know him.

*A hiker, perhaps. Had he left the cigarette butts on the cliff?*

He was maybe forty, heavily muscled but gone to fat. The man was wearing a T-shirt emblazoned with **Jesus is Coming (look busy)**, so she dismissed any thought he was associated with Tim. He looked like what he probably was, a lone camper escaping from the wife and kids, opting for the silence of the woods. He probably didn't know about the cabin tucked far behind her in the forest.

She decided it was best to keep it that way and remained hidden from sight as he moved from one side of the tent to the other to pound another stake into the hard-packed earth. He looked harmless but being a lone woman in a deserted part of the Alaskan wilderness did not dispose her to friendliness. Nonetheless, she relished this barest connection with another living, breathing human.

Having nothing better to do, she watched as he finished putting up the tent, gathered stones for a fire ring, and urinated on a tree. He had a large backpack from which hung a water bottle and a set of binoculars. She could see a bedroll in the tent and, she shuddered to realize, the stock of a rifle. Maybe he was a hunter.

*How did he get here?*

Leaning against a white birch with smooth reptilian bark twisting diagonally across the trunk, Roberta surveyed the surrounding trees looking for a car, although she couldn't imagine how anyone could drive to this spot. Given his girth, he didn't look like someone who had hiked in. But for all she knew, this area was covered with recreational facilities hidden by the trees, and people swarmed the woods looking for helpless animals to shoot, hapless fish to catch, or nature trails to trample.

Roberta hadn't realized how cool it had gotten until the man stopped and pulled on a camouflage jacket. As he built a fire, Roberta crept off, winding through the forest toward the cabin. She had gone quite a distance and judged it to be at least a couple of miles. She told herself he was not interested in bothering her. Now she no longer felt so isolated, but she also felt more vulnerable, believing it was possible for someone to stumble on her cabin. She had no idea how often the shack might be used and by whom.

* * *

Roberta occupied the long evening hours with chores, gathering sticks for kindling and small logs to replenish the woodpile, even though it was still stacked high on the side of the porch. She picked a bouquet of wildflowers, filled an empty soup can with water, and arranged the blossoms atop the rustic fireplace mantel before she ate her last tin of beans. Returning from the trash barrel where garbage was collected and eventually burned, she stopped in her tracks. Mingled with the breeze was the unmistakable odor of decay, that pungent, sharp smell of death. Unhappily reminded of the morgue in Juneau, she hurried to the cabin.

The impenetrable dark fell once more. Since she'd found the cigarette butts on the bluff and now spied the man in the woods, Roberta was less sanguine about not having locks. She was protected from bears and large cats, but a predator with opposable thumbs could defeat her limited defenses. She decided she'd place the old rocker in front of the door, wedging the back under the doorknob, before she went to bed. It wouldn't keep anyone out but she'd be warned if someone forced their way through it.

Before the stars came out, Roberta was startled by two cones of light that bounced up the dirt road, then suddenly snapped off. A large car, swimming through the gloom like a shark, pulled to a stop directly in front of the cabin. Because of the camper in the forest, she did not immediately think the obvious, and was beset by equal parts fear and anticipation. Then a blond head emerged from the vehicle.

At last! Tim!

She dampened a squeal, grinned like an ape, and covered the ground between the screened door and the car in seconds, the camper for the moment forgotten. Mindful of skunky armpits and stringy hair, she stuck out her hand when Tim approached and exhaled a shaky, "Hello!"

"Roberta. Good to see you," he said, taking her hand in both of his. "I had to hustle to get back so soon."

She felt like Eurydice to his Orpheus. They stood awkwardly for a moment, Roberta remembering their parting, the tentative kiss and the gentle embrace. She wondered now whether it was meant as moral support, or even a brotherly boost to enable her to withstand the hardships to come, and nothing more. Then again, she was still unsure she was capable of exploring the romantic possibilities. It was not that easy to turn her back on home and hearth. Could she discard her marriage, like a newspaper lining a birdcage, for a more wanton life? She smiled at the appropriate metaphor. After all, she had flown the coop.

She put sexual considerations aside as the trunk popped open and her thoughts shifted to food.

Tim asked, "You okay? Everything all right?"

Squelching the urge to complain about being abandoned without clothing, shampoo, or reading material, she said, "Sure, I'm fine. What's happening in Juneau?"

"We're close to shutting off the money pipeline."

"I hope that's good."

"You staying out of sight was essential, Roberta. It got everything rolling downhill. Like we thought, they're looking for you and making mistakes."

"What's going on?" She frowned and leaned toward him. "I don't understand."

"I can't tell you, but I want you to know that none of this could have happened without your cooperation."

Roberta's breast swelled with self-importance. Someday she'd know everything, but for now she'd wait, trusting Tim. "What's next?" she asked.

"We'll stay here for a few days until things can be wrapped up. We won't hear until someone joins us, since there's no cell service." He wagged his useless phone and threw it into the front seat of the car. "Help me with the stuff in the back."

Her mouth watered at the glimpse of fresh vegetables in the bag she hoisted from the trunk. Tim slung a small duffle on his shoulder, then picked up a heavy box and followed her to the cabin.

"I don't mind telling you, I'm half-starved," said Roberta. "Can we eat?"

"Of course. I haven't eaten either. I drove all day without stopping to get here."

Roberta turned on the lantern, which shed its weak light on food preparations. While Tim washed carrots, celery, and apples, Roberta unpacked the box. In addition to canned items that were a repeat of ones she'd become accustomed to, there was a bottle of shampoo, bar soap, toothpaste (but no brush), and a package of plastic combs.

She hesitated for only a moment. "Ah, Tim?"

"Yeah?" He was at the sink with his back to her.

"I hate to bring this up, it's such a nuisance, but—"

He turned to look at her.

"I've spent the last four days in these clothes."

He reddened. "Oh. Gosh, I'm such a dunce."

Roberta's only consolation was the thought that he obviously didn't have a woman in his life.

He rummaged in his duffle, pulling out clothing. He handed her a pair of boxer shorts, white cotton with Christmas candy canes, which did suggest someone of the opposite sex, and a couple of black T-shirts.

In this new world where she was roughing it, they would do quite nicely. “Thanks, really.”

He looked sheepish. “I should have realized.”

Roberta was used to men who couldn’t think beyond themselves.

While Tim ate soup she had no stomach for, Roberta devoured fresh vegetables in the form of a huge salad, the like of which she hadn’t seen since her last meal at the diner.

Tim also produced, wonder of wonders, a bottle of red wine. They each had a glass, served in mismatched jelly jars, and corked the rest. She vowed to help him make spaghetti the following day, and the wine would make it even more palatable.

Roberta sat back and smiled as he gathered dirty dishes and washed things up, so competent and self-assured. There was nothing so sexy as a man who knew his way around a kitchen.

“What can you tell me about your,” Roberta hesitated, “operation?”

“Only that it’s all going better than expected. Something will happen soon.”

“Have you found Carrie?”

His eyes did not meet hers. “No. But we will.” His moment of hesitation meant something, but she wasn’t sure what.

“Do you know what happened to William? Have any idea why he was killed?” William’s face as he lay on a gurney in the morgue flashed through her mind before she suppressed the image.

“No intelligence yet. All we know is his body was found in a ditch like roadkill. Two shots, one in the back that killed him instantly, one to the back of the head, execution style, to make sure.”

"Oh, God." Roberta struggled with a wave of nausea.

"Sorry. I shouldn't be so blunt."

Roberta bit her lip hard and tried to control her expression. She wanted Tim to think of her as tough and resilient. Then she was mystified. "William wasn't found in the graveyard?"

"No. Why should he be?"

"That's where he was shot," she said before his ignorance stirred her suspicion. *Why doesn't he know?*

Tim's head snapped up. "Where?"

"In Evergreen Cemetery." Roberta watched him closely.

Tim looked stunned. "What makes you think that?"

"I was there. During the shooting. Didn't he tell you?"

"Who?"

"Whoever you have inside the Police Department. Your mole? Is that what they call them? Or is he a spy?" It didn't make sense to her that Tim wasn't in the loop.

Tim looked uncomfortable. Or perhaps he was puzzled. "Well, the authorities are keeping all those details hush-hush. Maybe he overlooked that one."

"But he would know I was a witness, that I heard the shots and ran, and that I fell over William's body."

Tim frowned and seemed to search for a response. At last he said, "You know government work. Half the time the left hand doesn't know what the right hand is doing. Typical." He grinned. "I had no idea you were present during William's murder. What exactly happened?"

Hesitating only a second, Roberta decided it was just like the Feds not to have all the facts. "I arrived in Alaska with Mother's urn, you know?"

"Yes."

"I was visiting the cemetery, considering it for her final resting place. It was getting dark and about the time I was leaving, I heard shots."

"Shots at William?"

"Yes, but I didn't know that at the time. It was too dark to see anything, and I was frightened. I was hiding behind a tree for most of the action, paralyzed. All I knew was someone was shooting at someone else—William, as it turned out—and I closed my eyes as I heard a commotion that seemed to come from all directions."

Tim sat up straight, looking shocked.

"I ran out of there in a panic," Roberta said, blanching as she relived the sensations that flooded through her during the gunplay. "It was dark, I was scared, and he was so still." She frowned at the memory of falling over the body, bloodying her clothes. "I was certain he was dead. Within minutes the place was swarming with police."

"But they told me William's body was found miles away."

"It was?" She looked at him. "I don't know how to explain it. Is it possible he wasn't dead, got up, and was able to get away somewhere?"

"Maybe that's what happened." Tim's smile was more like a grimace.

"The police searched every square inch of the graveyard, all night long, and they didn't find him. I guess it's the only explanation."

"You're a mighty plucky gal, Roberta," he said, grinning.

Roberta grinned back. "I was terrified."

"Who wouldn't be? I'm in that position more often than I care to think about, and it's always, shall we say, invigorating to the point of heart failure."

For a moment, they smiled at one another, and Roberta shifted in her seat. When she lowered her eyes, she took in his square jaw, broad shoulders, and capable hands. She was confused. He should know more than she did, be more connected to the police investigation. Then his eyes convinced her that she shouldn't worry the petty details. Perhaps he wasn't really at the center of this operation, as she'd thought, but he was her savior on a white steed just the same.

"Oh," she said, remembering. "I saw a man in the woods today."

Tim's head swiveled, a look of surprise altering his face. His eyes probed hers. "What? Where?" Red crept up his neck.

Roberta pointed in the direction she'd walked that afternoon. "At least two miles from here, maybe more. He was camping, setting up a tent."

"What'd he look like?"

"Big guy. A mess of curly blond hair."

Tim looked angry.

"What's wrong?"

"This place is supposed to be remote. The idea was you wouldn't be found."

"He obviously wasn't looking for me. He's only a camper. Or a hunter." She remembered the rifle.

"I thought I told you not to go far from the cabin. I assumed you'd stay close by, be safe."

"I spent most of my time hiking. And I was safe. I always knew where I was. I was careful and didn't take any chances." She didn't bother complaining that she had nothing else to do for the past four days. She also decided not to mention the cigarette butts on the bluff, thinking it had nothing to do with her anyway.

"You didn't talk to the guy?"

"No. I kept out of sight. I'm not stupid." She didn't like his chastising tone.

He relaxed. “Of course not, Roberta. I should have known you’d go exploring, a smart woman like you, inquisitive and capable. I’m sorry. But I’m responsible for all this and if anything had happened to you…”

“It didn’t. I’m fine.” Roberta wondered what was really behind his concern before he changed the subject.

“What do you do in Indianapolis, Roberta?”

She tried to think of something more exciting to say than homemaker. “I’m writing a book.” It popped out without her thinking. There was that novella, which she’d thought a lot about and for which she had a general outline. And after all, that collection of recipes she was amassing could be developed into a cookbook.

“I can see that. You look like a writer, the creative type. What’s it about?”

“I’m not so creative.” She felt like a phony, considering the paltry bit of writing she’d actually done. She didn’t want to admit to a cookbook either. “It’s on nutrition.”

“You some kind of scientist?”

“No, I wouldn’t say that, either. But I have an extensive knowledge of food culture and organic food substances. I’ve done a bit of study on human ecology.” She hoped he didn’t know that was the new way of saying home economics, the department where her undergraduate major in clothing design was housed during her college days.

“What’s more important than food?” Tim lifted his glass and saluted her. “It’s all about chemistry, right?”

“And you, Tim? How long have you worked for the government?”

“All my life, it seems,” he said, averting his eyes.

“Have you always worked for the Treasury Department?”

“For the most part.”

"And for the least part? Did you have another life before?" Roberta asked.

"Nothing worth boasting about," Tim said.

Roberta decided that although he appeared to participate in conversation, he was quite practiced in revealing nothing about himself. "Where're you from?"

"It's best I don't tell you too much. But it can't hurt to confess I grew up in Florida."

"Florida? I would have guessed Texas, land of longhorns and tumbleweeds."

"Nope. Land of palm trees and oil spills."

They both laughed. Those charming laugh lines appeared. They called them crow's feet on women, she mused. Typical.

Tim stretched his long legs and let out a weary sigh. "Gosh, Roberta, I know you're starved for company, but I'm beat. Eight hours on the road from Juneau has given me an aching back."

Eight hours? Roberta did a quick calculation. The cabin must be almost five hundred miles from the coast. Was that even possible? From what she'd read about Juneau, it was not connected to anything inland; all roads were local.

He rose and stifled a yawn.

"I understand, Tim. Go ahead. You'll find your sleeping bag in my room."

Roberta reverted to type and bustled about the room to finish tidying up while Tim pumped water in the sink and readied for bed. Before she had things put away, he was upstairs and, no doubt, had sunk into blessed unconsciousness. Once he was gone, she indulged in a proper bath, heating water and lathering up the new bar of soap. She shampooed her hair and surreptitiously used Tim's razor, which she cleaned and dried with scrupulous care afterwards. Then she pulled on the boxer shorts and a T-shirt and washed all her clothing in the bathwater.

Once her jeans and blouse were strung out along the porch railing, she crawled into bed. She hadn't realized how nerve-racking it had been to be alone in the wilderness. And then, after discovering the camper, being not so alone after all. Tim's presence in the next room relieved her anxiety, and Roberta slept the long, peaceful sleep of the untroubled.

# CHAPTER 18

Roberta awoke to the excitement of Tim's presence. She scooted out of bed, saw his door ajar, and caught a flash of pale hair through the window as he entered the outhouse. She ran downstairs and retrieved her laundered clothes, pulling on the stiff jeans and limp blouse that had dried in the morning sun.

When Tim returned, he was already freshly shaved, and his hair was wet. There was a damp towel hanging on a nail near the sink. "Good morning, Roberta. I've heated some water for your morning wash." He grinned.

"Thanks. Did you sleep well?" Roberta asked as she lathered up the soap. "Have you recovered?"

"I believe I have." He glanced toward the shelves next to the stove. "Are you hungry?"

"Always," she said as he rattled pots and pans. She gave him sidelong glances as he whipped up hotcakes on a grungy griddle.

Even more appealing was the red apple she retrieved from the box he'd carried in the night before. Her mouth full, Roberta said, "This's so heavenly it must be forbidden. What should I think of a mysterious character who emerges from the woods with a magical fruit? Will you change the direction of the action?"

“Like the wicked witch?” he laughed.

The fresh fruit tasted otherworldly after her steady diet of canned soup. As she savored it, she smiled at Tim. She wondered what alterations this man with the red apples would make upon her life.

After a second cup of coffee, they took a rigorous hike. She admired his confidence as he angled across the land and through the trees. Only then did she realize Tim was familiar with the area.

“You know this place. You’ve been here before.”

She could tell he was considering how much to reveal. “Yeah. Used to come here as a kid with my folks. It belonged to a family friend.”

“On vacation? Or was your dad a logger or something?”

“He was something, all right.” His smile was rueful.

Roberta didn’t ask any more questions. “When I was a kid, our vacations were spent on my grandparents’ farm. I loved it.”

“What did they grow?”

“Some of everything. Big vegetable garden, acres of grains, mostly oats and wheat. Dairy cows, chickens. For a while, hogs.”

“Sounds like work. The farm still in the family?”

“My elderly aunt and uncle own it. But after they’re gone, I guess it will be sold to whoever is in the market for corn fields. I can’t imagine either of their kids wanting to live there,” she said, thinking of the endless flat land and the loneliness.

Tim broke his stride and turned to face her. “You anxious about home, Roberta?”

“Not really.” She looked him in the eye.

He stared back. “Your husband isn’t the type to worry?”

“He was on his way to an important meeting the last time we talked.” She glanced away from Tim to watch a dry leaf flutter between them, falling to earth.

"Now that you've," he hesitated, "run away, are you planning to stay? Or will you go back?"

"I didn't leave Indianapolis with any specific thoughts about that, but I'm thinking more clearly now, Tim. Yes, I think a shift in my life's trajectory is a good possibility."

Tim wrapped his hands around her waist and pulled her against him. She stood on tiptoe and tilted her face toward his. With no further ceremony, he pressed his lips against hers. She felt a jolt of pure pleasure. Then he kissed her eyelids and moved his lips down her neck to the hollow at the base of her throat until she was breathless. Roberta moaned.

"Oh, Roberta," Tim whispered.

She pulled at his belt and zipper. He struggled with her buttons at first but then whipped her blouse off over her head. They grappled with one another until they lay naked in the morning sun, tumbling on the ground with limbs entwined. Tim rolled her on her back and with one swift, powerful movement, plunged deep inside her.

Roberta cried out and dug her fingers into his muscled arms. Tim thrust his hips forward while she braced her heels in the hard earth and opened her body to him. She was oblivious to the hot sun on her bare skin and the rough plants that cushioned her backside as abandon swept her away.

Afterward, they lay exhausted upon the ground, which was at a substantial incline. With no effort at all, they could have rolled downhill in the springy weeds and rocky soil.

She smiled. "How is it we didn't end up at the bottom of this hill?" Roberta tried to move her arm, which lay upon a hard stone, from under him.

"Angle of repose," Tim said, lifting his weight from her shoulder.

She looked at him, questioning.

"It's an old mining term, means the angle at which detritus comes to rest."

She considered the word detritus: loose material resulting from disintegration. Ruins. Wreckage. She applied this not to herself, particularly, but to her marriage. Out of the destruction of her calcified domesticity, her passion for this stranger rose like a phoenix and soared on wings of forbidden desire. She folded her arms around Tim and snuggled against him. He looked younger with his hair mussed and his shoulders bare. Once more, they made love slowly, deliberately, as if they had all the time in the world.

# CHAPTER 19

For days, between food preparation and lovemaking, Roberta and Tim explored the surrounding area, he in the lead, she carrying the battered canteen and granola bars. He knew about the local vegetation and taught her which plants were edible and which were not, and how to tell the difference between a mountain hemlock and a western hemlock. Tim knew which trees were harvested and why. He also identified rock and mineral deposits, informing her of the local sand, gravel and quarry stone, things that might be used for construction materials. Increasingly, she wondered what he really did here as a kid in the rustic cabin. Maybe he worked alongside his father in a quarry or mine. Or perhaps they were logging.

She nestled against his bare chest, circling his right nipple with her finger.

"The area to the north of us is rich in jade, garnets, and fossils like the woolly mammoth," said Tim.

"I like your woolly mammoth," she giggled, snaking a hand between his legs.

He caught her wrist. "The lode deposits are available in several types, mesothermal gold, porphyry copper, magmatic segregation."

"No segregation sought at this moment," Roberta said, nibbling his earlobe. "But if you can think of a deposit you'd like to make…" She wrapped her legs around him and they wrestled playfully.

Tim seemed to know everything, and Roberta drank in every detail. "I can't decide whether you're a botanist or a geologist."

"Neither," he said with a grin. "Just a man with time to kill. This job consists of hours of boredom, moments of panic. There's plenty of time to learn about the place where I'm working."

But Roberta was unconvinced. His knowledge had the unmistakable resonance of someone born among these slopes and trees, someone who grew up scrabbling in this wilderness to survive.

They wandered through dappled forests and naked hills. From the cool, green silvered mornings to the misty blue dusks, they climbed over fallen logs, through thick, tangled vegetation, and across outcroppings of ancient rock. The sky was invariably clear, strewn with high white clouds. Faint breezes were warm by day and cool by night.

They stopped along a broad shallow river, its heavily silted water glistening in the sun. They sifted smooth stones and pebbles from the bottom through their fingers. Tim leaned toward her and placed his lips upon her throat, then laced her neck from crook to nape with kisses. He cupped her breast with his hand and they fell backward in the tall grass. They made easy love with a gentleness Roberta had never experienced. He explored every inch of her body with his fingers, brought her to ecstasy with his mouth. Euphoric sensations were so intoxicating it was almost painful. Her heart felt full, overflowing with desire for this man. Afterward, they lay upon grass warmed by their bodies and stared into the bright heavens.

"This stream starts in the mountains," he nodded with his head toward grey, snow-covered peaks miles away. "We should hunt for geodes—the Athabascans called them thunder eggs—filled with chalcedony and quartz."

Roberta noticed he didn't name the river. Despite all they shared, he kept part of himself unknown, as though always mindful of the job. He was like a dragon who guarded a bridge to understanding or knowledge, something shared only with the worthy who knew the secret word. She accepted that it had nothing to do with her, just his training. Or he was protecting her from information dangerous for her to know, as he'd said.

After hours of hiking, they made their way once again to the cabin. This time, they approached from behind. When they reached the gully, Tim suddenly stopped. Roberta turned to see a look of shock on his face and followed his gaze to the inukshuk she had built.

He spoke before she could react. "Someone's been here."

"No, Tim. I built them. I'd never seen one until I came to Alaska, and I was trying to fill my days." She felt silly and wondered if she should be embarrassed for having appropriated a traditional symbol that had spiritual meaning for native peoples.

He visibly relaxed. "Well, that's what inukshuk means you know. 'Somebody was here,' in an indigenous tongue. Gave me a start."

"Perhaps I shouldn't have. I know they're about marking a place of reverence or memorial for a beloved person." She hoped she hadn't violated some ancient code of behavior.

"They're also used for navigation or to indicate direction, to mark migration routes or where food or water can be found. You have no reason to be embarrassed. Seeing it startled me is all."

"I'm sorry."

He took her hand. "Don't apologize. I thought maybe I'd dropped the ball, failed to find a safe place for you. The idea that someone might have been here…"

“Well, I can assure you, sir, no one was.” She thought about the man in the woods again. “I was bored out of my gourd.”

“Your gourd? Is that some sort of Midwest expression?” He smiled.

“I don’t know. Guess so.”

They meandered to the cabin through spicy-scented leaves, hand in hand, laughing. Neither of them had mentioned the camper since that first night. Roberta imagined he was gone by now, back to the wife and kids.

At this thought, she felt a prick of guilt. She wasn’t surprised. A conscience often hurts when all your other parts feel so good.

## CHAPTER 20

Roberta lost track of time. She was unsure how many days they'd been at the small cabin and to her, it didn't matter. They rose with a sun that tinged the clear, pale world lavender and slept before the stars came out. When not probing one another physically or emotionally, they explored the woods.

Revealing his tracking skills, Tim showed her the scat of bear, rabbits, and mountain lions.

"Puma, right? Should I be concerned about going out without a weapon?" Roberta recalled her long walks in the woods, which now looked foolhardy, and was grateful for the gun Tim always carried.

"Pumas don't attack humans unless they're starving. But bears, yeah. When confronted, don't run. They've been clocked at over forty miles per hour. Best thing, if you can control your fear, is stand your ground and wave your arms. They don't see that in nature. They'll be scared and, with any luck, slink off."

They supplemented their canned goods with the edible plants available a few steps outside their door.

"I've always known about dandelions—tea, wine, cooking the greens or eating them raw in salads—but it never appealed to me," Roberta said with a grimace when she first washed the newly plucked vegetation Tim had gathered.

"City folk." Tim grinned. "Wasteful, paying for heads of tasteless iceberg from an antiseptic grocery while something richer in food value is growing in the yard for free."

Roberta thought about the toxins sprayed in her yard and those of her neighbors.

"And you drive hours through traffic to work and return home to use a stationary bike for exercise. What's wrong with this picture?"

Roberta imagined a suit-clad Brad arriving at the office sweaty from a commute on a bicycle.

"This is chickweed, good in salads or steeped in water. Likewise, nettles, shepherd's purse, and pigweed." Tim rummaged through the mess of greenery, identifying each plant.

Roberta was grateful Tim was able to improve their diet with fresh mixed greens, which they ate raw or added to the tasteless canned soups. She felt her life immeasurably improved by this knowledge and vowed to embrace it for a lifetime. She pictured herself in a calico apron like her grandmother, a basket on her arm, gathering edible plants as part of a simpler, more meaningful existence.

"We can trap rabbit if you've a taste for fresh meat," Tim said.

Roberta nodded, trying to keep a look of disgust from her face. Eating weeds was one thing but being responsible for gutting Flopsy was quite another. She imagined the calico apron covered with blood.

When the time seemed right, Roberta probed once more. "What do you think is going on in Juneau?"

"They're searching for you," said Tim.

"Do you think I should give myself up, get it over with? I have nothing to hide, after all."

"It isn't only the police, Roberta. It's the bad guys."

"The terrorists? Why? I still don't understand what in the world they want from me."

"They want the urn. Or, rather, what's in it."

"They still think I have it?"

"Of course. At least, we can assume that. Why would they think otherwise?"

"It's absurd." Roberta shook her head, puzzled. Shouldn't Tim have known about the theft from her room from whoever was feeding the Feds information from Craven's office, long before she told him about it? Something just didn't fit right.

"As far as they know, you were the last person seen with it."

"Someone stole it from my room. That person has it."

"How would they know that?"

"I don't know. What can I do about it?" Roberta said. "I have no idea who these people are."

"If you can produce the urn, we have people who can communicate with them, tell them where it can be found. That might move things along, if we catch them in the act."

Roberta sighed. "Like I said, it was stolen. If I knew where it was, I'd tell the cops."

He scrutinized her face, as if trying to read her mind. "Think, Roberta. Go back to that night. What do you remember?"

"Nothing, except getting thrown out a window." He was certainly unreadable. Didn't he believe her? After all, the absence of the urn was a sore spot.

To her, losing it seemed like one more failure, one more way in which she disappointed herself with regard to Martha. There wasn't one thing she could recall having done to earn her mother's devotion. Her childhood gifts—a pile of useless woven acrylic potholders, several plaster of Paris pinch pots, and a plethora of pasta necklaces strung on elastic cords—could never satisfy the debt that weighed upon her psyche. Of course, she'd tried to right the imbalance with smaller points of entry. She'd called every Sunday with news about the kids, her job, and any home decorating projects underway. She'd helped her mother move and even cleaned out the spice rack, consolidating jars and throwing out a can of allspice from the A&P, a purchase that predated Roberta's birth. They visited every holiday, never forgot her anniversary or Mother's Day. All of that paled in comparison to the large topic of a mother's love. It did nothing to alleviate the guilt she felt at having been such a despicable child. The arrangement for the ashes was her last and best effort to make amends.

After this uncomfortable conversation, Roberta refrained from asking about the money laundering, her mother's urn, and William's murder. She sensed that Tim had said all he was going to say. There was nothing more for her to know until it was all over, and the terrorist group was apprehended.

At night after dinner, they sat on the porch decompressing. Following each day of hiking, enjoying the crisp summer smell of dusty leaves and drying grasses, they shared their histories. Bit by bit, Tim revealed part of himself she would never have guessed.

"My dad was gone a lot. Really didn't know him as a kid, until I started working the summers with him." He rolled his glass of wine between his palms, as if adjusting a focus control into the past.

"So, he traveled? What did he do?" Roberta asked.

Tim didn't answer the question. "First memory. I was maybe three, couldn't have been more than four. He came in the front door looking like a giant. I was sucking my thumb. He grabbed me by the wrist and dragged me to the basement, put my thumb on the work bench, hefted an axe, and said, 'I ever see that thumb in your mouth again, I'm hacking it off.'"

Roberta was appalled.

"Guaranteed cure." Tim's grin was humorless. "Needless to say, I kept my thumbs out of sight when he was around."

A few uncomfortable seconds ticked by. Feeling she should say something, Roberta asked, "Is your father still living?"

"Nope. Killed in a bar fight. A couple of cops banged on the door in the middle of the night when I was eighteen. Mom opened up as I stood at the top of the stairs, where I could look down on them like in a dream. I can still hear that squeaky storm door, wailing like a banshee."

Tim seemed to be in some sort of trance. "The cop asked, 'Mrs. Westlake?' like he already knew."

Roberta wanted to comfort Tim but didn't move.

"Mom stood still as a stone. I'm not sure if she answered. He was a young guy, looked real nervous. 'Is your husband Charles Westlake?' he said. When she found her voice, she asked, 'Has something happened? Where's my husband?' She turned white as the lilies she bought for his casket."

Tim took a breath and closed his eyes. "Well, ma'am, I'm afraid he's expired,' the cop said, kind of mechanical, like he did it all the time and had his routine."

Roberta remained silent, unable to look away from Tim's hardened face.

"Christ! That was the word he used, 'expired,' as though Pop were an overdue library book or a carton of milk past its sell-by date."

Roberta had her own memories, stirring like moths flitting through the evening air. "My dad collapsed while standing at a vending machine buying a Coke."

"You know what they say," Tim grinned at her. "That stuff'll kill you."

"The can of Coke was included with his personal effects when they were returned to us." Together, they giggled with the grim laughter of the bereaved.

"Can't recall too many happy memories in the Westlake household."

"There's an oxymoron," said Roberta. "Memories are inherently sad. They represent something gone, something that's over."

"And a source of pain," said Tim, surprisingly bitter.

"Unbearable pain is a gift to us. It's the way we record the things that vanish, the way we imprint memory." Roberta recalled the words of the grief counselor she saw after her father died.

Tim repeated, "A gift?"

"Yeah, I know that's a grotesque concept," Roberta said, even as she realized the truth of it, remembering the tsunami of her mother's death. Too often, afterward, Roberta was ambushed with a suddenness and brutality that caused her heart to stop. Seeing her mother's forlorn slippers or discovering the Time magazine she'd been reading stashed under the bed was like a punch in the solar plexus. She gasped at the sight of a fingerprint glistening in a half-empty pot of lip balm.

"Why is there never enough time?" she asked as though Tim might have an answer. "You always think there will be an opportunity for it to get better, to be the daughter you want to be, to fix whatever is wrong between you. But our time ran out. There will be no more memories. I have to make do with what is left of what I thought would be a great deal more." They sat in silence for a few moments.

“How long’s your mom been gone?”

“Since 2009.”

“That’s a long time to still have her ashes.”

“I know. It’s just…” Roberta hesitated. “Something’s unfinished.”

Tim shrugged. “Isn’t it always?”

Roberta stared into the dark forest silhouetted against the twilit sky.

Mother. Roberta could imagine what she’d think about her current circumstances. She fixed her eyes on the stars hanging low in the heavens beyond the trees while considering her mother’s narrow, empty life. Her thoughts returned to the day of her funeral and a service devoid of dignity. The last time Roberta saw her mother, she lay in a box in an uncomfortable-looking pose wearing an orchid dress she remembered from Easter and an expression Roberta had never seen before. They were unable to maintain the fiction that she was peacefully sleeping given the rigidity in her posture that belied her true nature, her constant air of quiet resignation.

“How did she die?” Tim asked.

“Stroke.” Roberta turned to him. “And you know, I actually wish she’d died in a bar fight. Something more…real. I can’t help thinking that she faded away out of simple boredom.

“Were you with her?”

“No. My Aunt Ginnie was. She called me just before Mom passed to tell me her breathing was worrisome.” At the time, Roberta had turned the word over in her mind. Worrisome. Some worry? Not a lot of worry? Disturbing, troubling, disquieting? For herself, for Aunt Ginnie, or for Mother?

Tim asked, “Do you wish you’d been present?”

“I don’t think being there at the end would have made things better.” Roberta imagined herself keeping vigil at the hospital, her mother gasping with the deep, uneven breath of the dying. She didn't mind that she hadn't the opportunity to sit there and hold her mother's hand, for she knew, without being able to adequately explain it, that long before Aunt Ginnie called her from the hospital, Mother was already gone.

"It wasn't until after the funeral that I realized I had no idea who my mother was. Martha May Princezna was a woman who revealed nothing. Aunt Ginnie provided the only insight over the years."

"Was she older than your mom?" Tim asked.

"Yes. Mom was the youngest of six kids. Aunt Ginnie told me by the time she came along, my Grandmother was at her very worst."

"Drink or drugs?"

"Depression. According to Aunt Ginnie, there were weeks and even months when Grandmother Savage bathed and dressed her children and managed to have meals on the table. But there were just as many times, and those periods seemed endless, when she didn't come out of her room. Day after day, she'd lie in bed, unable to care for them." Roberta imagined her grandmother unable to eat, balled up in soiled blankets, coming out of her bedroom—for a drink of water, an aspirin—in wrinkled, dirty clothing, her hair tangled, purple shadows under her eyes.

Aunt Ginnie had told Roberta stories of the older children tiptoeing past their mother's room on their way to school after dressing and feeding themselves. They printed notes in childish block letters to slide under the door. Still in grade school, they were able to get themselves to the bus after Martha was haphazardly seated in the dining room with a box of cereal before they left for the day.

Roberta was overwhelmed with sadness, picturing her mother as a toddler. She must have passed the endless hours with books or toys left scattered across the squalid living room floor. She would have yearned for her mother's attention, especially when the cereal box was empty.

"Poor wee thing," Aunt Ginnie had said. "We'd come home to find nonsense notes that Martha had scribbled in crayon on a found piece of paper and tucked under Mother's bedroom door." Little Martha, too, had learned the only acceptable means of communication.

In the face of parental neglect, the older children persevered. They learned to operate the washing machine and, most importantly, the can opener. One of them stood on a stool to heat soup, green beans, or, if they were lucky, tinned stew. Aunt Ginnie had related those times of struggle, when they missed their absent father. Where was he? Roberta knew Grandfather traveled for work and was gone weeks at a time. Martha got lost in the shuffle, a tiny child representing but a footnote to a minor family tragedy.

Tim said, "Neglect is the most harmful abuse." He took her hand as she remained silent.

Roberta couldn't remember when she learned the worst. The discovery came long before the funeral, perhaps years after the Savage household was a distant memory. Maybe Aunt Ginnie had spoken of it, or possibly her mother had, when Roberta was too small to grasp its significance. Family lore whispered that Martha wasn't her parents' child at all, but the offspring of an unwed sister or cousin of Grandpa's. What else would explain why she seemed to be treated as a servant, why she was never included in family portraits, why she was disinherited when Grandmother died? Roberta would never know.

"Roberta, you won't make peace with her death until you figure out why you feel like you do," Tim said.

"I know why I hurt, Tim. I was never permitted inside. She was like fog. Or smoke. There was never anything to hold on to."

"I don't think that's it. You're angry, but you don't think you should allow yourself to be."

"Maybe. Mostly it's like I never knew her. She never shared anything that mattered, like fondly held beliefs or expectations. She shared no profound inner thoughts, flights of fancy, or childhood dreams. She'd been an enigma for all the years I was with her and now will forever and always remain a window I can't see through."

"Don't all kids feel that way about their parents, eventually?"

"No. You don't get it. It may not have been pleasant with your dad, but he interacted with you emotionally. He expressed anger and fear and longing. He subjected you to his feelings, to his wants and disappointments. None of that came from my mother."

"Perhaps she had a more interior life."

Roberta snorted with a mirthless laugh. Her thoughts flashed back to what Martha left behind. Once arrangements were made with the mortuary, the realtor, the movers, the auctioneers, and the thrift store, Roberta had sat in her mother's living room staring at the last boxes to be loaded into the trunk of her car. These were Mother's personal things that others were not to touch: the contents of her underwear drawer, the books from the shelf in her bedroom, and her jewelry box where broken beads rattled around like so many lost hopes.

And the journals. Boxes of journals. Martha May Princezna had written in one daily since she was thirteen.

It was not until weeks later, after Roberta had returned home and could reliably believe these things now belonged to her, that she picked up one of her mother's diaries, squared her shoulders, and opened it to a random page.

May 13, 1977. Went to store. Bought George cigs. High 63, low 51.

Roberta flipped through the pages of perfect script executed in a clear, strong hand.

July 22, 1978. Got gas. High 95. Low72.
August 15, 1978. Cleaned wallpaper. High 99, low 78.
August 22, 1978. High 93, low 75.

Roberta dug deeper into the box.

November 12, 1955. Went to school. Came home. Not too cold.
December 23, 1955. Can't wait until Christmas. Wish it would snow.
February 14, 1956. Did homework in arithmetic, Latin. School closed today, snow.
April 30, 1959. Spring Fling last night. Came home early. Light rain.
May 16, 1960. Watched TV. Played records. Warm.

And then deeper.

September 13, 2001. Watched TV. Rain. High 75, low50.
November 6, 2002. TV on the blink. Bought cigs. High 52, low 33.
November 28, 2003. Roberta came with kids. High 58, low 22.
December 2, 2003. High 45, low 32.

Roberta began to cry, and Tim put a sheltering arm across her shoulders.

"Hey, hey now." He squeezed her gently. "It is what it is. Don't get worked up about things you can't do anything about."

"I'm sorry. I'm a ninny." The memory receded. Roberta shivered and dried her tears on her sleeve. "It's just, who was the woman who gave birth to me? She left nothing behind to help me understand."

Sadness settled like ashes over Roberta's heart. The only thing Martha May Princezna, née Savage, contributed to posterity was a troubled daughter who, in turn, would leave no memorable mark.

Tim said, "Since when do we get it made easy? Not all parents leave a past."

Roberta wondered if he were thinking of his own father. "But kids can usually detect a pattern."

"Life's a bit more complicated than that. What exactly did you expect?" said Tim.

"That's a good question."

What Roberta expected of her mother, she didn't know. What she expected of herself was also a mystery. A grand romance, a stellar world-changing accomplishment, an earth-shattering discovery? Were that the case, she should have laid plans for a more meaningful existence. If she'd wanted a life that mattered, she shouldn't have gone to the local university, chosen a home economics major, and committed matrimony with the first man who asked her. She hadn't even bothered with a journal, given that she was no more imaginative or introspective than her sad, prosaic mother.

Roberta had thwarted her own early opportunities by marrying a man who had promise and then taking over the mundane requirements of life on his behalf. Modern conveniences, from the microwave to the computer, only enabled her to do more and more that meant less and less. Like her mother, Roberta was willing to sublimate any personal desires to please everyone else.

"It just makes me sad to think," she said, turning her tearstained face to Tim, "that the day my loved ones rummage through the belongings I leave behind, it will be more like a scavenger hunt than a treasure hunt."

* * *

Bedtime followed the long twilight. They slept together, having put both cots in the first room upstairs, one shoved against the other. Tim easily fell into an untroubled sleep.

Roberta noted the tide of his breathing and felt the weight of his body next to her. She wondered how long this idyll would last, he striding through the woods like a knight in shining armor, she toddling behind like a rescued damsel, carrying his banner and polishing his lance. She dispelled the uneasy thought that the excitement would someday end as she nodded off.

* * *

One tranquil night, a chill awoke her. Moonlight, along with a damp breeze, spilled into the room from the open window. She rose to close it and felt the itch of excess energy in the palms of her hands and the soles of her feet. She lay down again, but she knew it was no use. Rather than wake Tim, she tiptoed downstairs and sat on the porch step at the front of the cabin.

She watched the low moon rise high in the sky. It was only one-fifteen (thank goodness Tim had a watch), and she was certain she was awake for the duration. After more than an hour, she pulled on her jeans and shoes and took the path to the outhouse. Then she angled down the steep hill behind it to the gulley and stumbled upon the large rocks there. She followed along the bottom of the gulch for a few yards and went up the other side in a direction neither she nor the two of them together had explored. She wandered aimlessly, picking her way across the scruffy landscape.

Beyond the hardscrabble ground littered with dry weeds and loose stone, thick trees formed a dark barrier. Roberta ambled toward them and entered the shadowy forest. Broad paths of pine needles softened her step as she wound through the old growth trees. She kept the shadow-shrouded cabin in her sights as she moved along the edge of the woods. Now that Tim was near, she had overcome any fear of the wilderness. Their broad-ranging explorations never unearthed anything to be wary of, and her surroundings were now comfortable and familiar.

All was silence. The light, soundless breeze danced through the treetops. The sky was clear, the air crisp. Nothing on the ground responded to her step. Still, something as palpable as a whisper or a touch beckoned her. Drawn by an invisible presence, Roberta moved deeper into the shadows to stand among the towering trees. Wending her way forward, she spied a small, circular clearing ahead. She crept into the center and threw her head back, looking at the dark heavens high above. She wanted to howl at the moon. Feeling transported, she spun in a slow circle, like an ancient druid. It was magical. She had no shadow. She wondered if she'd lost it, as if this were Neverland and such things were possible.

Something stirred. Roberta stopped and stood still as the moonlight. Someone was with her in this enchanted spot. There seemed to be ghosts. Perhaps she'd found a fairy ring. An elfin dwelling or a haunted aerie. Roberta was not frightened, but she was not alone. Spirits inhabited this place.

She moved to the edge of the clearing and sat upon a mound of needles on the forest floor. Hugging her knees, she inhaled the damp woodsy smell while listening to the surrounding quiet. For a moment, she closed her eyes. When she opened them, something half-hidden by debris caught a moonbeam. She leaned forward, brushed at the leafy litter on the ground, and held the glittering object in her hand.

It was a silver earring with dangling arrowheads. The last time she'd seen it, it was flashing in the sun as Carrie ran down an alley in Juneau. Roberta felt a punch of adrenaline as awareness washed over her. A stinging sensation crawled up her face. She suddenly realized the pile of needles she sat upon had been combed up and repositioned recently. She clambered off it on her hands and knees. Hesitating only a moment, she rapidly raked the heap of loose material aside, exposing a plot of freshly disturbed earth.

Swallowing with difficulty, Roberta tore at the loose soil with her fingers. Then she stopped, fearing what she would find. She knew what was there. The scent of fresh earth, pine and, faintly, the putrid odor of death filled her nostrils.

Terror gripped her heart as tears stung her eyes and she took painful, gulping breaths. Something horrible had happened here. She had to tell Tim.

*Tim.*

A wave of nausea rolled through her gut. She sat on the ground again, wondering what Tim knew. He couldn't possibly be unaware. This was so clearly his turf, his operation. She went over the past several days of laughter and playful sex. If Carrie's body was buried there, he must have had a role in it. If so, what part had he played?

I can't believe he could do such a thing. Did he know when they…is he a monster?

Roberta's throat constricted with a queasy knot of fear. Stumbling toward a tree, she leaned against it and retched until her body convulsed with dry heaves. She looked in the direction of the cabin and then ran the opposite way. Low limbs tore at her hair and clothing, clawed at her arms. She ran until her lungs burned and a sharp pain stabbed her side. Catching her foot on a tangle of ivy, she fell headlong onto the hard ground. When she looked up, her face streaked with tears, the logging road was a few yards away, pale and dusty in the bright starlight.

*So, this is where the road leads.*

And it must go farther still, away into the wilderness where no one ever traveled now.

Roberta stood and brushed at her hair and clothing, wiping her wet face with the backs of her hands. She tried to realign the last few days. She'd accepted without question the idea that important things were hidden from her for her protection. But it was difficult to believe that Carrie's death was another fact that could compromise a federal investigation into laundered money and terrorist activity. She wondered anew why she had been spirited away to a cabin buried in the forest. She had never understood why being in Juneau was dangerous for her, why whatever was smuggled in her mother's urn compromised her safety. Who exactly wanted the urn and why did they believe she had it?

She questioned everything she knew about Tim. He gave every sign that he was in fact besotted with her, but now she wondered if this was all part of a clever plot to get close to her. More likely, the loneliness she'd been forced to endure was to make her feel dependent, to break down her defenses. She thought over their stay at the cabin and their ambling walks. Tim had avoided hiking in this direction. They had never come this far. She had to believe, if she was being rational, that Tim was at the center of this, and that he had full knowledge of what was buried in the clearing in the woods.

Taking a shuddering breath to settle her stomach, Roberta forced herself to think. What now? How did she protect herself when she didn't know why she was in danger? She opened her clenched fist. Carrie's silver earring shimmered in the moonlight. Roberta moistened her mouth and focused her mind. She must cover her tracks. If Tim was really dangerous, then she must not reveal that she'd discovered this burial site. Tucking the earring into her back pocket, she returned the way she'd come.

In frozen calm, Roberta searched for the clearing once more. It took so long to find she was beginning to think she'd lost her way. Then, there it was, looming ahead—the circle of trees and the fairy ring of bright grass where she was sure she'd felt an otherworldly presence. And perhaps she had. Roberta thought of Carrie, with the large, frightened eyes, as she replaced the dirt and raked the pile of pine needles atop the grave again.

Roberta angled through the trees and returned to the logging road to make her way toward the cabin in case Tim was waiting for her. He must not see her come out of the woods beyond the gulley behind the outhouse. By the time she rounded the bend, it was dawn. Tim was there, sitting on the front porch with a cup of coffee. She took a calming breath, composed her face, and stuffed her dirty hands in her front pockets. She turned the corners of her mouth up in what she hoped was a pleasant expression. He stood as she approached.

"You must have gotten up early."

"Couldn't sleep," she said.

"I was getting worried." Tim searched her eyes. "You out there with the lions and tigers and bears."

"Oh, my." Roberta forced a laugh. "I stayed on the road. Didn't realize it kept going for miles. Sorry." The smile felt frozen on her face.

"I made coffee."

"Thank God," said Roberta and she escaped inside, where, in the guise of rinsing her mug, she washed her hands of any evidence of digging into the earth.

She willed herself to return to the front porch, to lean against Tim's well-muscled shoulder. When Tim wrapped an arm around her, she felt his holstered gun. The hardness of it, so reassuring only yesterday, caused a tremor of fear.

"You're cold."

"Maybe a bit." She jabbed him with her elbow. "You could have thought to bring me some clothing, like maybe a sweater."

He visibly relaxed.

"I swear. Men." She tried to look him in the eye but couldn't.

"I'll make it up to you by fixing breakfast in a minute," he said, smiling.

The cold gripping her heart made it difficult to project the warmth and affection she'd felt until two hours ago. They sat in silence. He was guarded.

"A penny for your thoughts," he said at last.

*Two pennies for my eyes,* she feared. "I'm just weary this morning."

"Then let's get some breakfast into you."

When Roberta heard him working the pump in the sink, she sidled across the porch and opened the metal cabinet. As she suspected, the new shovel was crusted with dirt and the pick ax was gone. She then went to the outhouse. Once inside, she slid the silver earring out of her back pocket and felt its weightlessness in her hand before tossing it into the toilet.

Roberta's mind raced. She went over the way she'd met Tim, his intense interest in the urn, and his genuine shock when she told him it had been stolen. She saw his clandestine visit to her room in Juneau, where he looked the space over thoroughly, with different eyes. He wasn't really looking for a bug. He was confirming she didn't have the urn. And he offered no proof that the police were after her when she fled. She wondered how far they were from civilization really. She now doubted there were any animals in the woods to be wary of other than the two-legged variety. It appeared Tim wanted her to be where she was now, alone and feeling vulnerable. Like a landed fish, she felt herself floundering, struggling to breathe and regain control of her quivering body. Her handsome prince had turned into a very large toad.

After breakfast, they went hiking, Roberta this time in the lead. She ambled toward the gulley behind the outhouse, to test Tim. He took her hand as they skirted the top rim, leading her away from the forest behind it. Sauntering again in that direction proved she was right. Tim casually guided her beyond the trees that hid the small clearing to a hillock. So now she knew. When they reached high ground, Tim caught her in his arms.

Roberta flinched, biting her bottom lip hard to control her urge to flee. Fear clutched her entire body.

"Hey," he said, frowning. "Are you okay?"

Roberta leaned her forehead against his arm and said, "I don't feel so well. I'm kind of faint." She could not look at him. Surely her lies would show on her face, like Pinocchio's nose. All her passion and desire for this man had turned to terror, making her mouth dry, her stomach quiver, and her legs weak.

"Maybe it's the sun. It's gotten hot. Let's get you inside." Before moving on, he produced the canteen and insisted she drink.

Roberta let him support her weight as they returned to the cabin. She glanced at the car squatting on the road where it had been the whole time, covered with dust. It looked more like a useless pumpkin than a vehicle in which escape was possible. She did quick calculations. The keys might be in the ignition. The cell phone was still on the seat, she was certain. The chance she could slip away in it was possible. Tim would have put in enough gas to get back to Juneau. She didn't believe she could survive in the wilderness if she fled on foot. The car was her only hope. If not that, she could use a fairy godmother about now.

Inside, Tim pumped another cup of water for her and made her sit in the rocking chair.

"It could be my cooking," he said with a grin. "You've been my guinea pig all week."

"I'm sorry. I've a headache and I'm sore all over. God, I hope it isn't the flu."

He catered to her all day until the sun set and the twilight slowly faded. Then he insisted she go to bed. She lay there, terrified, thinking what to do next. Hours later, Tim crawled in bed beside her and put a possessive hand on her hip. She pretended to sleep.

Roberta hadn't meant to doze but was jerked awake when Tim rose in the middle of the night. Hearing the screen door squeak, she ran to the hallway window to watch Tim cross the front yard like a ghost and lean against the car, looking at his watch. After a moment, he stood at attention and walked down the dusty road, his shadow black against the pale ground. He held something that looked like a long rifle in his left hand.

Tim looked down the road as headlights illuminated the trees and bounced toward the cabin. Before the big dark car pulled up and stopped, the lights snapped off. A large man exited the car while the motor continued to rumble softly, and the two men spoke. Both were merely shadows, the newcomer facing toward Roberta. Something pricked at her memory. His silhouette was familiar.

Then she recognized the way he moved, his lumbering quality, the set of his broad shoulders and big head. It was the man in the woods, the camper. Roberta's heart felt like a stone. Anguish clawed at her insides, and she blinked away sudden tears.

After speaking together but a moment, both men got into the waiting car and drove silently up the dusty logging road, disappearing beyond the trees. Roberta knew where they were going. She pulled on her jeans and shoes and ran out of the cabin and behind it, through the gulley, and into the woods that surrounded the clearing she'd found only that morning. Entering the forest, she paused a moment for her eyes to adjust to the inky blackness. She felt her way forward more by memory than sight. Creeping along the perimeter of the woods until she found a path among the old growth trees, she ducked through branches, her footsteps muted by the blanket of needles and damp leaves.

Roberta heard the two men before she saw them. Bending low, she crept from tree to tree, guided by the sound of their voices. Given the casual tone of their conversation, they were not concerned about being overheard.

Roberta crouched a few feet outside the clearing. Suddenly, their faces leapt into view as Broad Shoulders struck a match to light a cigarette. Then they were thrust into darkness once more. Roberta stopped breathing as she huddled against a tree trunk in the shadows.

"…can't tell," Tim was saying.

"You should've beaten it out of her," said Broad Shoulders. "Knocked her damn teeth out."

"I fucked her instead. She'd tell me. The cow's in love."

"She might be smarter than you think."

"Doubt it. If she had the stuff, she'd suggest we cash it in and escape to a desert island somewhere. She's a fucking romantic, the stupid bitch. She doesn't have it."

"Still. What's to lose? We're gonna off her anyway."

"That's more your line. But maybe you're right. Last ditch effort."

Roberta's senses telescoped and panic overwhelmed her. She fell into a trance, immobilized by dread. She didn't know how much time passed or what Tim and the other man said to one another. She stared, wide-eyed, not daring to move.

*So, it was the urn he wanted, after all. Playing house was just a clever game to get me to give it up*. Tim had been playing at some kind of Stockholm syndrome routine, keeping her isolated and frightened, ensuring she would identify only with her captor and do anything to please him.

A sudden shift in the cloud cover flooded the clearing with moonlight. Roberta shook herself out of her stupor. Her mouth dry and her palms wet, she shrank into the darkness, eyes riveted on Tim and his companion. Cigarette smoke wafted to her on the night air, triggering another memory. With a shock she realized Broad Shoulders was the man who'd thrown her out of the window. How had she been so dense? It was all so obvious to her now.

*Think! Focus, or else I really am a stupid cow.*

Tim handed Broad Shoulders what he'd carried away from the cabin. The shovel.

"We'll get rid of her tonight," Tim said. "I'll take one last shot at making her give up the urn, scare the shit out of her."

"Why do I have to do all the dirty work?" said Tim's accomplice, taking the spade.

"I'll do the hard part. All you have to do is dig."

"You driving back?"

"Nope. I'll walk, leave you your car," said Tim. "I need to think through a strategy. Build up to it."

Roberta shuddered and pressed her palms to her thudding chest. As Tim made his way to the road, Broad Shoulders flipped his cigarette butt into the dirt and ground it with his heel. So, she realized, he'd been the watcher in the woods. She'd been under surveillance the whole time. She had never been alone. The big man, camped in the forest close by, spied on her from the bluff. The entire charade had been a ruse to get her to cop to having the urn and the valuables it contained.

He sank the shovel into the hard-packed earth and grunted. The sound of her own grave being dug jerked Roberta to attention and she scurried away from the clearing.

*How much time do I have?*

Once out of earshot, she sped in the direction she'd come, calculating how long it had taken her to walk the road from the clearing to the cabin that morning. Twenty minutes, maybe. No more than that, and for Tim it could be less. She flew across the gulley behind the outhouse, her mind racing. Inside the cabin no more than sixty seconds, she grabbed Tim's denim jacket, her blouse from the back of the rocking chair, and the half-full canteen. No time to fill it. She raced to Tim's car, ripping open the door.

No keys.

She grabbed the cell phone lying on the seat before rocketing across the road, down the slight incline, speeding into the trees, moving roughly perpendicular to the rutted lane. Run, Goldilocks, run. You're a sneak and a thief, and you've upset the tidy orderliness of things. The bears are dangerous and will eat you alive. She now recognized the menace in that tale.

Roberta had the laser focus of a hunted animal. She moved straight into the woods opposite the cabin and turned sharply to run parallel along the dirt track toward the highway. She still had no idea how far that might be. A mile? Thirty miles? Tim had exaggerated the distances to make her feel more isolated and vulnerable. She'd been such a half-witted fool.

How long she had before Tim came after her, she didn't know. Once he got to the cabin, he would look for her, first upstairs and then in the outhouse. He might wander about the road and the surrounding area for a few minutes, thinking she couldn't sleep and had taken a walk. When he noticed the missing jacket, the canteen, the phone, he'd know. If she'd failed to close the car door, it would signal an immediate alarm. She ran harder.

Her head pounded and her spirits sank. Tim was a tracker. And he knew these woods. She had to get ahead—way ahead—if she was to stay alive.

Roberta's panic was like a spur. But Tim would expect her to follow the road toward the highway, just as she was doing. She'd have to take risks. Forget fairy tales and their warnings. She'd have to stray from the path, chance getting lost in the woods, and brave the wilderness without leaving a trail. Roberta's perspiring skin was clammy, but she shivered in the cool morning air and kept on moving.

Her legs burning, she stopped and sagged against a tree to nurse a stabbing pain in her side. She gulped air to calm her racing pulse and listened. After taking a mouthful of stale water from the canteen, she turned on the phone. No signal. And only ten percent of the battery charge remained. She put it on airplane mode to preserve power. She had to find a signal. Her life might depend upon it.

She sniffed the air like an animal. The forest had a humanless feel, a disturbing quiet. She imagined Tim tracking her like a Native

American, as she'd seen in the movies—silent, efficient, and relentless. She had been zigzagging in and out of the trees, moving farther from the rutted road than Tim might have expected. She had to be bold. She embraced the wilderness as her salvation.

Roberta looked behind her at the way she'd come. In the distance, she could see the dirt road, high above her now. It's possible there were telltale signs of her passing. Tim might be able to pick up her scent like a predator. Catching her second wind, she sped on, charging into and around the trees. She scrabbled over stony outcroppings that jutted like teeth from the landscape. She encountered gullies, some deep enough to require that she skirt them, others she barreled through, down one side and up the other. When she could no longer run, she walked, or sometimes sat to catch her breath. During her escape, the sun had risen and now was sinking again. She'd been on the move since before daylight, stopping only to slake her thirst or listen for her pursuers while she kneaded the sharp twinge in her gut.

Roberta stumbled and scrambled, falling more than once, tripping on tangles of weeds, stepping into unexpected holes. She panted, her mouth open, the rasping breaths making her throat raw. Stinging and biting insects arrived with the long twilight. She coated her exposed skin with dust to protect it. Scratches covered her arms and ankles. Her feet burned with the pounding abuse they'd suffered.

She stopped again to drink from the canteen. Her muscles and lungs ached. So tired her knees were giving out, she couldn't run any longer. And traveling in darkness was too risky. Without the sun or the ability to see the moss on the trees to suggest direction, she would probably wander in circles. Maybe that's how Tim would catch up with her. She looked back at her path through the forest. She needed to get off the ground. She shouldn't bed down where man or beast could find her.

In the lingering light from the setting sun, Roberta looked for a good climbing tree. Ducking under the draping branches of a huge hemlock, she could nearly stand in the tent-like space beneath. Given the limb structure, which grew like the spokes of a twisted wheel, Roberta figured she could climb ten or fifteen feet up and perch high above the ground, draping her arms and legs across the branches to rest.

But first, she had an idea. She grappled with the blouse tied around her waist. She tore at a button, making sure a piece of fabric clung to it. Then she walked forty feet ahead, into a small clearing, leaving evidence of her footprints. Placing the button on the ground in plain sight, she then backtracked to the accommodating tree. Should Tim be following her, and if he was really good, he would find the button and keep going forward.

She climbed, struggling to haul herself nearly twenty feet up between thick branches, to where the limbs were a bit sparse and almost too small to hold her weight. After scraping her flesh on rough bark and broken twigs, both of which grabbed at her hair, she parked her bottom on a narrow branch and threaded her legs through others, settling her chest and head against the trunk. She used her blouse to cushion her face against its bristly surface. Then she pulled Tim's jacket across her back and shoulders, wrapped the arms around the trunk and tied them, holding herself in a kind of sling. This arrangement would allow her to relax, even to sleep.

Exhaustion overtook her the moment she let down her guard. Ignoring the needles and nubs that jabbed through her clothing, she allowed her head to slump forward and her body to sag. Before she sifted into a wary slumber, she remembered what they'd said, Tim and the stranger, in the clearing in the woods.

*...you should've beaten it out of her.*

*She doesn't have it.*

All they ever wanted was the urn. Every intricate detail, all the clues over the past weeks, spun, whirred, and clicked into place. No wonder Tim knew nothing about William's death or the theft of the urn. He wasn't with the Treasury Department nor did he have any connection with the police. It was all a lie. She should have trusted her intuition, and paid heed to her suspicions that Tim wasn't who he claimed to be.

They were the bad guys, the supposed 'terrorists' who transported gems in the luggage of unsuspecting travelers, the ones seeking Roberta because the urn went missing. She had been an ignorant patsy. Now that the spell she'd labored under was broken, she saw Tim for the evil, wicked trickster he was. Roberta was always smarter than she gave herself credit for.

Avoiding thoughts of the more painful revelations she'd overhead in the clearing, she succumbed to an uneasy sleep.

# CHAPTER 21

The rustling of leaves jarred Roberta awake. The rosy shimmer of dawn brightened the eastern sky. Her mouth felt like cotton and her eyes were sticky, but both popped open as something or someone moved around below. Her stomach knotted. A swarm of gnats swam around her head and caught in her hair. Her face heated with panic.

Roberta sensed rather than saw someone beneath her perch. She peered through the boughs to find a glimpse of who or what moved across the forest floor. Shuddering, Roberta spied a flash of bright hair.

*Tim.*

She clutched the tree trunk and willed herself not to move. The sound of furtive footsteps floated up to her. She could not see well but knew Tim was moving in the direction she had gone last evening before she doubled back. He would find the button. She glanced toward the dirt road. Almost lost in the shadows, the large dark car glided silently along, keeping pace with Tim as he tracked her through the wilderness. Of course, the man who had thrown her out a window would bring his car, would move in concert with Tim. First, they would want confirmation that she ran in the most logical direction, toward the highway. The button would provide that. Then they would set a trap somewhere along that route, where she would have to seek help to return to civilization.

Roberta considered backtracking to the cabin along the old logging road. That would be the last place they'd look for her. But then what? There was no means of communicating with the outside world, no transportation unless Tim conveniently left his keys where she could find them, and no handy huntsman nearby to save her if the wolves returned. She might as well stay up a tree, as long as she knew where they were. Confident Tim was yards beyond her hiding place, she shifted on her narrow branch to relieve the ache in her rear and the stiffness in her legs. Her clothing was limp with damp.

The car had moved farther down, almost beyond her sight. Then she saw Tim scrambling up the steep side of the road toward it. Three hundred feet away, and on higher ground, he was roughly level with her. Roberta was shocked to see that although she was hidden from below, the sparse upper branches left her exposed to view from where Tim stood now, scanning the wilderness with binoculars. He made a slow turn, from right to left, starting at the sheer wall of rock that bordered the dirt track. Terrified that he would see her clinging to the tree, she reached upward and pulled a branch above her head across her face and torso. Remaining as still as her trembling body would allow, she watched him study the vast forest.

He paused. The lenses of the binoculars were pointed directly at her. She stared, not daring to blink, still as the dead.

He stood motionless. Glass and metal flashed in the morning sunlight. *What does he see?*

Tim lowered the binoculars, hesitated, then threw himself into the front seat of the car, which sped off toward the highway with a lurch and a spray of dust. Roberta moistened her mouth as she took a deep breath.

Shaking the tension from her muscles, Roberta descended from her hideout. Hunger gnawed at her insides. She searched for chickweed, goosetongue, and purselane, as Tim had taught her. He might come to regret revealing the few survival skills she'd gleaned from him. For the moment, she was ahead of the game, as she had successfully evaded her pursuers and knew where they were.

Roberta drank the last of the water and dined on edible greens. Some leaves were bitter, others sweet or tangy, but all were fortifying. The blackberries she found were sour but welcome. She felt strength return to her limbs as she strode forward, now following Tim. Most essential to her survival was the one thing she couldn't find behind in the shack—a cell phone signal.

Roberta plunged farther into the woods, going roughly south according to the moist green side of the trees and the sun that rose on her left. Should she lose sight of her only signpost, the dusty road, she could still be guided by the damp mossy growth. Her fear of walking around in circles, getting lost in the wilderness, felt less of a threat.

She pondered how far she might be from the highway and how heavily traveled it was. She cocked her head and listened for the sounds of traffic. What she heard was the trickle of water. Her thirst had grown as the sun tracked toward noon, so the discovery of water buoyed her lagging confidence. She followed along a dry ditch and found a very broad, shallow stream with a heavy burden of silt rushing ahead of her. The water did not look potable, and she regretted not having anything to strain the dirt out of it.

*Improvise.*

Undaunted, Roberta positioned the canteen upright between two rocks and unscrewed the top. Scooping muddy water with her blouse, she used the tightly woven fabric to remove the heavier silt. Almost clear water dripped through the cloth to trickle into the canteen. Before it was full, she drank. It was gritty and tasted of dirt but quenched her aching thirst. Afterward, she filled the canteen to the top, rinsed the grit out of her blouse, and washed her face and arms. Draping the wet blouse around her neck atop her T-shirt, she picked up Tim's jacket and the canteen and started walking once more, moving into the trees.

She drove forward at a steady pace, the road no longer in view. Battling spiders' webs and biting flies, she ducked under branches and stepped high through the undergrowth. She ate berries again, drank again, and forged ahead, sometimes running if the terrain allowed, until the sun came to rest just above the treetops. Then she walked some more in the endless twilight.

* * *

By nightfall, Roberta had been on the move for two full days. Contemplating how many miles she'd likely covered, she decided probably no more than a car could go in two or so hours. Rather than being discouraged, she was invigorated. It was only a matter of time.

She would not despair or even consider the possibility she was going nowhere. She would conquer this wilderness. The bad guys would not win. Playing upon her feelings of vulnerability, Tim tried to make her believe it had taken eight hours to drive from Juneau, which she now realized was another lie. None of the roads led that far outside of Juneau. Even if she was that far from civilization, Roberta worked it out in her head like a middle school math class word problem: if a five-foot, five-inch-tall woman walked three miles per hour and started out in the Alaskan wilderness four hundred miles from Juneau, how many hours would it take…

She sat on a fallen log in a dim shaft of sunlight and raked her fingers through tangled hair, dislodging bits of bark, leaves, and insects. Then she pulled out the phone. Still no bars and now only nine percent of the battery remained. Keeping it on airplane mode to save the charge,

Roberta was tucking it into her back pocket when she heard a noisy thrashing somewhere behind her. She whirled around, fear hitting her like a shovel to the face. Before she could react, a huge bear barreled out of the trees. She stood as if paralyzed.

The large, shaggy animal lumbered toward her. It stopped when it registered her presence, and their eyes locked. Rumbling with a low growl, the bear then swung his head from side to side. The hair stood up on his back and neck, and his ears sloped backwards. Roberta was frozen with horror. Panic turned her legs to water. The bear stood and snarled, baring its yellow teeth.

*What did Tim tell me about bears?*

The bear roared and charged toward her, covering the distance between them in a second. Terrified, Roberta fell backwards over the tree trunk and tried to duck beneath it as the animal stopped a few feet away.

*Don't run!*

Roberta knew she couldn't outpace the bear and stifled the urge to flee. Running would only trigger the animal's killer instinct.

*Don't look like prey!*

She crawled half-way under the trunk as the bear stood on its hind legs and roared again. He swatted at the ground with a huge paw and snuffled and snorted, growling low in its throat. Roberta fancied she could smell its foul breath.

The fallen tree was only a trap. Roberta scrambled from under it, did a diving somersault, and stood holding a small branch with dead leaves clinging to it.

*I must stand my ground or I'm a dead woman.*

She tried to make a low, fierce growl of her own, but it came out a high squeak. Finally managing to sound like a yodeling fog horn, she raised her hands high over her head and waved them, holding the branch.

The bear paused and took a step back. Roberta shifted her eyes to the bear's chest, not wanting to suggest a challenge or threat. She pulled at the blouse draping her neck and waved it high in the other hand. Looking wary, the bear took a few steps to the side. Without a backward glance, it lumbered into the trees at the same spot from which it had appeared.

Shaking violently, Roberta stared at the place where the bear retreated into the woods, picked up the jacket and canteen, and stumbled in the opposite direction. The adventures of Goldilocks took on a whole new meaning, fraught with peril.

After a few yards, she broke into a run. It had the salubrious effect not only of distancing herself from danger, but also of dispelling the panic that shattered her nerves. She ran until her chest heaved with the struggle to breathe, and her legs cramped.

When she stopped, she collapsed on the ground and laughed hysterically until tears came. She rejoiced in being alive, wondering at her luck. She'd ducked bullets, been thrown from a window, kidnapped, chased into the wilderness, and now menaced by a bear. And she had survived. She couldn't possibly have known what was in her future when she left home with $12.39, a credit card, a broken bracelet, and her mother's ashes.

Focusing on her anger as motivation, she thought of Tim. She recalled his hurtful words, burning with humiliation.

*She'd tell me. The cow's in love.*

*She's a fucking romantic, the stupid bitch.*

She wanted more than to survive. Roberta smoldered with the desire to slay the dragon. She wanted Tim Westlake, if that was his name, to get his just deserts. He should rot in jail or get a needle in his arm if he was involved in the deaths of William and Carrie. But now she needed to find a safe place to sleep. She darted into the woods again, alert to new dangers. The need to survive trumped embarrassment, all regrets, and her lust for revenge.

# CHAPTER 22

Roberta opened her eyes to intense darkness. She shifted her aching body and moved her arm from a twig that had been stabbing her flesh. Staring into the night sky, she listened with every cell of her body. Nothing stirred. Attuned to her surroundings, Roberta felt like a wild animal wary of dangerous predators, yet open to opportunities. She felt like a cat, once a pampered pet, who had been lost and was now feral.

At daybreak, Roberta dropped to the ground from a branch only ten feet up, its major advantages being a leafy screen and a broad limb for her rear end. She quenched her thirst but before foraging for berries, she stretched her arms and legs and pulled the phone from her hip pocket. Turning off airplane mode, she angled it in different directions.

*I have bars!*

Roberta hit 911 and squealed when she heard a woman's voice.

"911. What's your emergency?"

"Help! Please help me! I'm lost! I'm wandering in the wilderness somewhere outside of Juneau." Breathless, she spoke as rapidly as possible fearing she would lose the connection. "My name is Roberta Blankenship. I'm lost! You have to help me!"

"Are you in a safe place?"

"No! No! I'm being chased by two killers! And there are bears!"

"Where are you?"

"I don't know. I was kidnapped," Roberta said, putting the most generous spin on her predicament. "You have to help me! Call the Juneau Police Department and inform Craven," she realized she didn't know his first name. "Chief Craven of the Juneau police."

"Can you stay on the line?"

"Yes! But my battery is about to die. It won't last. Help me! You have to do something to help me!"

"Can you identify any landmarks?"

Roberta spun around three-hundred-sixty degrees as Tim had earlier, scrutinizing the terrain. "Trees, nothing but trees, dammit!" Her voice sounded like a squeak through a plugged nostril.

"Is there anything to clarify your location?"

"No! There's nothing. Just miles and miles of wilderness. There's no way to orient myself." She fought back tears and clutched the phone. A violent tremor seized her and she struggled to focus. "I—I'm near a logging road that leads to a highway." She tried to remember if she'd seen a sign or something identifying which highway they'd taken. All the roads were local, nothing went farther than the next settlement or commercial site, or wherever they needed access. There couldn't be that many. "I was taken to a cabin. I don't even know how long it took to get there."

"Are you near the highway now?"

"I don't know! Can't you find my location with the phone? Use the cell tower?" There was some term they used on all those cop shows. Triangulate. Did you need three points on a map to do that? She ransacked her brain for a way Craven could find her. She should've thought this through long before now.

"Do you know which direction you were going when you left Juneau?"

"I was forced against my will." Roberta's hands trembled as she offered this half-truth. "It was dark. I have no idea." Roberta relived her flight from the city. There was no sun and she had no clue about how to read direction by stars. She didn't want to waste her limited battery power on useless speculation, but she was desperate to give the woman on the other end of the line helpful information. "Please! Please call Chief Craven in Juneau. Or connect me with the JPD! Let me talk to someone there."

"I'm afraid I'll lose you. You must stay on the line."

The woman's voice faded and Roberta lost every other word.

"No! No, no, no, no. Stay with me!" Roberta screamed.

"Can—call—help—know…"

"Can you call me back? Did you ID this number?"

"—not," the woman said. "—blocked."

"No! No, don't go." She gripped the phone as if it would strengthen the connection. "Give me the number for JPD. I'll call them."

The phone crackled, hummed, and went silent.

Roberta shook it and pressed the 'on' button, angling the phone in different directions once more. The screen was black. It came on for a moment, but again no bars appeared in the display. The battery charge was now two percent. She turned on airplane mode once again, allowing her tears to flow.

Don't fall apart, Roberta told herself. At home, tears might elicit concern, exasperation, or consideration, but not here. Here, everything was reduced to simply one thing: staying alive. She wiped her face with her shirt sleeve and decided to be encouraged. Now Craven would know what had happened to her. She didn't just run from a murder charge but was kidnapped. They would now look for her if they weren't already. And the dirt road intersected with a highway that led to civilization. All she had to do was keep walking. And avoid Tim. And the bears.

She hoisted the jacket and canteen and scurried once again into the woods. In this area, she encountered more brush. Not all the trees were firs, her step was not cushioned by a carpet of needles, and the sunshine that filtered through the leafy canopy allowed a liberal growth of sticky bushes and long grasses. She stepped higher in the undergrowth and put her feet down where she couldn't see beneath. She thought of snakes and small creatures with lots of teeth and attitude.

Wading through cotton grass, yellow flowers, and vines that tangled around her feet, Roberta stumbled upon a small sunny meadow sliced by a narrow stream of water. It didn't appear to suspend major amounts of silt but was barely moving. Was it safe to drink? She looked about, at mountains in the distance and the acres of trees. Unable to imagine what might contaminate it, she refilled her canteen.

The sun was high and Roberta relaxed along the bank, setting aside her worries. Taking off her shoes for the first time in more than two days, she discovered she'd worn blisters on both heels. Now that she knew they were there, they throbbed and stung. Rolling up her jeans, she dipped her feet into the ice-cold water and gasped with the shock. She forced herself to immerse her legs up to her calves, for the cold eliminated the misery in her flesh. She rested her feet on the muddy bottom and wriggled her toes. Surrounded by a thick layer of silence, Roberta lay backward upon the long grass and closed her eyes.

The last time she'd languished upon the ground, Tim had pressed himself into her and she'd wallowed in his attentions. She had fallen victim to some kind of enchantment, as if she'd pricked her finger on a magic spindle. It was all too clear another sort of prick had done her in.

Since the sun was hot and Roberta exhausted, she tried to nap but couldn't. She was cautious and aware, focused on any sound or movement signaling danger. She sat upright and peered between her knees at her reflection in the still water. She was startled at the thin face that stared back at her. Her hair was flat and tucked behind her ears, and her eyes appeared hollow. The sagging T-shirt revealed her collar bones and sun-burnt neck. She frowned at her brown arms and legs. She'd grown tough and thick–skinned, like the vegetation in arid climates.

Roberta not only looked like an entirely different person—thinner, darker, freckled—but also felt different. For days, she had not pined for her home or her children and husband, as women always do once they escape their loved ones' demands. She did not think of friends or family, responsibilities or longings, the past or the future. She thought only of the here and now, and what it took to survive. She felt strong. Her limbs were muscled and well-defined. She was alert. And, yes, she was brave.

Roberta pulled the shoes onto her wet feet and stood, listening with an ear angled in the direction she was going. She hoped to hear traffic on the highway or pick up signs of human activity. There was only the sound of the living forest, the rustling of insects, the occasional chatter of birds, and the ever-so-slight babble of water. Looking across the landscape, she distinguished the different trees, the rich green of hemlock, the paler cedar, the blue-green of spruce, the yellowish birch.

On the far left, a bright flash of reflected sun seared her eyes.

*Binoculars!*

A jagged blade of fear pierced her body. Roberta jumped like a rabbit and dove into the woods. Had they seen her? She hunched low and wove a path through the brush. She drove herself farther into the interior, tearing through thick bushes, ignoring the brambles that grabbed at her limbs, her arms and legs pumping.

Panting for breath, she stopped to listen. Someone was thrashing through the undergrowth behind her. She veered left moving toward, she prayed, the highway. Even a second's hesitation brought the sounds of her pursuers closer. She embraced her panic and doubled her efforts, picking up her speed. She ran now without worrying about the noise. She heard them following close behind. Could they see her? Terror clutched at her heart.

There was no place to hide. The trees were narrower, their limbs barer, the ground more open despite the tangle of vegetation. Not a ditch, fallen log, or outcropping of rock provided cover. She had to outrun them. Her mouth twisted in a grimace, the canteen banging against her hip, she threaded her way through the forest. She heard feet pounding. Glancing behind her, she saw only the violent shaking of saplings and branches. She searched the ground for any refuge. When she saw a thicket of bushes ahead, she dove into them, hunkered down, and held her breath.

Her body shook and her eyes bulged as Roberta peered through the thick leaves at the path behind her. The thrashing stopped. For a moment, she thought she'd lost them. Then a shaft of sunlight was broken by a shadow. She heard the unmistakable sound of swishing grasses as someone stalked nearer.

Roberta shrank against the earth, smelling the damp, rotting leaves and the musty odor of mold. Her eyes were riveted to the path she'd taken. There might be telltale signs of her hiding place. A ripple of dread shuddered through her when Broad Shoulders suddenly stepped into view only yards away and crept forward.

He glared in every direction, then lifted his hand and signaled to his left. Her gaze followed his and she saw Tim sidle out of the trees. Both men had focused on a spot beyond where she hid. But they knew she was no longer running. They were stalking in silence, hoping to flush her out.

Roberta huddled in fear as her pulse pounded in her ears. Opening her mouth wide, she swallowed air as her lungs fought for oxygen. Rough, prickly twigs poked and tore her flesh. She shivered, closed her eyes, and laid immobile with fright.

When Roberta dared to look once more, their backs were to her. They inched forward, signaling to one another. It appeared they were walking in a circle, but the circle did not include her hiding place. Should she sit tight or should she run? She glanced behind her in the direction she'd come. The path was overly exposed, and it was so quiet—they would be alert to any movement. Instead, she scooped damp leaves to scatter over her legs. She buried her hands and face in the loose debris littering the ground. If they turned in her direction, they might see her from a different angle. She stayed put.

She lay still for hours, unable to hear Tim or Broad Shoulders. They, too, were waiting. She lifted her head from the humid earth and scanned the surrounding trees. They could have angled around behind her. Or they might be ahead. It wasn't clear which direction offered escape. There were two of them, double the danger. With the sun low in the sky, the evening insects chattered, and the night birds tuned their songs. Roberta's muscles ached with tension, and her skin crawled.

Night fell. In the darkness, Roberta took a long pull from the canteen and moved her stiff limbs. She was grateful for the cacophony that serenaded the dark, contrasting with the silent, motionless day. She considered picking a direction and moving on, but she decided to hunker down. How long would they wait? Were they waiting even now?

Roberta decided to find out. Easing outside the thicket, she felt along the ground and found a half-rotted stick covered with lichen. It was light but had enough heft to sail some distance. She would have to choose her target carefully so as not to expose herself. To her right, the trees, backlit by a starry sky, thinned a bit, offering fewer obstacles to a hurling object. She held her breath, drew back her arm, and followed through. The stick somersaulted through the air.

Roberta ducked again into the thicket before the stick shattered against a tree trunk several yards away. A bright light punched through the darkness and circled through the forest only thirty feet from Roberta's hiding place. Tremors arced through her body as she flattened herself once again. The beam of light raced through the trees, moving up, down, and around, like the orb of a giant beast. Roberta squeezed her eyes shut and balled her fists to keep from shaking.

At least she knew where they were. Or one of them, anyway. Her other pursuer could be in another part of the woods, guarding against her flight. She feared she'd revealed she was still there as well.

She remained alert for hours, her ears straining for sound, her eyes focused on any movement in the darkness. During the night, a sudden wind had chased the clouds from the sky and bright moonlight dappled the forest. Dancing shadows camouflaged both the hunter and the hunted.

At some point, Roberta slept. She jolted awake at dawn as something small disturbed the tangle of leaves growing at her feet. A rodent skittered past her and into the dirt a few feet away. She looked left and right, up to the tops of the trees and down across the tall grasses. She dared not stretch her aching muscles or turn to look over her shoulder.

She didn't know how long she could she sit here, undiscovered, but hoped they would decide they'd lost her and move on. She doubted she could creep away while they remained behind, searching for her. Dismayed at sensing movement behind her, a chill dimpled her flesh.

With a sudden jerk she found herself launched upward and exposed to the weak morning light. Huge hands gripped her arms and shook her until her teeth rattled. Broad Shoulder's angry red face was inches from her own.

"You bitch!" he snarled. "Westlake. Over here."

## CHAPTER 23

As she yelped in terror, Tim ran out of the trees a few yards away, zipping his pants. He wore a victor's smile as he approached and grabbed her by the shoulders.

"I don't know what you think you're doing, Roberta."

"Trying to stay alive," she said, shaking with fright.

"By running into the wilderness? We expected to find your carcass out here. I'm surprised you weren't killed by a bear."

"There's a lot that might surprise you." Roberta struggled to adopt a defiant attitude while her insides turned to jelly. She didn't know yet how to play this, how to stay alive.

She could tell Tim was thinking the same thing, how to work the situation to get what he wanted. Watching him consider his options, indecision flickering across his face, she tried to project a toughness she didn't feel.

To her shock, he embraced her. "What were you trying to do, running away like that? I thought I'd lost you."

He said it as though she'd fallen out of his pocket. Was he serious? Should she play along? Her focus sharpened and she sorted through the possibilities. Nothing good would happen if she willingly returned to the cabin and the grave dug in the clearing in the woods.

“Forget it, Tim. How dumb do you think I am?” Her humiliation overcame her fear.

“I don’t know what you mean,” he said, his facial expression one of calculated innocence.

“If you want to know where the urn is, and whatever is in it, ask Sasquatch here.” She jerked her head at Broad Shoulders.

The big man twitched, contorting his face with an ugly frown.

Tim blanched, looking startled. “Wha—what?”

She fixed him with a pointed stare. “This is the creep who threw me out the window and put me in the hospital. When I hit the ground, the urn was on the dresser in my room. When the police searched for clues afterward, the urn was gone.”

Tim looked at Broad Shoulders, his face sharp, his eyes wary.

“She’s crazy,” the other man said. “She’s got it. She’s trying to get us to go at each other.” He turned to Roberta with a sneer. “Bitch!”

It occurred to Roberta that it did her no good to convince Tim that his buddy had taken it. That would leave her in that hole in the clearing. She’d better rethink this.

She lifted her chin in defiance. “Troglodyte!”

Broad Shoulders grabbed her by the throat with one hand and squeezed. She managed a strangled cry, trying to breathe, as her eyes watered and her head pounded. She grappled with his hand with both of hers. Before she lost consciousness, he let go, dropping her to the ground. He kicked her in the stomach and grabbed her by the hair, pulling her head back. “You tell him where it is,” he shouted, spittle flying in her face.

“Okay! Okay! Please, stop.” She groaned with pain.

Tim put up a hand to ward off another blow. Broad Shoulders let go and her face hit the dirt. Roberta had to think fast or lose everything. The big guy wanted her, the only person who could implicate him, dead. Tim wanted her alive only as long as he thought she knew where the urn was. She had to return to Juneau where the police were looking for her, where she might have a chance.

"All right. I'll tell you where it is," she said, whimpering.

"Tell me now, Roberta." Tim grabbed the collar of her shirt and jerked her to her feet, balling his hand into a fist.

"I will," she pleaded. "I will. Please don't hit me."

"I'm listening," said Tim.

"I have to show you. I'm not sure I can describe where it is. Where I buried it."

"Why didn't you tell me before, Roberta? That you know where it is? That you had it?"

"It was illegal, what I did."

He frowned and searched her face for lies.

"I didn't want to spend the money for a plot and the burial, you know? So, I buried the urn myself in a lonely spot in Evergreen Cemetery. It would be hard to describe, to tell you how to get there, but I could take you. Only I know how to find it."

Tim hesitated, thinking. She hoped it sounded just stupid enough to be the truth. Roberta looked at Broad Shoulders. He knew she was lying. But he couldn't admit that to Tim without blowing his cover. He would be anxious and off-kilter for the duration of this ordeal, not knowing what she might say. She was counting on it.

Tim looked at her with suspicion. "So why didn't you tell me in the first place? When I told you what was in the urn and what was at stake?"

Roberta plucked up her nerve. "Well," she hesitated, "then our association would have been over. You'd have the urn and I'd be on my way back to Indianapolis."

Tim snorted. "You thought you'd be going back with the jewels, you mean. You wanted them for yourself."

Roberta felt lucky. He bought her story, thinking she was as larcenous as he was.

"Do you have any idea how to fence jewels, Roberta?" He jeered at her.

She allowed him to believe anything he liked, as long as he bought the bit about buried treasure. He let her go and she limped pitifully before them on the way to the car. She tried not to hyperventilate, avoiding an image of her body lying in the forest, cooling to ambient temperature.

The three of them wound through the high grasses, slender trees, and across the narrow stream to the car parked in the middle of the dirt road. That revealed to Roberta no one ever traveled there, that the cabin and surrounding area were abandoned. She looked for any distinguishing signs to identify that specific place. There was nothing but the road itself.

They bound her hands with duct tape but did not blindfold her. That told her something else: they didn't expect her to survive to tell her story. They tossed her into the back seat and then slid in the front, Tim at the wheel. The car growled to a start and moved forward, bouncing in the ruts, going no faster than twenty. She saw her reflection in the rearview mirror. What a mess! A pale bruise darkened her left eye, fingerprints marked her neck, and her stringy hair and sun-burnt face were covered with a fine layer of dirt. Her T-shirt and jeans were filthy. And she smelled like fear.

She watched the digital clock on the dash. It took twelve minutes to reach the highway. This time Roberta committed everything to memory, if for no other reason than to recover Carrie's body. And she also realized it demonstrated faith in her survival. They turned right onto an unmarked two-lane blacktop. The first sign she saw about fifteen minutes later identified it as Basin Road with an arrow pointing to Juneau. One-hundred and ninety miles. Not so far. Not eight hours by any stretch. She'd slept on the way to the cabin and had no clear sense of the distance, and Tim no doubt wanted her to feel she was miles from anywhere. He had fooled her from the beginning.

Roberta watched the broad, grassy fields dotted with purple flowers slide past, framed by snow-covered mountains in the distance. Cumulonimbus clouds sailed through the blue sky, backlit by the morning sun. The rugged splendor did nothing to dispel her anguish.

Once she was able to calm her racing heart, she studied her captors. Despite his foray into the wild, Tim was still trim and neat in his black T-shirt and slim jeans. Regardless of his cherubic face, Broad Shoulders looked like an unmade bed and smelled like a sour washcloth. Both men seemed big and strong, even without their weapons.

Evil should manifest itself in some obvious physical trait. Then she might not have been so taken in by Tim with his dumb story about terrorists, so full of holes. Searching her room for bugs. What a crock! When he abandoned her in the woods with no way to get in touch, it should have tipped her off. And the spy in the police department, only an idiot would believe that. She gritted her teeth in disgust, marveling that she'd not seen the menace in Broad Shoulders when she spied him out there in the woods. She should have listened to her intuition. Something kept telling her the whole thing smelled.

Tim pulled into a gas station. Roberta listened to the ticking of the engine as he stepped out of the car. "Wait here," he said to his accomplice as he left them alone.

Roberta watched him as he headed toward the men's room. She hoped he was stricken with some malady. Diarrhea. Urinary incontinence. Syphilis. No, she rethought the latter. The pleasure she'd taken in their sexual escapades had dimmed in her memory given recent developments. None of it was real except for her humiliation. Anger swelled deep in her soul and gave her courage.

"You," she said. "What's your name?"

"Fuck you."

"We'd better make a plan, you and I."

"Yeah? Why so?"

"You have the jewels. I know it and you know it. You'd kill me, but you can't manage that without Tim being suspicious. When I get to the cemetery, there's nothing there. What are we going to do? We are, whether you like it or not, in this together."

He sat very still, thinking about it, as Tim approached and stuck his head in the window. "Benny, better take her in and let her get cleaned up." Then he popped open the gas cap and shoved the nozzle into the tank.

"Hey, Benny. My name's Roberta," she said as he came around to the back, cut the duct tape that bound her hands with a small but wickedly sharp knife, and pulled her out of the car. She read once that if you engage your kidnapper personally, tell him your story, tell about your family, he could see you as an individual, making it more likely you'd survive.

"Somehow, you're going to have to let me escape. There's no other way," Roberta said when they were out of earshot.

"Or I can make sure you die."

"There's that, but it's more difficult to explain."

"I push you off a cliff and tell him you jumped."

"Is that the way it is? So, why don't I convince Tim you're the guy right now? Why not? What's in it for me to protect you?" Then she understood something else. Benny had been the shooter in the cemetery.

She'd seen only shadows, heard low voices. But now that she'd met him, she knew. Everything made a bit more sense.

"You see, I got it all figured out." She spoke quickly, as they made their way to the restrooms across the broken concrete. "You were in the cemetery, right? You shot William. You guys decided to keep the loot for yourselves and followed me to the gravesite, expecting I would reveal the burial location. Once you knew who I was and William told you my mother's name, you had all the information necessary to recover the gems. So, you didn't need William anymore. You double-crossed him."

Sweat broke out on Benny's brow.

"When you couldn't find a record of the interment, you followed me around. What were you planning, to beat it out of me, what I'd done with the urn? When you broke into my room, it was there on the dresser, so you threw me out my window and took it."

He licked his lips.

"And there's Carrie. What did you do? Convince Tim that she and William had stolen it for themselves? Is that why she was so scared? Is that why you murdered her? So she couldn't talk?"

He swung her around to face him when they got to the ladies' room door, out of Tim's sight. "You shut the fuck up. You're not telling anybody a thing."

She followed his darting eyes, tiny slits like a pit bull's, under a sloping forehead and his incongruous mop of blond curls. He didn't know how to get out of this. That would be up to her.

"Listen, Benny—"

He jerked her onto her toes by her arm and growled in her face. "Get in there and clean up. Don't think about locking the door and making a racket. We'll blast it open." He gestured toward the gun under his jacket. He pushed her into the restroom.

Inside, the concrete block was painted a sickly green. Small, filthy, and windowless, it stank of pine disinfectant with notes of stale urine. After relieving herself, she turned the faucets on full blast. There was no hot water and no soap, but she ducked her head under and scrubbed at her face and scalp with her hands. Looking in the rectangle of wavy, polished metal that served as a mirror, she combed her hair with her fingers and at least felt cleaner. There was nothing to be done about the soiled clothing hanging limp on her increasingly slimmer frame. She lifted her shirt and touched the tender spot on her rib cage where a black and purple bruise the size and shape of a footprint had appeared.

She and Benny walked back to the car where Tim waited behind the wheel. This time they didn't bother to bind her wrists. She sat in the back with the child safety locks on, where she plotted an escape. In no time they would be in Juneau. The sun wouldn't set for hours. She could only imagine what they might do. Maybe they wouldn't wait until dark, as the cemetery was quite isolated. Or it could be busy. She'd lost track of whether this was a Sunday or a weekday. Though she'd become adept at determining the time by the sun, she'd lost all notion of the days of the week, a strictly man-made convention not linked to any natural occurrence. For a week she'd lived like a pioneer, then for three days like a Neanderthal.

If they bound her hands again, that would present a problem. She could try to strike a deal that would appear to ensure her cooperation. If she asked for a cut of the loot, and they agreed, they might assume she'd be a willing participant. They'd be in this together. Of course, they'd kill her anyway, regardless of their promises.

She stared at Benny. He was lost in thought, as though it were unfamiliar territory. He was probably the first in his family without a tail.

Roberta turned her attention to Tim. Could he really kill her in cold blood? She tried to imagine she meant something to him after all they'd experienced together. She had been an adoring lover, following after him with the big-eyed devotion of a golden retriever. He'd taught her things, soothed and supported her, seeming more like a father figure except for the sex part. She willed him to do some soul-searching in the hope he'd find he had one. At the same time, she knew it was hopeless. He'd been using her the whole time.

Her eyes shifted to Benny again. She prayed he was staying on task, trying to figure a way out of this for both of them.

Don't let your tiny mind wander, Benny. It might get lost.

Roberta felt tremors in her legs. She calmed her quivering insides by remembering Martha's patient, sensible response to all adversity: take it a step at a time, do the best you can, and a solution will often present itself. Everything happened for the best. Roberta tried to fit her particular circumstance into that equation. If she got herself killed, that wouldn't be good for anyone. For the first time since Tim and Benny wrestled her into the car, she thought of her children. Denial had kept her emotions in check. Now, with tears stinging her eyes, she wondered if she would ever see them again.

Tim slowed the car. They were on the outskirts of Juneau. Roberta felt enormous relief being in sight of other people and normal human activity. She'd felt lost and alone for a long time. Hope flowered in her breast.

"Want to get a bite, Benny?" asked Tim.

A Burger King loomed ahead on the corner. As Tim moved into the left lane and the turn signal blinked, Roberta's mouth watered. She hadn't eaten anything but weeds for three days.

Roberta wasn't sure she'd actually get to participate in the meal. They probably wouldn't feed a dead woman. This, more than anything, made her want to cry.

They went through the drive-through and ordered four burgers, fries and cokes. She was bereft of hope until Tim threw a sack in her lap and handed her a soda. She was overwhelmed with gratitude born of Stockholm Syndrome. He must still love her, after all.

She devoured the sandwich, allowing the grease to run through her fingers, and wiped ketchup from her mouth with the back of her hand. She ate as if it were her last meal. And for all she knew, it was.

They sat at the far end of the parking lot while they consumed their food. After he collected the trash, Tim got out of the car to toss it and then went to the men's room again.

"Benny?"

"I told you, shut the fuck up."

"We're in trouble. Both of us."

He didn't turn to look at her, only stared straight ahead.

"You know I have no clue where the urn is. What'll we do when I get to the cemetery? How long do I march around providing false leads before Tim catches on?"

"He won't believe you."

"No, he won't. And he'll bludgeon me until I tell him what I know. When I'm on the verge of death, he won't think me capable of lying. Then you'll be in the soup. I'll be forced to tell. I really don't want to tell, Benny."

He turned to face her. "It'll be me doing any dirty work. You won't be able to speak once I hit you."

She blanched.

"I know how to kill you with my fists. He'll be pissed," he smiled with a curl to his lip, "but what can you do? Shit happens."

So that was his plan. When Tim realized she'd snookered them, Benny would "accidentally" beat her to death. Roberta was on her own. Anguish constricted her throat and she struggled to take a deep breath, settling her stomach. She didn't want to toss up the only meal she'd had in days.

Tim sauntered across the blacktop toward the car. She could just tell him now about Benny. But if she did, then neither of them would have any reason to keep her alive. Her only choice was to wait for the opportunity to escape once they entered the cemetery.

They drove around Juneau until dusk. Cars, pedestrians, and storefronts blurred by Roberta's window as she focused on where she was and what she might do to save her life. She hadn't a clue. When they pulled, creeping, past the graveyard, she realized they'd been waiting until it closed for the evening. Although the wrought iron gates stood wide open, a sign indicated that Evergreen Cemetery was open from nine to six on weekdays, nine to nine on weekends. She assumed it was a weekend day, and that Tim hoped to minimize the possibility of encountering visitors inside by waiting until after hours.

"Better not leave the car near the entrance," said Tim, as he turned into the nearest side street and parked. His eyes met Roberta's in the rearview mirror. "Don't want anyone to become curious about someone being in there this late."

Benny opened the back door and dragged her out without a word. He didn't give her a chance to assist but plopped her on her feet on the graveled roadside. She looked about the empty street and darkened homes. Tim opened the trunk and retrieved a short-handled shovel.

Nausea rolled through her at the sight of it. They quick-stepped toward the cemetery entrance and ducked inside.

She stood between Tim and Benny in the cool shade of a large pine. Death stood in her shadow, rattling his dry bones. A surge of adrenaline kicked her emotions into high gear. Goosebumps danced down her arms while cold grew heavy in her chest.

Tim pulled back his jacket to expose his gun. "Okay, Roberta. You're on."

She shivered from head to toe and turned toward the three paths that led into the interior of the graveyard. "Let me think. I took the right-hand path. I'm pretty sure." She started toward it.

"Don't try to be funny," said Tim.

Roberta glanced at Benny. "Nothing about this is funny except for maybe Bozo here. But it's been God knows how long, and I'm half-starved and fully terrified. If I'm having trouble remembering, it's nobody's fault but yours."

Tim got an ugly look on his face as she picked up the pace. They stayed close behind her, Benny carrying the shovel. Panicked, she looked in every direction. She had to get out of this cage. She was in desperate need of a plan to save herself. Trapped and hopeless, she felt like she was locked in a room and asked to spin straw into gold.

Darkness fell gradually, leaving a purple haze. Deep shadows loomed among the gravestones. The large monuments, topped with angels or crosses, threw menacing shapes in the gloom.

"I buried it on top of a freshly dug grave," Roberta said, making it up as she went along. "I only had a trowel. It's not like I could enter a graveyard in broad daylight with an urn and a shovel." She thought this sounded quite believable.

Roberta walked with purpose along the path she'd taken weeks ago, right before Benny chased William down and shot him. She passed the tree where she'd cowered in the groundcover. The orange marker placed by the police was still there. Her insides felt like they might drop out.

"It's someplace off to the left here." Roberta pointed. "It was a new grave, like I said. It shouldn't be hard to find. I'm confused, not sure where I am."

"You'd better get sure," said Tim. "You try anything, you're in trouble."

Roberta was certain she was in trouble whether she tricked them or not. She felt perspiration prickling her armpits. She licked her dry lips and tasted bitterness in the back of her throat. She glanced at Benny, whose face was a blank. He looked tense, probably wondering what was next. His stake in the outcome of this little adventure was as big as hers.

"It's somewhere over here," she said, taking a route perpendicular to the path and down a row of more recently erected headstones. She stood a better chance of finding a freshly dug grave in a newer section of the cemetery.

She walked on, farther into the graveyard, searching for an escape. She was terrified that her only exit might actually be in a grave of her own. She remained aware of the shovel in Benny's hand and the gun at Tim's waist.

"You'd better be finding that grave, Roberta," Tim muttered with menace.

"It's here, I swear. It looks so different now. It's been too long. I vowed never to forget the name on the stone where I buried Mother, but I have. I'd remember if I could just think a moment, had some time."

"You don't have time, Roberta," Tim said.

She whirled on Tim and Benny. "Maybe you'd like to tell me just what I do have." She spat the words at them. "What's my incentive to find it? I'm a dead woman the moment you have that urn."

Tim slapped her across the face, almost knocking her off her feet. "It's the difference between having your skull bashed in or a swift bullet to the temple, my dear."

Roberta fought to regain her balance, shook off the blow, and kept moving. The sun was gone now and she wove through the pale, moonlit night, the men following like evil, ugly ducklings. She found her way forward blocked by an almost invisible wire fence sagging across their path, weed-choked and rusted. On the other side, the earth fell away into a steep slope covered in tall grass. Her spirits lifted.

"Now I remember. It's not far from this fence. I think it's up this way." She led them to the right along the fence and up a slight incline. Tim searched the ground while Benny kept close to her, no doubt looking for an opportunity to shut her up for good. She eyed the slope beyond the fencing for a likely place to jump. As if conjured by a fairy godmother, a grave covered with baskets of faded flowers appeared ahead.

"There it is!" she cried with compelling confidence, pointing. "That's it!"

Both men dropped their guard and swung around toward the grave. At the same moment, Roberta dove over the fence and dropped several feet, her fall broken by brush and thick grasses. She tucked her head and knees and rolled downward.

Shouts and scrambling erupted behind her. "Shit!" Tim said, and she heard thrashing sounds that meant they were coming after her. She rolled faster.

Benny grunted. Tim swore again, but his angry voice was now more distant.

Roberta kept rolling, rocks and bushes bumping and scraping her arms and back, a bruising fall that seemed to go on and on. It was one thing to fall off a cliff and roll downward like a log, it was another to try to stay on your feet in pursuit. She had the advantage. Maybe they would just let her go, believing the new grave held what they wanted. Or Tim would dig, and Benny would come after her. Benny would insist upon pursuit, knowing she could expose him. He'd think it was safer to catch and kill her rather than let her get away.

Roberta didn't ponder the more positive options or allow them to prevent her from running as though her life depended on it. She came to a sudden stop against a large tree, which she hit feet first with some force. Hearing their voices behind her, she popped upright and ran, she hoped, toward the road they drove in on. She was disoriented but chose a direction, operating on pure adrenaline, fear stinging her into vaulting over rocks and fallen tree trunks. She ran along the edge of a grove of trees, knowing she could get lost in them, not wanting to be pursued again in the wilderness. She had to find the road.

She gasped for breath. Her muscles burned. She focused on getting to some populated place instead of whether Benny or Tim—or both—were close behind. She reasoned they wouldn't shoot her. Gunfire would invite attention they could ill afford, and they couldn't kill her before they were sure they had the urn.

The rugged terrain suddenly leveled, and she saw lights ahead. Encouraged, she redoubled her efforts although a pain in her side threatened to cripple her. She pushed herself forward toward a small city street.

The first car whizzed by, speeding up as she waved her arms practically standing in the middle of the pavement. The second vehicle, a wheezing, rattling truck, stopped.

She wrenched open the passenger door and threw herself inside. “Go! Go! Take me to the police. I’ve been kidnapped!”

The truck ground forward even as the driver gaped at her, his eyes wide. “You okay, ma’am? You need a doctor?” Wearing a ball cap and a soccer jersey, he looked like a high school student.

As the truck sped away, Roberta closed her eyes and collapsed against the seat. She struggled for air while grasping her aching sides. Only when the fear drained away could she feel her bruised and bleeding body.

# CHAPTER 24

Roberta ended up in the hospital once more. The bustle at the police station and the swift ambulance ride were a surreal blur. She'd been sedated but not knocked out while they taped her bruised ribs, stitched up a gash on her arm, and x-rayed her limbs. Despite that, exhaustion, malnutrition, and relief seduced her into a dreamless sleep.

The sun lit her room like an operating theatre when Roberta came to, vaguely aware of bandages, an IV, and Brad sitting beside her.

As she opened a sliver of an eye and blinked against the glare, Brad jolted out of an exhausted stupor and stood over her.

"Roberta?"

"Wha—" She had difficulty moving her lips.

"Are you okay? Are you in pain?"

She groaned at the stiffness in her body while gathering up her strength to stand. "I have to pee."

Brad helped her swing her legs over the side of the bed and struggle upright. She took several tentative steps, then shook him off. "I'm okay," she said, as she dragged her IV stand into the bathroom and closed the door.

As she washed her hands, the toilet making a whooshing racket as it flushed, she stared at herself in the mirror. She didn't recognize the slim, bruised face that blinked back at her. She needed a shower and a week at a spa. It occurred to her she might actually get a week in a hospital bed.

When she opened the door, Brad was waiting anxiously on the other side to help her back into bed. His hair was too short, like his pants, which always showed a bit too much sock. He looked drawn and tired and was obviously stressed. She guessed the anger would come later.

Brad searched her face. “You look terrible.”

*Is that all you have to say?*

“Thanks,” she said. “Good to know the romance isn’t dead.”

“I didn’t mean it that way. You’re all beat up.”

“That I am.” She settled against her pillows, her limbs heavy.

“Do you need something? What can I do?”

*Too little too late.*

She motioned to the pitcher beside her bed. “Get me some water.”

As Brad poured, he watched her out of the corner of his eye, wary, as if she might burst into flame.

“What’s going on, Roberta?” he asked after a long silence.

“I wish I knew.”

“I don’t understand any of this.”

*Great. He’s going to whine.* “That makes two of us.”

“You can’t possibly mean you don’t know what is happening or why.”

“Nevertheless.” She glared at him in the bright light.

His jaw flexed with exasperation, or maybe bitterness. “You came to Alaska of your own free will, didn’t you? You took your mom’s ashes, drove to the airport, and boarded a plane.”

“I did indeed.”

“And you have no explanation?”

“None you would understand.”

Roberta felt power surge through her. She didn't have to explain anything to him or to anyone else.

"Okay. I assume some day you'll include me in your plans."

"I'll send you an engraved invitation."

He shook his head. "Roberta, I know I don't get what's going on, but I *am* trying."

"You certainly are." She suppressed the urge to bite him.

Contempt wasn't typically part of her arsenal, but it felt right in the moment. They sat and stared at one another as if across a great divide. She had no idea what might come next. He shifted away from her, an agonizingly familiar gesture.

"I called and called. You didn't answer my messages."

"I was busy making changes in my life. I didn't call back because you're one of them."

He sighed. "You're not being fair, Roberta. Can't we discuss this?"

"I'd like to see things from your point of view, but I can't seem to get my head that far up your butt."

Brad looked shocked. "I'm attempting to be reasonable here."

"Reason has nothing to do with it," she said. "And I don't have any easy answers. If I did, I'm not sure I'd bother sharing them with you."

The longer he talked, the angrier she got. *It's a good thing I don't own a gun.*

Brad stood in silence for a few seconds before his shoulders sagged and he turned to look out the window. He sighed once more, this time with resignation. When he turned to her again, he looked like a sorority girl without a date to homecoming.

"I've taken the time to fly all the way to Alaska, cancelled my classes for the week, and undone my schedule, so the least you can do is talk to me." When she didn't answer, he mentioned the lawyer she'd hired to keep her out of protective custody, who was apparently out of town; complained about the food in the hospital cafeteria; and expressed his desire to be at an important Promotion and Tenure meeting sometime next week, so they should wrap things up here, if you don't mind.

She felt the weight of twenty years of pent-up rage. "Is that all that concerns you, your precious meeting? What about me and what I've been through?" she said, fighting back tears.

"About that, Roberta." He looked at her like she was an unfamiliar bug. "There's a police officer guarding your door. What have you gotten yourself into?"

"I haven't gotten myself into anything. I've been kidnapped, assaulted, and generally inconvenienced by some asshole thugs that nobody seems to be concerned about." She collapsed against her pillows in disgust. "What about these bruises on my face and neck? Do you think I've been to a garden party?"

Seconds passed as she frowned at him. This was her husband. He should feel some sense of outrage.

"Doesn't it bother you? That your wife has been brutalized?" Disbelief spread through her like a slow poison as the silence lengthened. Perhaps the heady Alaskan air worked like a magic potion and had changed her from a Midwestern housewife into something wicked.

"Chief Craven said you were lost in the wilderness, living rough."

"You don't believe me."

"Of course, I do. But…"

"I'm your wife." Roberta was incredulous. "What have they been telling you? Despite what they think, you'd believe these male yahoos rather than the mother of your children?" She wanted to pummel him with her fists but laughed hysterically instead, folding her arms tight across her bruised ribs. Brad backed away, his face turning red.

"You really think I'm a smuggler? For Christ's sake, a murderer? Is that how you see me after all these years? You haven't defended me, assured them of who I am? What are you thinking, that I've gone bad like a lost potato under the kitchen sink?"

"Of course, I've defended you!"

"Then why is a cop standing outside the door, huh? I bet he's not here to protect me but to protect the world *from* me." As she spoke, she knew something else. Chief Craven and his minions weren't likely to spend any time trying to discover the truth. They'd already made up their minds, and her injuries didn't suggest anything to them but a woman who'd been lost in the woods. She was alone in this thing. And they wanted to pin a murder on her. A week in the hospital might turn into a lengthy stint in jail. That grim prospect deafened her to anything but her own anxiety chattering inside her head.

Brad kept talking. He indicated several women's magazines he'd picked up for her. He moved a vase of daisies closer to the bed. Maybe he mentioned Laura and Bradley Jr., or even Tinkerbelle. It's possible he waxed poetic about the adverse repercussions of bad tenure decisions. She wasn't sure because she'd stopped paying attention. His stream of boring babble threatened to become a flood, and Roberta had the despairing sense that Brad had sprung a leak and, until the plumber came, there was nothing to be done about it. That person arrived in the form of a Patient Assistant who rattled in with machines and computers on a pole tangled with wires.

"Hi. I'm Courtney, your PA. I'm here for your vitals."

She chatted a bit, smiling, oblivious to the tension thickening the atmosphere while taking Roberta's temperature, pulse, and blood pressure.

After Courtney left, silence filled the room. Brad was no doubt sorting things in his head, rearranging the facts, looking at the new patterns.

When he reached for her hand, she moved it beyond his touch. “Roberta,” he said, his tone apologetic.

“Just go, Brad, please. Can’t you tell I don’t want you here?”

He hesitated a moment, thinking something over. “Chief Craven wanted to talk to you as soon as you were awake.”

“I bet he does.”

“I’m to let them know.” He looked like a dog who’d just peed on the carpet. He moved toward the door and stepped out of the room.

*Really? That’s it?* Roberta was reminded of why she’d left home. Or one of the many, many reasons. *Where are the kids? I could be dying here. He should fight with me like he cares!* A cerebral man, always excessively polite and attentive to decorum, was so annoying at times like these. How did she end up with a husband who ate his pizza with a knife and fork and color-coded his socks?

There was a flurry of activity outside her door. Several minutes passed before a nurse entered.

“How’re we doing today, honey?” She was cheerful and efficient, getting another pillow and blanket for her. “Are you in any pain?”

“No. Where’s my husband?”

“He’s been here all night. You didn’t see him?”

Roberta declined to answer, as the nurse seemed to be distracted. When she exited, Roberta caught a glimpse of Brad in conversation with the cop stationed outside her room.

*Traitor.*

Before the door closed, Chief Craven, looking starched and polished, stepped through it. “Well, Roberta.”

Uh-oh. Fears confirmed. She blinked at him, waiting.

"That was a stupid thing for you to do."

"What was? What did I do?"

"Run away like that. Better to stay here, face the music, rather than flee. Where exactly did you think you could go? There's nothing but wilderness out there."

She stared, mouth agape, and cried, "I didn't flee! I was kidnapped!"

"Kidnapped." He repeated the word, but it wasn't a question. His face was a blank, his voice skeptical.

"Yes! Taken against my will." By now she was able to declare this as if it were true.

"You got any evidence of that, Roberta?"

"Are you always so dense or are you making a special effort?"

"Then enlighten me, if you would."

She spilled the whole story: Carrie in the café, Tim Westlake and his search for stolen jewels, the dirt road to the cabin, Benny with the big shoulders, the grave dug for her in the clearing in the woods, the return to Juneau, and the harrowing escape from Evergreen Cemetery. She conveniently glossed over how she got to the cabin in the first place and her relationship with Tim, which shed a different kind of light on everything.

He stood, impassive, his hand on the stiff bedside chair, his eyes hidden behind dark aviator glasses. Given his attitude, she might have been developing a case for a separate universe existing in the drinking water. At one point she wondered if he was still listening.

"So that's it?" He stared at her while she blinked in the sunlight.

She felt like she was being interrogated in a small cell under bright, menacing lights. Her ribs ached. It was difficult to take a comfortable breath. "Isn't that enough?"

"Like I said, you got any proof?"

*Not all men are annoying. Some are dead.*

Suddenly, Roberta remembered. "I made a 911 call. Didn't you get it? I had Tim's cell phone, and I finally got a signal. They must have called you. It should be recorded."

"Yeah, we got that, Roberta. Sounded like someone frantic, lost in the woods, cold and hungry, nowhere to go. You see, Roberta, we figured that's what a person in your position might say, to explain things. Know what I mean?"

She thought for a panicky moment before saying, "The phone. Where did the phone come from? It isn't mine. They must have the number, right? Can't they trace it?" Then she remembered the number was blocked.

But she detected a glimmer of a question in his face. Ha! She had him. He hadn't thought of that. "And I can find the cabin I was held in with your help. Where did the canned goods come from? How did I get there? You haven't found any record of my renting a car, have you?" She pushed on, her mind skipping around like a needle on a scratched record. "And there's a fresh grave in the clearing. I can take you there."

"So, there's another body?"

Roberta saw him tense. Now he was hooked.

She hesitated only a moment. "I don't know that for a fact, but something is buried there. I found Carrie's silver earring. And there's a second grave dug, too, but it's empty because it was meant for me. Why would I do that? Wouldn't that prove what I've been saying?"

"Well, Roberta, you make some good points. We can certainly check out that cabin, especially if, as you say, we need to recover another murder victim."

"Why, thank you, Chief Craven. That certainly takes a load off my mind." She made no effort to keep the sarcasm out of her voice. "And I appreciate the security at my door. My kidnappers are likely trying to find me to make sure I can't implicate them."

Craven did not correct her rationale for the armed cop in the hallway, that he was to keep others out rather than her in. He smiled, no doubt trying to put her off guard.

"Okay, Roberta. We'll check out your story. Mr. Blankenship is unable to provide any information about plausible criminal activity."

*Brad? Give me a break. That Quisling.*

"And what criminal activity would that be, Chief Craven? Just what am I supposed to be involved in?"

"Smuggling drugs. Cancer on our society. Especially when you see that ordinary, middle-class folks like yourself get caught up in it. It's a shame, really."

"It's also absurd," Roberta said. She was startled to hear his surmise about drugs. Perhaps he was right, and the jewels Tim talked about was just another lie. "Chief, my kidnappers said my mother's urn was used to smuggle jewels. Drugs were never mentioned."

At this, Craven peered at her and seemed to be piecing together parts of a complicated puzzle. "When exactly did you meet William and his companion?"

"At the airport the day I flew into Juneau. July 30."

He pulled out his phone and swiftly typed something into it, obviously looking something up. "Jewels, you say?"

"That's what I was told," she said.

"That would be an interesting connection, Roberta."

"What? What would be an interesting connection?"

Craven rubbed at his jaw while staring at her, thinking, no doubt wondering if she was an unwitting victim or part of a smuggling ring. "There was a major heist in Seattle, a really big snatch. Much of the loot has been recovered, but a lot of it is being found piecemeal, kind of here and there, in Alaska. We were wondering how they got the stuff out of the lower forty-eight. Could be—"

"My mother's urn was probably used to ferry stolen goods across the border. Doesn't it make sense?"

"I don't really know, now do I?"

"Doesn't it stand to reason that they would target someone like me? Can't you see I'm an innocent bystander?"

"Or maybe you're part of a gang of thieves, Roberta. Drugs or jewels, Roberta, it's a shame."

"The real shame is when the police don't protect and serve the taxpayers who pay their salary." She felt her face heat with anger.

"More reason you should help us, Roberta. Tell us the truth. You are wasting time and money."

She narrowed her eyes and snorted. "The cabin, Chief Craven. Look for that cabin."

* * *

That afternoon, a police sketch artist and an officer with a large map of Juneau and the surrounding vicinity had set up shop in her hospital room. She did what she could to describe Tim and Benny after going through several books of mug shots without success. She might just as well have been looking at the Glamour magazine Brad had so thoughtfully purchased for her. Tim knew so much about the area, she felt in her gut that he had a long history in the state of Alaska. But she had no reason to believe Benny was local. After all, she herself had no prior connection. She revealed every nugget of information she possessed.

"All I know is we returned to Juneau on Basin Road," she told them. "As we rolled into town, the sun was going down on my left over the mountains."

"Up in that area, there's a web of old logging roads," said a young officer. "You remember anything to identify the one you were on?"

"Trees and more trees," said Roberta. "I did pay attention to the time it took us to get back here. It was about three hours once we left the dirt road for the highway."

"That certainly narrows it down," the officer drew a circle on the map in red. After taking her statement, they packed up their mug shots and maps and left her alone with Brad.

They had no more to say to one another than teenagers on their first date.

"How're the kids?"

"Fine," he said. "They're concerned about you."

*There's a first.*

"What are you doing here, Roberta?" A dejected sigh ricocheted around the room. "What's happening?"

He sounded so forlorn, she let go of her combativeness for the moment. "Honestly, I don't know, Brad. I couldn't be cooped up at home anymore is all."

"Why?"

"Just...nothing. What's there for me?"

"Might I be so bold as to say your family?"

"Yeah. And where does that get me? I'm ignored, put upon, and taken for granted."

"I work really hard." Brad started whining. "I do everything I can to support you and the kids. I bring my paycheck home."

His words jump-started her anger. "That's the oddest apology I've ever heard," she snapped.

He blinked at her.

"I've just had enough." She glared at him. "Enough of you, the kids, of Indianapolis. Of doing the same thing over and over, going nowhere." The image she conjured was not a merry-go-round, but a rocking chair, one of constant, rhythmic movement remaining in place.

"There's more to life between the wedding chapel and the rest home than," she waved her hand in a way that encompassed everything, "what I get." A sudden picture of her aged self sitting alone on a single bed, tracking the days with a pill box, startled her.

"I give you all I can."

"That isn't what I mean. It isn't about money, or stuff, or anything like that."

"So, then what?"

"I'm sick of myself. Sick of what I do, what I know, who I am. Sick of my life. My whole friggin' life!"

"Then we'll change things. When you come home…"

*I've got to get out of this cage before I gnaw off a limb.*

"I don't plan on going home."

Brad looked as though she'd slapped him. He stared at her, seeming to take a long step back in his head. Again, she watched him reorder his thoughts and calculate the new possibilities.

"I'll stay here or go to California or Wyoming or Florida. Anywhere but the Midwest. For all I know, I'm going to jail, and from my perspective even that is better than Indiana."

"But, Roberta…"

"I want to sleep," she said, closing her eyes. "Get out."

Brad hesitated, shuffling from foot to foot.

"I mean it." Her voice rose to a high pitch. She picked up the Glamour magazine, which served only to remind her how inadequate she was in feminine desirability, and threw it at him. He flinched, deflecting it with a raised arm, and it flopped at his feet like a wounded pigeon. He left on the run, followed by a loud snick of the door latch.

She collapsed into her pillow, wincing in pain. She shouldn't be surprised. He was as estranged from her as she was from him. How else could she have had sex with a stranger and feel no sense of remorse? Tim, the son-of-a-bitch. That bastard! Her dignity was pierced by his duplicity as she recalled in vivid detail the scene in the clearing in the woods.

*...I fucked her instead...the stupid cow's in love...*

*...she's a fucking romantic...*

This, more than the beating he'd allowed Benny to give her, more than the disdain with which he treated her after hunting her down like an animal, angered Roberta. A wave of outrage bubbled up in her throat. Contempt for him was like that of an aging queen who'd been scorned for her beautiful step-daughter. A murderous surge of energy and resolve throbbed in her head. She would cut his heart out.

Roberta narrowed her eyes and balled her fists. She had no intention of being charged with Tim's crimes while he got away. She was not about to wait for the police to figure it out. They had their culprit, as far as they were concerned. Even now, as they went through their lackluster search for clues, they did it with no urgency or sense of real curiosity. She was the only one who cared enough to get at the truth. Finding that cabin, and Carrie's grave, was the only way to be exonerated.

She slid out of bed and, wheeling her IV with her, cracked open the hallway door. The armed uniformed officer had his back to her.

*How can I get past him?*

She opened the cabinet to search for her clothing. She found nothing but her dirty running shoes. She'd never be able to escape the premises in her hospital gown. Maybe she could find some discarded scrubs. Tying her robe around her, she opened the door and went through with her IV stand as though it were perfectly natural.

The officer turned toward her. "Um, ma'am? You can't leave your room."

She laid it on thick, limping and leaning on her pole. "Oh, please. It's so claustrophobic in there. If I can get some fresh air down in the lounge, I'd feel so much better."

He stood in her way. His name badge said "Corporal Pike."

"I beg you, Lieutenant Pike," she said, promoting him. "Only down the hall? I'm going stir crazy. You can watch me walk down and back. Please?"

"I was told to keep you in your room."

Roberta hung her head and looked up at him with the most pitiful damsel-in-distress expression she could muster. "Just for a moment?" If she were the witch everyone thought she was, she ought to be able to cast a simple spell.

He glanced down the broad hallway with its polished floors and blinked. "I guess it would be okay, if I walk with you."

*Swell.* How was she to find a pair of wayward scrubs with him tagging along? "You're a prince, really," Roberta said limping forward, the cop trailing behind.

As she made her way toward the other end of the floor, she glanced left and right, committing the layout to memory. Exit stairs at the end. Elevators in the center near the nurses' station. Public restroom, unisex. Staff room, requiring the swiping of an identification card. Another broad door with a sign: Staff Only.

She faltered, leaning heavily on the railing along the wall.

"I think I'm going to be sick." The cop took her elbow, casting a nervous glance toward her room.

"Let me stop in here a minute." She pushed against the Staff Only door and made her way inside, the cop standing a mere three feet away.

Her eyes at once lit upon two large plastic tubs, each with a white lid. She ignored the one marked 'Trash' and looked inside the other indicating 'Laundry.'

*Yes!*

She stared at a pile of balled up scrubs in white, turquoise, and navy blue. She dug into the depths of the container, ignoring thoughts of MERSA, C-diff, and other infectious diseases. She doubted Alaskan medical centers were yet dealing with Ebola, dengue fever, or hantavirus. Undaunted, she rummaged to the bottom and came up with a pair of pants and a shirt, both the dark blue worn by respiratory therapists and other techs, marked 'S' for small. She quickly pulled the pants over her hospital socks and rolled the legs above her knees. She folded the top flat and tucked it inside her robe. She glanced in the mirror to see that nothing showed, and then opened the tap on the sink to splash water upon her face.

Roberta opened the door, her hand pressed against her forehead, and leaned against the nervous cop. She said, "I'm too weak. Please take me back." They shuffled to her room only a few yards away.

Alone once more, Roberta planned her escape. Hiding the stolen scrubs on top of the tall cabinet across from the bed, she took off her bandages and showered as well as possible given she was tethered to an IV. While soaping up, she gingerly avoided her injuries and took stock. Nothing too serious, a few stitches, the bruised ribs, which were the worst, painful and debilitating. Afterwards, she rewrapped the elastic bandages as well as she could.

Snapping together her gown and popping into bed again, she waited for the night shift to come at eight. She knew her stay in the hospital would be short, and she'd probably find her battered body decorating a jail cell soon enough. She couldn't let that happen.

"How are we feeling tonight, Mrs. Blankenship? I'm Becky, your PA tonight."

"I want to sleep, please," she said.

"The nurse will be here to take your vitals, get you a sleeping pill, and we'll be out of here." She aimed a laser beam at her wristband and fiddled with the IV. Another young woman brought ice water, retrieved another thin blanket from a drawer, and asked, "You need another pillow?"

"Yes, thank you," Roberta said with a smile. She was the very essence of docile cooperation.

When the nurse arrived, she handed over a white paper cup containing a pill.

"I'm not sure I need that. I'm exhausted."

"Take it," she said, using the tone of a drill sergeant. She looked like a cross between a prize fighter and a Mack truck.

Roberta tossed it in her mouth but put it under her tongue as she took a sip of water. As soon as they left the room, Roberta spit the pill into the trash can. Before she could decide on the timing for her exit, the door slid open with a whisper and a shadow approached.

*Brad. Uh-oh.*

She pretended to sleep.

Now what? He probably expected to sit by her bed all night. She considered including him in her plans and dismissed the thought immediately. He'd be no help. He'd already made buddies with the police and, goody-goody that he was, would not condone her actions, let alone participate in them.

*I need to get rid of him.*

Roberta blinked as though coming out of a healthy sleep. "Brad, what are you doing here?"

"Keeping you company."

"But I just want to sleep. You should get some rest." She assumed he had taken a room somewhere.

"I need to be here." He looked forlorn.

*Crap. This is a hairy nightmare with gum stuck to it.*

"But it won't do for both of us to be exhausted. You should go."

He pulled up a chair like he planned to stay for the long haul. "Don't you want to hear about the kids?"

*Not really*. "You've talked to them?"

"Of course, but I haven't told them anything. I mean, I didn't want them to worry and after all, what could I say?"

*What an ass*. "Apparently, the only thing you can think of is 'Your mom's a murderer.' Tell them the cops have me, no worries."

"Roberta."

"And why shouldn't they worry? I almost died, not that you care."

"I do care. Of course, I do," he said, not managing any sincerity.

"Then why do I feel you're not really on my side?"

"I *am* on your side…"

"Brad, I reiterate! I've been a victim of thieves and murderers! And now falsely accused of God knows what. Why aren't you indignant? Why aren't you challenging them, telling them they're wrong about me?"

"Chief Craven seems to be a reasonable guy…"

"No, no. That's not it. Why aren't you raving mad, defending me?" Her nails dug into her palms.

"It'll all come right eventually. We have to let them play through."

*Jesus Christ, golf metaphors*. "You must be dreaming! Do you think they have the wits to find their own dicks?"

"Hey, what's going on in here?" It was Mack Truck, who seemed to grasp the situation pretty well, standing in the doorway. "We can hear you at the nurses' station."

"Oh," Brad said. "Sorry."

She trained her glaring high beams on him. "You shouldn't be riling her up. I just gave her a sedative."

He said, "It's that she…"

"You need to leave," she insisted, standing like a fortress with hands on her hips. "There'll be plenty of time to harass her in the morning. Right now, she needs to rest."

Brad jumped like he faced a nun with a gun and sprinted toward the door. He turned to say something, but the nurse barked, "Leave now. Do this later."

Tears sprang to Roberta's eyes. She was awash in gratitude. Mack Truck turned to her and in a soothing voice said, "You rest now, hon. Don't think about husbands and other idiots tonight."

Undone by the act of pure sympathy she'd been thirsting for, Roberta said, "Thank you. If I hadn't already gone through that phase in college, I'd kiss you."

The nurse grinned then turned all the lights out and breezed through the door, her white uniform like a sail.

Roberta counted to ten before she tore at the tape that anchored the IV and removed the port from her wrist. Stanching the spurt of blood with her gown and a bit of pressure, she hobbled into the bathroom to dress in the stolen scrubs and her tennis shoes, fearing at any moment the door would open and admit whoever kept the hospital humming all night long. Roberta moved quickly, having thought it all through. She put on the shower cap the hospital had provided, pulling it down to her eyebrows, and yanked on a pair of latex gloves from the dispenser beside the sink. She rummaged in the trash to find a paper facemask. Turning it inside out and pulling it over her nose and mouth, she suppressed a shiver of disgust.

Opening the hallway door a crack, she peeked outside. The cop was standing a few feet away with his back to her again, looking at his smart phone. Down the hall to her right, a gaggle of medical personnel dressed in hospital garb meandered toward her end of the floor. As they passed her door, she squared her shoulders and angled out to join them, walking with purpose, her head held high. She didn't look back to see if Officer Pike had seen her or registered anything amiss. When she reached the shadows at the end of the floor, she knew no one was watching with anything like suspicion. She stood for a moment, reviewing her options.

Taking the hall to her left, she fled down the stairway to the floor below. Every step jarred her painful ribs, so rather than going down several stories using the stairs, she pushed through the door on the next landing and made her way to the elevators near the nurses' station. Her pulse raced as she watched the digital numbers count down. Every second might bring disaster. It was possible she had only moments before her absence was discovered. The door slid open and she joined a young couple, the girl visibly pregnant.

Fifth floor. A white-coated doctor stepped inside and turned his back to her. Roberta bit her lips and swallowed to dislodge the lump of anxiety in her throat.

Fourth floor. Two hospital workers in turquoise uniforms joined them. Precious seconds ticked by as the doors slid shut. Roberta stripped off the gloves and wiped her sweaty palms on her thighs as she huddled behind her companions.

First floor. The elevator bounced to a stop and the door shuddered open. Chief Craven, his face impassive, stood on the other side.

# CHAPTER 25

Roberta nearly stopped breathing. As everyone stepped out, she followed close behind the two scrub-clad employees, her head down, her bruised face still covered by the shower cap and surgical mask.

Please, Lord, don't let him see me.

She dared not glance back as she sped toward the double doors to the parking lot, any thought of the pain in her side secondary to the panic in her breast. She had to put as much distance between herself and the hospital as possible. Within a minute or two, Craven would discover her absence, the on-duty cop would get a tongue-lashing, and there would be an APB out for her across the city.

*Where am I?*

Roberta broke into a kind of hopping trot to favor her painful ribs, angling toward the street. Once on the sidewalk, she realized her get-up would attract attention rather than disguise her now that she'd left the hospital grounds. She pulled off the plastic cap and paper mask, balled them inside the gloves and tossed them in the gutter. In addition to regular clothes to avoid attention, Roberta needed money and, first and foremost, she needed a car. She had to get to her room before the cops had a lookout posted every place she'd ever been. Making it to downtown Juneau, and soon, was essential.

Noticing an old sedan creeping in her direction, she stepped into the street and waved. Once more, she commandeered an unsuspecting driver to aid her. She was reminded of Blanche DuBois, always depending upon the kindness of strangers. With cars.

She asked the elderly man behind the wheel to drop her near Bullwinkle's Café. Chatty and obliging, he was delighted to help a frantic woman whose car wouldn't start get home to her children before the babysitter turned into a pumpkin. Roberta was now a few quick steps from her room. The big question was whether there was a cop already there keeping an eye out for her. Craven could have mobilized his forces already, but she had to take the chance that he had not.

Approaching the building from the south, she kept to the shadows. Moonlight spilled through the trees, flooding the roadway and storefronts in a pale glow. Except for the cars passing on the cross street ahead, she saw no activity. No one lingered on the sidewalk, and no patrol car idled out front. In case they were cleverer than that, she took every precaution.

Roberta sidled up to the building and crept through the darkness to the rear. She tried the back door, but it was locked, as she'd assumed. The mechanism was a deadbolt requiring a key to open from the outside, but inside, you merely had to flip the lever from right to left. She picked up a stone about the size of her fist and tapped it on the small glass pane nearest the lock. After several tentative efforts, each successively harder, she managed to shatter it, the splintering of glass echoing through the night. Startled, she stepped into the shadow of a scraggly pine. When no response was forthcoming, she leaped to the door, put her hand through the broken window and unlocked it. She slid inside and plastered herself against the wall for several seconds, listening for unfamiliar sounds. Everything was silent. She tiptoed up the creaking stairs and hesitated at her door. She didn't have her key. It would be in her purse, which she'd left at the diner when she fled from Juneau with Tim.

*Now what?*

She could go to the diner. In fact, she must, to get the small sum of money she had. After all, she was going to find that cabin and get to Tim. But something else occurred to her. Benny had opened her door through brute strength. She did a quick calculation, his height and weight, versus hers. She put her fingers against her bandaged ribs.

*Maybe not.*

Still, Roberta pressed her shoulder, pushing as hard as possible given her injuries, against the door and turned the knob. To her amazement, it popped open under modest pressure.

For a moment she stood in the center of the room, dazed. She shouldn't have been surprised that the lock was compromised after Benny's break-in. Lucky for her it was. A light from outside swam across the dark walls and she stepped to the window to peek around the sash. A police cruiser slid to a stop at the curb. Alarm swept through her.

She grabbed a pair of jeans, T-shirt, and a long-sleeved blouse from a hook on the back of the door. As she closed it behind her, she saw shadows looming in the vestibule below. Seeing no way to get down the stairs and out the back, she scurried to the bathroom at the end of the hall instead. Stepping into the tub to huddle behind the shower curtain, she hugged her clothing close to her body and held her breath.

"It's quiet," said a man with a rumbling baritone, sounding bored. Careless footsteps clomped up the stairs.

As far as she could tell, there was only one cop. He must be talking on his phone.

*Knock, knock, knock*. How thoughtful he was to rap his knuckles on the door. She heard the handle rattle and the hinges squeak as he opened it.

"Nobody here. Wasn't even locked. No sign anyone's been around. Nothing." He wandered about, his muffled voice droning on although she couldn't make out the words. Sounds of shuffling. He was opening drawers, the closet, looking for clues, evidence of her presence. Silence followed. He must be listening to instructions. He might be talking to Craven himself.

The cop's footsteps approached the corridor, where he seemed to stop outside her door. She heard a sudden snap, and a beam of light hit the curtain. She froze, fear sizzling in her veins. The cone of light crawled down the hallway and bounced to the right and the left, up and around, probing the corners of the bathroom. Roberta heard boots on the stairs.

"It'd be stupid to come here if you ask me. They ought to focus on the airport. He'll have us checking the cruise ships for stowaways if he thinks of it." No, not Craven, apparently. The front door banged shut with a rattle of glass. She was relieved he hadn't thought to check the back one with its broken window.

Roberta slumped on the side of the bathtub, waiting for the jolt of adrenaline that had pierced her body to calm. As a vein in her temple throbbed, she tried to focus all her senses. She needed to get out of there. Someone else who lived on her floor could arrive at any moment. It was best that no one saw her.

Roberta yanked off her scrubs and pulled on her jeans, T-shirt, and long-sleeved blouse. She was grateful the latter was dark green with a lime pin stripe, good for hiding in shadows behind buildings and in back alleys. She wadded up the discarded items and shoved them under the ancient claw-foot tub.

She sneaked into her room again, crept to the window, and looked at the patrol car sitting at the curb. The headlights lit up the street in front. She'd leave through the back the way she'd come. Roberta glanced at the clock. It was a quarter after ten. Fantasy would be closing up the diner.

# CHAPTER 26

She kept to the back of the buildings until she came to the cross street, and then sauntered across with a few tourists who were drunkenly weaving their way from the tavern on the corner. Once she reached the far side, she disengaged her shadow from theirs and sped down the alley to the diner. From behind the dumpster, she saw Fantasy put ketchup bottles into the fridge and gather the salt and pepper shakers. Peeking around the side of the building, she spied no police vehicles. She did see, however, a lone customer sitting at the counter, apparently loath to leave Fantasy's orbit. Roberta waited. Feeling another presence, she looked behind her to see Snarfblatt, staring at her with his inscrutable yellow eyes.

"Hi, buddy," she said, bending down to scratch his battered head.

He moved just beyond her reach before lumbering with a stiff elephantine gait across the alley. Cats understood cruelty, but not affection.

It wasn't long before the screen door squealed and closed with a bang as Fantasy lugged out the trash.

"Fantasy," Roberta hissed from the shadows. "Fantasy!"

Stepping backward with a strangled gasp, Fantasy dropped the garbage bag with a heavy clunk.

"It's me. Roberta." She leaned forward into the light from the back window.

"Crap! You scared the bejeesus out of me!"

"I'm sorry. Really. I didn't mean to frighten you."

"What are you doing back here?"

If Fantasy was asking an existential question, Roberta was clueless. She said instead, "Not to put too fine a point on it, I'm hiding from the cops."

"The cops?"

"Have they been here? Asking about me?"

Fantasy hesitated, which told Roberta all she needed to know.

"I didn't do it, Fantasy. I've been framed."

"For that guy's murder?"

"That and smuggling, terrorism, and probably obstruction of justice or evading the law, something like that." Roberta grabbed the girl's hand. "You have to help me. I'm the only one who can clear myself. Nobody believes me."

"Gee, Roberta," Fantasy stuttered, "I—I don't know." She glanced nervously toward the street.

"Look, I won't get you in any trouble, I promise. I'm in desperate need of some wheels and my purse. I left it here, remember?"

"Sure. Donna put it in the kitchen. We didn't think to give it to the police, and they didn't think to ask. It's yours. Of course, you can have it." She looked over her shoulder and motioned for Roberta to come inside, where they stood in the dark pantry behind the kitchen.

Roberta checked to see that the restaurant was empty before she spoke. "When's the last time they were here, the cops?"

Fantasy relaxed. "That cute one stopped about twenty minutes ago. Told us if we saw you to call and let them know. He said you escaped from the hospital?" She reached behind her to the hooks where they hung the aprons, lifted Roberta's purse, and gave it to her.

Roberta rummaged among the contents. "It was that or be thrown in jail." She quickly counted her cash. It amounted to about seventy dollars and some loose change. She shoved the bills in her pocket.

"Fantasy, you've got to loan me your car."

Fantasy balked at the suggestion, her eyes wide. Roberta didn't blame her. Aiding and abetting was a serious crime. "Look, you can stay clear of this. Just loan me the car and then call and report it stolen tomorrow. It would be understandable that I would take your car. They can't blame you."

"I don't know…"

"I'll give you this," Roberta fished the broken bracelet from the bottom of her purse, a gift from Brad on their tenth anniversary. "The clasp is busted, but the coin shop that buys scrap gold will give you two hundred dollars at least." She had no qualms about discarding this piece of jewelry, as it wasn't the only thing broken and not worth keeping.

Fantasy's misgivings wobbled as she held the heavy chain in her hand. "I don't like to take your things."

"Come on, Fantasy. It's yours." Roberta folded Fantasy's fingers over it. "I'm not a criminal. I've been caught up in something having nothing to do with me. I'm being targeted unfairly. And you could use the money."

"Okay, I guess." Fantasy stuck her hand in her front pocket and reluctantly produced her car keys.

"It'll be fine, honey, swear to God." Roberta held the wad of jangling metal and plastic in her hand. "You need me to take off the house key?"

"No, better not. That'd be suspicious. I keep one hidden in the garage." She smiled. "I can tell the cops I was drunk and left them dangling from my door. Serves me right."

"You're a true friend, Fantasy." Roberta gave her a hug, grateful for her deliciously inventive mind. "Can I drop you at home?"

"No, don't bother. It's a nice night for a walk. It's only about five minutes."

Roberta figured it was best that Fantasy not be seen with her. "Trust me. Nothing bad will come of this."

* * *

Roberta slid into the driver's seat of Fantasy's ancient blue Honda Civic and pulled down the alley. The car had half a tank of gas, but she thought she'd better fill it. She wasn't sure how far the cabin really was or how easy it would be to find. She could think of nowhere else to start but there if she was to track Tim down. And if the cops managed to follow her, she could show them where she'd been held captive and lead them to Carrie's body to corroborate her story.

Tim and Benny might've hung around long enough to dig up the fresh grave she'd led them to at Evergreen, but they would have fled by now. Although she doubted they would return to the cabin, given that's the first place she directed the authorities, she might be able to find clues regarding their whereabouts. It was pointless hanging around in Juneau, either in jail or out on bail, waiting for the incompetent cops to decide she was guilty.

She pumped gas and bought bottled water, praying that the cops hadn't been by with her picture. She purchased a two-pound bag of salted peanuts and a Butterfinger, one to keep up her strength, the other her morale. She'd have bought additional supplies if she'd had more money or dared use her credit card. Only after Roberta had taken off in the

Honda again did she regret not buying a flashlight or, better yet, a small knife. Once on her way, she'd felt the need for some kind of weapon even though she blanched at the thought of going mano a mano with Tim or Benny. She shivered.

In the darkest part of the night, she reached Basin Road. Since the Honda's odometer didn't work, she tracked her mileage using the dashboard clock. At the 7-Eleven at the intersection of Basin and Gastineau Avenue, she recorded the time. She would maintain a steady sixty miles per hour. If she accurately recalled that harrowing return to Juneau, the first sign she saw shortly after entering the highway from the dirt road leading to the cabin indicated 190 miles to Juneau. Once she'd driven that distance, she would start looking for the road to her left. She steadied her nerves by relaxing her shoulders and setting her jaw.

As she drove, she doubted herself. She'd been terrified when caught, driven back to town a captive, battered and starving, her life in jeopardy. Would memory deceive her? Her mother's steady voice drifted into her head.

"Always do your best, dear, and things will work out."

*Really, Mom?* She wondered if William's or Carrie's mother had told them the same thing.

With the windows down and the cool night air lashing at her, Roberta flew across the even pavement, encountering no one coming toward her, no one behind. Her headlights illuminated the deserted highway, bouncing through the vegetation crowding the shoulder and catching the glowing eyes of small animals hidden in the long grasses. The shadowed foliage that blanketed the terrain, smooth and unbroken, disappeared into mountains rising black against a moonlit sky.

Deep in the Alaskan wilderness, she studied her surroundings looking for anything familiar, shifting her focus from the distant hills to the dark wall of rock on her left. Her mind was riveted on every detail. Her eyes on the road, she entered a kind of trance. The white lines induced a kind of fever as the asphalt sped beneath her. Visions appeared: Tim's bare shoulders. Benny's fists. The inukshuk on the edge of the gully. Time ticked by as she gripped the wheel.

Roberta jerked herself out of her reverie and looked at the clock. She'd been driving for a bit more than two hours, about 120 miles. After only another hour, she'd have to pay close attention to the web of intersecting dirt roads that led into the interior of Alaska's wilderness.

Perceiving a flutter deep in her gut, something inside tightened and began to grow. What was she doing out here in no-man's land in the middle of the night? She passed several small dirt lanes on her left. To the right the road dropped into a shallow ditch, and low-growing vegetation rolled to the mountains in the distance. Not a recognizable tree, stone, or distinguishing topographical feature broke up the vast space. Only the rocky fortress of the mountains rising to hem her in, unchanging and vaguely menacing, appeared familiar.

In another few miles, she encountered the sign she'd seen on her return to Juneau with Tim and Benny and felt a frisson of excitement. She stopped her car and looked in the rearview mirror. Juneau, 190 miles. Now she knew the road to the cabin was near, but doubt bubbled up. From this direction, everything looked different. The view had altered, with the rolling prairie over her right shoulder. She passed the first dirt road. Too early. They had driven for a few minutes before encountering the telltale road sign. For how long, she wasn't sure. She wished she had a better sense of the distance or the time it took to get there.

Roberta slowed and searched the darkness. Maybe she should wait for dawn. She couldn't see much beyond the ghostly pale dirt lanes that disappeared into the hills on her left.

After another twelve miles, Roberta stopped at a road around a curve. She backed up a few feet and angled the car to shine the headlights on it. It had a distinguishing characteristic that all the others did not: tire marks in the dust. She scrutinized the surrounding trees and low-growing brush. Yes, this had to be it.

*I'm here at last. Now what?*

The cabin was at least five miles from the highway along the rutted track. She didn't want to walk the entire way or to drive right up to the cabin big as you please. She had to stash the car somewhere nearby and go the final distance on foot. She turned in and after three miles or so, crept along searching the areas on both sides for a likely spot to hide the Civic. To her right she spied a break in the trees and nosed into a mostly flat space, rolling over bushes and narrow saplings.

It was black as pitch. Roberta shifted her gaze about the trees and scrub, dark against a darker sky. Emotionally keyed up for the last few hours, she now embraced a deep exhaustion. Rather than go fumbling about in the dark getting lost, she decided to rest. Tilting the car seat backward, she tried to get comfortable and closed her eyes.

She startled awake when it was still dark, feeling achy and damp. Birds had begun their morning song while she worked the kinks out of her limbs.

Dawn was breaking as Roberta scavenged small leafy branches to hide the car from the road. When the sun peeked above the horizon, she grabbed her purse and set off through the trees toward the cabin. She felt foolish tramping through the wilderness carrying her large, mint-green summer bag, but she needed the water bottles and the stash of food. God only knew how long she'd be out here or what she might find.

Roberta walked almost two miles before the cabin loomed ahead in the pale morning light. Keeping to the trees across the road, she inched as close to the shack as she could without a chance of being seen. She sat behind a slim mountain hemlock and stared through its draping boughs. The cabin had a dejected look. If someone were there, she thought they'd be up and about by now, lighting the lantern, firing up the stove, opening a window. It was beginning to warm up. Roberta peeled off her shirt and used it to cushion her rear.

She felt like a spy, a hunter-tracker, or a predator. She felt powerful and capable, driven by an intensity of purpose and righteous indignation. By putting one foot in front of the other, she would do what was necessary to absolve herself of guilt or blame despite the lack of confidence projected by her diffident husband and the lazy devices of the local police. She rejected any thoughts of how this might look to Chief Craven, who no doubt would see her return to the cabin as proof of her guilt. She had to trust that Carrie's body and other evidence would support her story. Besides, she had nowhere else to go.

Her stomach rumbled. Roberta rummaged for the Butterfinger and tore at the wrapping. She was only halfway through it when she decided she must be crazy. Tim and Benny were long gone by now. They wouldn't be there, the first place the cops would look if she'd been able to persuade them of her innocence.

Still, something in the cabin might offer clues to where they'd gone. Hanging her bag on her shoulder, Roberta wound through the trees the way she'd come. Out of sight of the cabin, she sped across the road and into the trees on the opposite side. She angled toward the outhouse and surveyed the surrounding trees. No sign of anyone or anything. She listened. Nothing. Running across the rocky terrain to the shack, she looked into the only window in the back. Everything was still and bare. The musty old quilt was lying across the arm of the rocking chair where she'd left it. She slid across the porch and inside the cabin, peeking out the front window. There was no one out there watching. She listened for noise from upstairs.

She looked about the room, her pulse racing. The floor and furniture were furred with dust. Several cans of soup and an empty saltine box occupied the shelves above the sink. The wildflowers she'd placed on the mantle days ago were shriveled into a tangle of black, lit by a single shaft of light from the front window. The woven grass barrette she'd made the first day of her seclusion in the wilderness was lying under the table. She retrieved it, caught her hair up, and fixed the piece at the crown of her head with the pin.

Was that a creak from upstairs? She stifled a squeal and shrank into a corner.

*No. It's nothing.*

Roberta pressed a palm against her thumping chest and tried to moisten her dry mouth. Then she tiptoed upstairs to assure herself that no one lingered in the shadows waiting to grab her. The door to the first room squeaked as she opened it. Only the metal cot with the dirty ticking mattress and a small, decrepit table anchored the room. The second room was equally bare. Then she noticed both sleeping bags were gone.

*So, they've been here.*

Roberta stood in the shadows and stared out the bedroom window. Now she knew they were out there somewhere. Waiting. They had to be. They hadn't yet found what they wanted. She surveyed the forest for a glint of those binoculars. She didn't feel safe in the cabin, but she would have to wait until dark to leave.

* * *

The lonely hours passed. The sun climbed high, and then sank slowly behind the trees, a brilliant sunset backlighting the cabin and the stand of firs around it. When hunger gnawed at Roberta's spine, she dared not light the stove. She dived into the peanuts, filling the cabin with their scent. Washing salt from her fingers, she spied the small folding knife beside the sink and tucked it into her back pocket.

Once darkness fell, Roberta took the old quilt and entered the woods across the road, intending to bed down below the sheltering boughs some distance from the road, hidden from sight in all directions. She had no clear expectations. Maybe Tim and Benny would show up, or maybe it would be the cops. If not, there was nowhere to go, nothing to do about her predicament. She felt not only lost, but as if she'd made a poor decision by coming here.

She folded the quilt double and lay upon it, trying to keep from thinking about what would happen to her if no one believed the truth. She'd end up in jail. Stranger things had happened. She felt the air come in waves, ribbons of warmth and cold. She smelled dew and heard the cacophony of night creatures tuning up in the dark. The heavens seemed like a huge bowl, embracing her, protecting her. She felt herself hurtling through space, spinning and tilting to the dictates of some ancient and impenetrable law. She felt rather than heard the echoes of distant times and lost peoples.

Roberta sat up, suddenly alert. She felt a prickling of her skin. Someone was nearby. She closed her eyes and lifted her nose to the shifting air. Fire. She smelled smoke. Roberta got to her feet under the fir tree, hunkered down as if ready to flee, and watched the shadowy landscape for any movement.

*Where? How far?*

She strained all her senses, hearing only the insects, feeling nothing but the falling dew. The silent trees, dark and forbidding, failed to reveal any secrets. The scent of burning wood on the air alone announced danger.

Roberta eased on her dark shirt once more. She slid her feet into her tennis shoes and cleaned up the scattered litter—two empty water bottles, the crumpled candy wrapper, the rest of the peanuts—stuffing everything into her purse. She rolled up the quilt and tucked it under a bush. She felt for the small knife in her back pocket.

The green bag. It almost glowed in the dark. She crept to the first line of trees along the dirt road and hung it on the highest branch she could reach. She took several seconds to locate a few stones to form a tiny inukshuk at its base so she could retrieve her purse afterward.

After what? she thought. Roberta hesitated. If she followed the scent deep into the woods, she'd need a way to get back. She retrieved her bag and dug the peanuts out before leaving it behind.

Roberta wound her way through the trees across the pine-needle covered ground, leaving a trail of legumes as she went. Instincts led her eastward, away from the cabin. She looked ahead, her eyes and ears alert to danger. She kept to the trees and the shadows. Her feet made no sound.

Drawn like a bird of prey to a kill, she felt a heightened consciousness, an almost supernatural awareness. Weaving through the trees, around bushes, boulders, and rivulets of trickling water, she lost the scent of fire time after time, then picked it up for a split second, just enough to guide her onward. Roberta looked backward at her trail. The peanuts glowed in the moonlight but would be noticeable only to someone really looking for them. She drove forward, ducking under hanging boughs and vaulting over fallen logs.

Then she heard voices. They drifted on the heavy air, mingling with the currents. Crouching, hidden by darkness and the dense underbrush, Roberta made her way toward them. She stopped and squatted on all fours behind an outcropping of rock.

Tim and Benny sat on folding camp chairs in front of a two-person camouflage tent, heating a small pot on a campfire ringed by stones. They both slumped low in their chairs, bundled in down jackets against the cool evening. They spoke to one another, their baritone voices rolling like drumbeats toward her. She was unable to distinguish words.

*Now what?*

She'd found them but wasn't sure what to do. And why were they here? Of course, this is the place they knew, the place that was familiar. And they were unlikely to go elsewhere as long as the jewels were still out there and they thought they had a chance of retrieving them. But she knew they would avoid the cabin. She also imagined one of them always looking out, using the binoculars, to be warned if the authorities showed up.

She watched. The night deepened. Against the black forest, the orange campfire glowed and illuminated the two huddled figures. They drank coffee and ate something out of cellophane bags.

Suddenly, Tim stood, his lean, rangy frame silhouetted against the dancing fire. Roberta shrank against a boulder as he moved about, rearranging things and dousing the flames, sparks swimming through the air like fireflies. Childhood tales of the fantastic came to mind, of gnomes, trolls, dwarves, and Rumpelstiltskin. Gremlins and goblins inhabited her head as she watched the dark figures shift against the dying yellow light. As they readied for bed, Roberta felt the weight of her own exhaustion.

She put those thoughts to rest. With grim determination, she decided to do the only thing she could. Roberta had to return to Juneau and tell Chief Craven where they were. She would help them find these thieves and murderers and prove her innocence.

With any luck, they'd still be here when she returned. It would take half a day to get to Juneau and back, if she could even persuade the cops to come. She was awash in frustration, angry at the powerful men who seemed to thwart her at every turn.

Roberta closed her eyes to think. The car. Of course, they had to have stashed a car nearby, then accessed the campsite on foot. They must have hidden it along the road, just as she had secreted the Civic. She felt an encouraging spark of hope. Find the car. She'd disable it somehow and make sure they couldn't get far. When the police came, they could trace the car to its owner. It would provide additional proof of her story.

Crouching low, she followed the trail of peanuts through the darkened forest. Several times she lost her way, turning the wrong direction, tripping over logs or rocks she hadn't encountered before. But she backtracked to pick up the trail once more and sped toward the cabin and the dirt road. It seemed to take hours in the dark, but at last she came upon the narrow lane in front of the shack.

She hadn't seen any sign of their car on the way there, so she turned left and kept going uphill, past the cabin toward the clearing in the woods. Although her discovery of the unmarked grave had been days ago, fear shook her as she thought about what Tim and Benny had planned for her. As she threaded her way up the incline through the trees next to the road, she imagined a narrow, dark hole, smelling earthen and damp, dug next to Carrie. Roberta contemplated the very real possibility that the ground might swallow her up and she'd never be seen again.

Something gleaming in the moonlight caught her attention, reminding her of Carrie's silver earring. But this time it was a chrome bumper hidden in the trees well off the side of the dusty track. Roberta waded into the weeds and pulled aside several strategically placed branches. She circled a dark grey older-model Buick: Benny's car.

*Bingo.*

She tried the door, but it was locked. Swell. No way to raise the hood. She stared at the ground for a moment, then thought of her knife and had the bright idea of flattening the tires. Opening the blade, she tried to sink it between the treads on the left front one. Impossible. She tried a stabbing motion. The blade bounced back without making a mark. This was harder than she'd imagined.

*Okay, nothing.*

Roberta returned the knife to her back pocket and repositioned the barrette which had loosened from her upswept curls.

She decided that getting under the hood was her best bet. She searched the ground for a large rock, and with some effort, she dug one out of the hard soil, breaking her nails and skinning her knuckles. The small stone was heavy and difficult to handle, but she hoisted it above her head and heaved it. Although aimed at the driver's side window, it hit the door panel instead. The blow reverberated through the night air, startling Roberta with its thunder. Alarm shot through her. They might hear. But maybe it wouldn't occur to Tim and Benny that their getaway car was under assault. She couldn't worry about that now. She had to finish what she'd started and get out of there. The fourth blow shattered the glass, and Roberta reached through it to unlock the door, a heartening minor victory.

Grappling under the dash to release the hood, she struggled even more with the catch to lift it up. Roberta stared at the engine, battery, and radiator not knowing what to do. She wasn't sure what exactly would prevent the car from running. She pulled at the wires connecting what she thought was the carburetor, trying to disengage them, but without success. She tried in vain to pry the caps off the battery cells, bruising her fingers. Eventually she yanked at the fan belt and managed after some effort to saw through it with the small knife. She imagined it couldn't run, even for a while, without a fan belt. Or, maybe it was the alternator belt. She wasn't sure. Roberta finally decided to leave the driver's door cocked open, letting the dome light drain the battery. She hoped it didn't shine like a beacon through the forest, warning her foes of danger.

This was all taking too long. The hair rose on the back of her neck. Someone was coming. Tim could be making his way through the trees toward the car as she labored. Panic tasted like vomit rising in her mouth. She needed to get as far from the car as possible. She swung around, searching the dark shadows surrounding her. She felt it. She knew something wicked was near and getting closer.

*Run, run, run.*

She darted into the trees again, crouching low, moving toward the cabin. Staying near the road, she threaded a path alongside it until she spied the haphazard inukshuk pointing the way to her purse hanging from a branch. She retrieved it and slung it over her shoulder on her way to the blue Honda.

*Now, to get the cops.*

She became bolder as she neared the car. Her nerves buzzed with excitement at the thought of returning to the police station in Juneau. She waded through waist-high weeds toward the vehicle hidden in the brush, but as her hand reached for the door handle, she felt herself fly through the air and hit the ground. Terror bubbled up as the air was knocked out of her. Her bruised ribs burned with excruciating pain. Someone grappled with her arms and hands as she heard a whoop of triumph.

Jerked to her feet, she came face to face with Cute Cop and, unfortunately, Officer Pike. Terror was replaced by gratitude.

*Thank God! The cavalry has arrived.*

"You won't believe this," Cute Cop said into a two-way radio attached to his shoulder.

The speaker crackled with indistinguishable words.

"We got her. Out on one of those old logging roads. The stolen car was hidden in the high grass."

Roberta snorted in dismay, her relief replaced by annoyance. "Listen. You have to help me," she said, gasping for air. "They're back in the woods, hiding out."

She realized her wrists were bound behind her with plastic zip-tie handcuffs. Pike was holding on to her upper arm, being unnecessarily rough. He no doubt got a shellacking for losing her at the hospital, and this was payback.

The radio crackled again, but this time she recognized Craven's voice.

"Get back here pronto. Her…jewels…urn."

Roberta struggled against her restraints. "Listen to me. You have to hear me out. The bad guys are camping in the woods. You have to get them. They've settled in for the night, but they might be gone by morning. I can lead you to them." But neither cop responded. She was slammed against the car and Pike frisked her from shoulders to ankles.

"Put a cork in it, lady."

"Listen," she pleaded. "Listen to me, please."

"You have some fairy tale to tell us?" said Cute Cop.

"No, no. You have to believe me. I'm innocent. The murderers and thieves you want are camped in the forest. They're not thirty minutes from here on foot." As she said it, Roberta hoped she could find their campsite again. It had gotten even darker once she'd found the road. But the cops had flashlights. They'd be able to pick up the trail of peanuts.

"Grab that purse," said Pike. "Let's see what's in it."

They had their back to her as Roberta realized the quick pat down had failed to discover the knife. It was still floating in the bottom of the back pocket of her now baggy jeans.

"There's nothing here," said Cute Cop, clearly disappointed in the contents of her mint green bag.

What are they looking for? Roberta wondered.

"They're not on her, that's for sure."

It was the jewels, of course. Somehow, she had to convince them that Tim and Benny were nearby and that they were the real criminals. She had to get the cops into the woods rather than take her back to Juneau where she would have a tough time explaining herself.

"If it's those jewels you're searching for, I know where they are," she said.

Both cops turned toward her and searched her face. "Yeah?" said Pike. "We were thinking maybe you did."

*Okay, Roberta.*

She reached deep within herself.

*Now, you have to be Scheherazade.*

She had to make something up, tell a tall tale to stay in play. "Yes. I'm the only one who can help you. They're back that way, hidden far into the forest."

"And we should believe you because?"

"Why else would I be out here?" said Roberta. "It's not for my health. It's not remotely in the direction of Indianapolis."

The cops looked at one another, uneasy about accompanying her anywhere. Clearly, neither had the authority to think outside the box, or in this case, a jail cell. They'd been told to take her in. Taking the initiative was not in their tool kit.

"Call Craven," Pike said.

The intercom crackled again. "Damn," said Cute Cop. "Reception is crap out here."

"Hello? Hello? Ten-forty. It's Pike again. Let me speak to Craven."

Buzz. Snap. A distant, unintelligible voice floated on the night air.

While both cops stared at the communication system as if willing it to be cooperative, Roberta slid her manacled right hand into her back pocket until she had the pocketknife.

"Hello? JPD? It's Pike. I need to talk to Craven."

The communication system hummed, cracked, and snapped.

With both hands tied behind her, Roberta could easily open the blade and free herself. But then what? Running once again through the wilderness had no appeal. Unless she could lead them to Tim and Benny's camp. But they wouldn't confess to anything, and these cops had already had her pegged as the criminal. She could imagine Tim, with his smooth banter, talking his way out of any difficulties she could throw his way.

She could take them to the cabin, but that didn't make much sense, either. It wouldn't prove anything except she'd stayed there. Roberta was tired. She would, instead, lead them to the clearing in the woods, to Carrie. Opening her grave would expose more questions and get Craven out here. She closed the blade on the knife and tucked it into her pocket once more.

"Come on, guys. What harm will it do? You've got me. Why not take me back with the jewels? You can be heroes."

She saw this particularly appealed to Pike, who no doubt needed to recover his honor with the higher-ups. They stared at her and then looked at each other. Cute Cop, with the air of a man who was born on third base and thought he'd hit a triple, said, "We don't need to be heroes." He had no reason to exert himself. He hesitated, thinking for a long moment.

"But if you've got the stuff, no reason not to take you and the proof back with you."

Good. She had them.

"You're right. Why make another trip? And coming back here is the last thing I ever want to do," Roberta said. The discovery of the body would ramp up the investigation, lead to Tim and Benny, and hopefully, to her exoneration. That was the most positive face she could put on it. She pushed from her mind more likely scenarios, one of which was the cops believing she had killed Carrie, too.

Cute Cop and Pike led Roberta toward the road. With her wrists bound, she was awkward. She stumbled a couple of times and stepped in a hole, but Cute Cop held her by the arm and steadied her toward their cruiser, which was obscured by dark shadows. She felt the heft of the knife bounce against her right buttock and was reassured that she had options. It seemed like old times when they pushed her into the back seat. She was downright tired of being manhandled by cops and criminals alike.

She couldn't believe she was here again. Was it that blasted karma thing? She must have done something awful in a former life to deserve this. Had she killed Lincoln? Ordered the hit on Pearl Harbor?

"It's about two miles," said Roberta, "to the cabin. All the proof you need is buried in a clearing in the trees behind it."

The police car inched forward on the dusty, rutted road, the headlights bouncing through the trees and across the track, illuminating the way. Their beams finally came to rest on the decrepit shack as they pulled into the front yard. The lights snapped off and they were plunged into a world in tones of grey.

The three of them exited and stood for a moment. The building looked dilapidated and forlorn, its shingled roof sagging, just as it had when she'd first arrived. Hopefully, Tim and Benny were still just a short distance away, hiding in the forest. Or maybe they'd been warned by the headlights and were long gone. She could smell their dormant fire, the cold ash and lingering smoke. She thought about taking the cops in that direction, following her virtual breadcrumbs, smooth legumes glowing in the pale moonlight. Instead, she fixed her eyes on the trees behind the privy.

Something wasn't right. No good would come of this nighttime foray into the woods. Perhaps Tim and Benny were waiting for them. Something was. Roberta's chest tightened, and she took shallow breaths to minimize the pain in her bruised ribs.

Each cop took an elbow and led her toward the cabin steps. Panic flickered somewhere inside her. The small structure didn't hold any charm or promise of adventure. All she felt was menace.

*By the pricking of my thumbs, something wicked this way comes.*

"Okay. Where're we going?" said Pike.

Roberta squeezed her eyes shut and tamped down nausea. She'd come this far. She shouldn't be afraid. Not now. "We need to go around back, into the woods behind the outhouse."

They skirted the cabin to climb the incline leading to the clearing. The pebbly ground was unnaturally bright in the moonlight, and the trees ahead were a solid block of shadow. As the three of them made their way around the gully, small stones dislodged and dribbled down the sides of the narrow fissure in the earth.

*Is that a whisper?*

Roberta controlled a shiver of anxiety as they approached the forest.

*Someone's here.*

Why was she so frightened? She was with cops, and they had guns. Nothing in the trees could harm her.

*Perhaps Carrie's ghost haunts the clearing.*

A wave of anxiety clutched at her. Perhaps the idea of digging there to prove her innocence was a bad idea. More likely, facing the real possibility she'd be blamed for Carrie's death made her queasy. Or maybe Carrie wouldn't take kindly to being disturbed.

Roberta and the cops plunged forward, she in the lead. Cute Cop flicked on a flashlight to illuminate a narrow path through the darkness. Roberta moistened her mouth and licked her dry lips. Horror thrummed in her veins, making her knees weak, her legs like water. She stopped. It felt like an invisible but impenetrable wall, as palpable as a thorny thicket, barred their path.

"Which way?" asked Pike.

"Let me think," said Roberta. "I need to get my bearings."

*If you go into the woods today...*

The spirits of this place watched. A thousand eyes bore into her back and upon her manacled hands. Roberta trembled, fearing the ground would heave and quake at being defiled. Their presence was a violation.

*If you go into the woods today, you'll get a big surprise...*

Roberta threaded a path through the ancient firs. She ducked under low boughs and angled past large boulders that stood like sentinels. The cops lumbered behind her, weighted by their utility belts and a sedentary lifestyle. Then there it was: the clearing.

She stopped abruptly.

"Is this it?" asked Cute Cop.

Roberta's feet felt rooted to the ground. She was sure Hades himself would split the earth and carry her like the mythical Persephone to the underworld, where she would live a kind of half-life. She had entered some perilous realm.

*If you go into the woods today, you won't believe your eyes...*

"No," she whispered, staring at the mound of debris on the edge of the treeless plot. "We must not…"

Then a flash of fire seared her eyes and a loud boom cracked, shattering the silence. Cute Cop spun backward and hit the ground. *Gunfire! Christ, this is where I came in!*

"What the hell…" yelled Pike, pushing her to his left as they dove into the brush.

Another shot thundered nearby. Pike clambered toward his partner, but Roberta panicked and tried to run. Awkward with her hands tethered behind her and disoriented in the darkness, she stumbled into the clearing and fell, rolling herself into a ball on the ground. Someone grabbed her by the shoulder and yanked her to her feet. Then an arm came round her neck and she was dragged, her feet scrambling to find purchase, into the trees.

"Keep your mouth shut," Tim rasped through gritted teeth. He put a gun to her temple. The cold metal felt like a hot iron. Overwhelmed by terror, she no longer felt the pain in her ribs.

He tightened the grip on her throat, and she fought for air. Roberta closed her eyes and struggled against him.

His breath was hot and labored next to her ear. She heard Pike moving in the trees across the clearing. Or it could be Benny. He was probably out there in the dark.

Tim dragged her into the old growth. She felt the forest crawling with creatures, alive and panting, their eyes shining, and their gaping mouths full of sharp teeth. Furtive movements, sounds of shifting through leaves and brush, came from all directions.

For a moment, everything stopped. The sky darkened, shadows gathered, and a great whooshing sound enveloped them. She could see nothing but felt as though some giant beast hovered overhead, buffeting them with the hot wind of its foul breath. Tim backed into a thicket of trees and loosened his grip. She breathed more easily and was able to angle her body forward, away from his. He jerked his head from side to side and up, searching the trees. Now he held the gun in front of her, whipping it left and right, following it with his eyes, ready to fire at anything that moved. She was certain he was as frightened and confused as she was, his senses overloaded. A great, deafening wind tore at their clothes.

Tim positioned her between him and the menacing dark. She didn't know if using her as a shield was a smart thing to do. She wasn't sure the cops wouldn't shoot her. If Roberta could make herself understood above the harrowing noise, she'd tell him that. But she did the only thing she could do. She inched her right hand into her back pocket for the knife. Opening the blade while Tim's attention was riveted upon the alarming sounds surrounding them, she pressed it against the plastic restraint binding her wrists. The blade wasn't sharp enough to make it easy. She pressed it again and again against the plastic ties, using a sawing motion, hoping Tim wouldn't notice. Given the awkward angle and her distress, she sliced her wrist with shallow cuts before the tether was loosened enough for her to wrench one hand, oiled by her own blood, free.

Wet fingers compromised her grip on the knife and it slipped from her grasp.

*No!*

Her heart sank as the knife hit the ground somewhere behind her.

Roberta felt her pulse pounding in her ears. Desperate, she sagged forward and down, trying to recover the knife, when Tim jerked her upward, tightening his arm around her neck once more.

The barrette she'd attached to her hair had loosened from her tumble of curls and rested against her forehead. The artistic bit of frippery held in place with a stick dangled before her eyes. The hair pin, six inches long and whittled to a point at one end, was front and center.

*Can I get it without Tim realizing?*

Darkness, earsplitting noise, and confusion distracted him. Tim glared beyond her into the trees and up in the air at the chopper that bore down on them. A blinding searchlight circled through the trees near their place of refuge. His mind was surely focused on how to stay alive, how to get away, how to use her to his advantage. Roberta, her movement deft and sure, reached with her right hand and drew the sharpened implement out of her hair.

Confidence flooded through her. She now had the advantage of surprise, of being lean and strong, and of having honed a prey animal's sensibilities. Having been hunted, she could run like a gazelle and dart like a rabbit. Her head whirred like clockworks. What should she do once caught in the jaws of a predator?

Slay the dragon. She had now entered a world of good and evil, where these were not abstract concepts. And no magic would save her unless she had the wit, heart, and courage to do what was necessary.

*Mirror, mirror on the wall,*

*Just who am I after all?*

With the hair pin grasped in her right fist, she conjured her anger, which erupted like a corpse in a shallow grave. With her other hand she grabbed the gun as she jabbed the stick over her left shoulder, blindly aiming for Tim's carotid artery. The sharpened implement plunged deep into his left eye instead.

Tim screamed. Roberta let go of the stick and struggled to hold onto Tim's gun with both hands. He squeezed off several wild rounds until a clicking sound signaled the bullets were spent.

Then the woods exploded. From every direction, a swarm of creatures descended upon them, and she and Tim were caught by the chopper spotlight like bugs under a microscope. Roberta and Tim were separated. She offered no resistance, giving herself up to the thunderous roar, blinding lights, and grappling hands. Voices shouted, men grunted with either effort or distress. Flashlights snapped on and bright beams raked the trees. Shadows bounced about her until lanterns lit up the forest.

She entered a kind of trance, a spell of enchantment transporting her to a place of mysterious solitude. The magical journey was complete. She had emerged not a victim, but victorious.

* * *

She found herself once again sitting in the back of an ambulance. She sipped tepid coffee while emergency lights strobed upon the cabin, making it pulse with a ghastly red glow. The helicopter that appeared out of nowhere had taken Tim, bloodied and hyperventilating, from the scene. The Big Bad Wolf didn't seem so scary anymore.

Benny was handcuffed and secured in the back of a police car. He had been found peacefully snoozing in the camouflage tent at the end of a trail of peanuts.

While a medic bandaged the superficial wounds on her wrist, Roberta spoke words of comfort to Cute Cop, whose first name she learned was Devon. He lay upon a gurney with a minor head wound. The bullet that grazed his skull would earn him a medal but no lasting ill effects. She looked up to see Chief Craven, who materialized out of the darkness.

"Well, Roberta."

"Chief." She was as calm as the archetypal wise woman in a fable. She had shed her symbolic red cape and run with the wolves.

"You led us on a merry chase."

"I'm not going to lie, Chief Craven. I'm grateful to see you," she said, gesturing to the hubbub surrounding her, "and everyone else." She'd come to realize that the woods were full of cops, searching for her, when she'd stumbled upon Tim and Benny.

"And we're grateful to get our hands on you." He pushed his glasses up on his head and fixed her with a steely glare. "There are a few holes we need you to fill in."

"Am I still suspected of something? Do I need a lawyer?"

Craven held up his hands as though she'd pulled a gun. "What you say will be strictly off the record. We have enough evidence to put these two guys away. We've recovered the gems, which are connected to a whole string of thefts, and are confident of going up the line to capture the brains of this outfit. These jewel smugglers, and the fencing operation for a nationwide ring of thieves, is now down for the count." They moved away from the medics and Cute Cop to lean against a cruiser out of earshot. "You've been part of something important."

"I'm no longer a suspect?"

"You never really were. I know you think we're idiots, but we were trying to keep you safe. A whole task force has been after this band of smugglers for almost a decade."

"And the terrorists?" Roberta asked.

"What terrorists?"

No terrorists. As she'd suspected, this was a gang of selfish plunderers with no political agenda. It figured. She'd been snookered, but good. "I guess I was misinformed."

"We haven't discovered anything like that. Nevertheless, people across America and Canada can hang onto their valuables a bit longer until the next group of burglars are sucked into the vacuum. For now, thieves will have to rely on their friendly neighborhood pawn broker, so it's a bit less lucrative and a lot more risky."

"A never-ending story, I'm sure," said Roberta, feeling marginally better about her role in bringing closure to this unfortunate episode. At least the bad guys would get what's coming to them. "You said you had questions?"

"The most pressing being who's buried up there?" Craven motioned toward the clearing in the woods.

"If it's a young woman with short black hair wearing one silver earring, her name is Carrie. I don't know her last name or anything about her, except she's part of this." She waved her hand in the general direction of the cabin.

Roberta then reminded him of meeting William and Carrie in the airport once again. "William and Carrie stashed the jewels in the urn. Apparently, they knew someone was looking out for them in Juneau and dared not carry the stuff in themselves. I was an unwitting mule." Roberta thought that's what a carrier of contraband was called.

"When I got to Juneau, they sent someone to the Goldrush Hotel after it, but I'd moved my room."

"That checked out. The innkeeper made a police report."

Roberta rolled her eyes. "I guess they couldn't figure out where I was. But days later, they thought I'd buried the urn, so William and Benny went to Evergreen Cemetery to unearth it. What didn't occur to those yahoos is that I hadn't had time to arrange a burial, and despite what I told William, I hadn't even made up my mind to bury Mom, as opposed to scattering her ashes somewhere."

"So, William and that guy," he indicated Benny, "went to Evergreen for the urn, ignorant not only of the time it takes to set a headstone but a lot of stuff. So, what happened?"

“I’m not sure, but my guess is that William was either trying to impress the higher-ups or was getting pressure to recover the loot and assumed finding the grave would be a piece of cake. He knew my mother’s name and I’d told him I planned to bury her in Juneau. Evergreen is the only cemetery within the city limits. Maybe they followed me there,” it occurred to her once more. “They probably wondered why I’d be going if not to visit my mother’s grave.”

“So why the gunplay? Why was William killed?”

“Benny must have decided to keep the jewels for himself. William revealed where they could be found. It seemed easy. He offed William and planned to return to dig up the urn and keep the gems. The bosses would assume William had taken them. No one would be the wiser.”

“And the girl in the woods?”

“I assume they killed her because of William. If she got scared enough she might spill her guts. They got to her before she could tell what she knew. She was only a bit player, and either William was important to her or she thought she’d get the same treatment as he did. She and William also might have been part of a plan to keep the jewels for themselves and realized Benny’s double cross. She was a loose end that had to be tied up, one way or the other.”

“And all this time, the urn is in your room.”

“Either there or in Benny’s possession.”

“What’s your take on why William’s body wasn’t found at Evergreen?”

“I think Benny moved it so that a spotlight wouldn’t be trained on the graveyard as a crime scene. He needed to return to find the buried urn and didn’t want the cops interfering.”

“So, while you were alerting us to the gunplay, he was out there moving a corpse.”

"That's the only thing that makes sense. And later, when he couldn't find a grave for my mother, Benny came looking for me. The original plan may have been to beat the information out of me, but the urn was sitting on my dresser. He tossed me out the window, took the urn with the jewels, and then played it like he knew nothing, pointing the finger at William, who was conveniently dead."

"And the tall guy? What's his role in this?"

Roberta had the grace to blush. "He was the brains, I think, at least at this point in the game. He kidnapped me, more or less, telling me he was with the Treasury Department and that they were monitoring a terrorist plot. He convinced me that staying hidden in the cabin was for my protection. All the time he thought I had the urn, having discovered the jewels. He was unaware of Benny's double cross." Roberta reminded Craven of her return to Juneau only yesterday. "No one believed that I'd been kidnapped, so I had to go after the evidence myself."

"Unnecessary, Roberta. We'd have found Westlake, or whatever his real name is. You jumped the gun, so to speak." He shook his head. "This could have been a lot easier if you'd stayed in the hospital in Juneau and let the professionals come out here to track these guys and recover the body in the woods. But you have the truth on your side, and everything you told us makes sense."

Roberta sighed with something like relief.

"So, Roberta, is there anything else we should know?"

Oh, yes, she thought. There was so much more, but nothing she would speak of. If you know there is magic, you can face any future. If you believe you are powerful, anything is possible. If Roberta had learned anything, it was to put the most optimistic spin on whatever she must accept. She smiled.

Craven said, "Now you need to come in and make a statement."

"So, you're not going to hit me with an obstruction charge?"

"Don't tempt me," he said with a grim face. "Thought I'd save the taxpayers a few dollars and send you back to the lower forty-eight."

As if, thought Roberta. No one was going to make her do anything. But it was just as well. Juneau didn't feel like someplace she belonged anymore.

Then she heard the beep beep beep of the ambulance backing up. It reminded her of the dryer, the dishwasher, and myriad small appliances in the little colonial in Indiana. She was homesick. And she had new lessons to impart to her children. It also occurred to her for the first time that, no matter whom you live with, they eventually annoy you. Maybe she was being too hard on Brad. The anger and discontentment she felt should never have been directed at her husband and the kids; the turmoil was all from within. So, she was going home.

Suddenly, something else struck her. "Chief Craven, where are my mother's ashes?"

"Well, you see Roberta, we found the urn in the back of the big guy's car, hidden under the spare tire, but it contained only the jewels. I'm sorry. And we have to keep the urn as evidence until all this is settled."

Roberta felt like all the wind had been knocked out of her. She had to accept, at last, what she'd known all along. Poor Mother! Her ashes had been dumped in the garbage at a Tim Hortons in the Seattle-Tacoma Airport. And then Roberta grinned. What an astonishing close to an exceedingly quiet and conventional life.

It seemed fitting somehow that a woman who never dared do anything the least bit extravagant or outrageous should figure in so unorthodox an end, flying across the country to be scattered at an international crossroad by jewel-smuggling murderers. The ultimate in shape-shifting transformations was achieved despite a less than dignified, not quite happily-ever-after ending.

Tears sprang to Roberta's eyes. "There you go, Mom, free at last. Ashes to ashes."

# CHAPTER 27

Roberta stood quietly in a place she'd never expected to see again: her own kitchen, where she pored over a document that brought her life into focus. She'd returned to Indianapolis, to the small white house that withstood the blow of her sudden departure, and planted a mountain hemlock in honor of the most terrifying and amazing time of her life. She contemplated it now as she looked backward. So many of her questions had been answered.

Having extinguished her inner turmoil, and embracing the familiarity of home, she finally was able to have a heart to heart talk with Brad. They sat across from one another at the kitchen table.

"It was—transformational," she said, trying to explain her Alaskan experience. "I've grown and accepted who I am. Now with this," she gestured with the form she held, "I've reconciled with my future and my past. I wanted you, more than anyone, to understand. Brad, I've overcome obstacles to my happiness, something Mother was never able to do."

Roberta's quest to know her emotionally unavailable mother, a purpose she realized only after her return, had driven her to look carefully into the public record. She'd gone online and requested her mother's birth certificate from the Morgan County Court House. She now had the answer to everything in her hand.

Brad touched the edge of the torn envelope she grasped. "You've discovered something important, haven't you?"

"Yes, I have." Roberta sighed and read details from the paper she'd been sent. "Martha May Princezna née Savage was, according to this, the daughter of the man who raised her, my grandfather. But her mother was one," she stumbled over the pronunciation, "Alexandrina Gianopoulos, age sixteen, unmarried, from Hamilton County."

"Oh," Brad uttered, the lone syllable weighted with portent.

Roberta sat back and stared at the ceiling, shaking her head. "We always knew he was a man who expected life to revolve around him and to do exactly as he pleased, but this is unbelievable. He forced my grandmother to raise his lover's child."

Brad took her hand in his.

She leaned toward him, excited. "Brad, it explains everything. The facts of Mother's unfortunate birth, and what it suggests about her upbringing, has freed me—us—from this nagging, harmful, unspoken history."

Later that afternoon, Roberta placed the document in a drawer next to the woven barrette she kept as a charm, a remembrance of her experience, and felt a calm she'd never known before. She believed compassion for everyone involved, not just for her mother but also for Grandmother Savage, would lead to healing. She also saw her flight to Alaska in a new light. What drove her to leave was a search for something Roberta had lost in herself. Now, having found the last piece of the puzzle, she was made whole. Her mother's tragedy need not echo through successive generations.

Roberta hung the only photograph of Martha caught in the same frame with the mother who reared her, the picture she'd retrieved from the fireplace all those years ago, where she could see it every day. She hoped never to forget the thicket of family secrets that burdened everyone, those who were innocent but betrayed.

"Poor Mother," she said trailing Brad into the living room. "And Aunt Ginnie and the other children. Think what they must have suffered. I imagine Grandmother Savage had no emotional resources to protect herself from such an abusive husband." Roberta's eyes teared at the photo of her grandmother looking like a wraith, her vacant stare signaling her withdrawal from the world. Now that Roberta knew Grandfather Savage and Miss Gianopoulos, however unwittingly, were the authors of the sorrow and dysfunction visited upon Roberta's past, the anguish reverberating through the years like a wrenching howl of pain would end.

She was glad Brad said nothing, but placed a comforting arm about her shoulders instead.

"It's something I've felt all my life, Mother's unhappiness. I just didn't know where it came from." She wiped away a tear.

"I'm proud of you," Brad said. "You've exposed all this—those hidden truths—to the light. It's like in a fairy tale. You've dispelled the curse."

She grasped Brad's hand. "Now I understand why my mother couldn't love me."

* * *

Sitting at the kitchen table on an autumn afternoon, Roberta sang to herself. She took comfort in the cool breeze that scattered scarlet leaves across the backyard as she finished homework for a course in fabric design. Brad watched a football game with Brad Jr. as Laura and Laura's new husband tinkered under the hood of Roberta's car. Families abide. They put up with her going back to college and her plans to start her own business like it was another harebrained scheme of hers, just as they forgave her for escaping into the Alaskan wilderness to find her past. They listened to her wild tale as if she were delusional and then got on with their lives.

She didn't mind anymore, but their inability to understand now made her thoughtful. She faced an important truth, that the only knowledge worth seeking was an understanding of one's self. She was no Goldilocks. The way forward did not lay in finding the exact middle path between opposites, finding that which is "just right." Like Dorothy who sought the witch's broom, she had to risk everything before she could see what was truly of value. Her future would not be discovered in the excitement embodied by a different place or another person, or the calm inherent in withdrawing from responsibility, but in the center of herself, her heart, and the creation that flowed within.

Roberta recalled the stories of her childhood. Fairy tales would have her believe that peace and joy can exist only on some condition, upon following certain rules:

Don't go into the woods.

You must not stray from the path.

Don't question authority.

Beware of a wolf in sheep's clothing.

You must be home by midnight.

Don't talk to strangers.

Only innocence and goodness are rewarded with undying love.

"Screw that," she muttered with a smile. She knew by this time that only by driving off-road, unmasking the wolf, and questioning everything could she detach from the merry-go-round of disappointment, anger, resentment, and depression. She closed her notebook and held it against her heart. The time for secrets was over.

**Acknowledgements**

As with most books, mine was not created in a vacuum. I had the advice and support of an amazing writing group, Company of Writers of Columbus, Ohio, which has taught, nurtured, and supported me throughout my writing career. The members are honest, direct, creative, and astute. My enduring thanks go to Pat Brown, Erica Scurr, Leslie Robinson, Elizabeth Sammons, Lacy Cooper, Ken Leonard, Dianne Moon, Bob Garrett, Angela Palazzolo, and Sue Rudibaugh.

I am grateful for family and friends who read my work, carve out and preserve valuable time for me, and provide feedback. But above all, I am beholden for the inspiration they provide: John M. Newman, Alexis D. Newman, Gregory A. Newman, Lisa Johnson Newman, Amy Clifford Millsap, Douglas Millsap, Kathi Godber, Deedy Middleton, and Alexandra Glover.

I am fortunate to have an excellent partner in Draft2Digital Publishing and wish to thank particularly my editor, Liv Birdsall, for her taste, patience, and good sense. She keeps me on track and adds clarity and consistency to my writing.

Any merit this novel has is due to the contributions of many people. All shortcomings are mine alone.

***Other titles by Phyllis M. Newman…***

With Edgar Allen Poe, Sherlock Holmes, and the nineteenth-century detective novel as inspiration, teenaged Kat Carson, detective-in-training, ferrets out a killer. The clues lead to romance, mayhem, and self-discovery in this noir mystery set in sunny Hollywood, Florida.

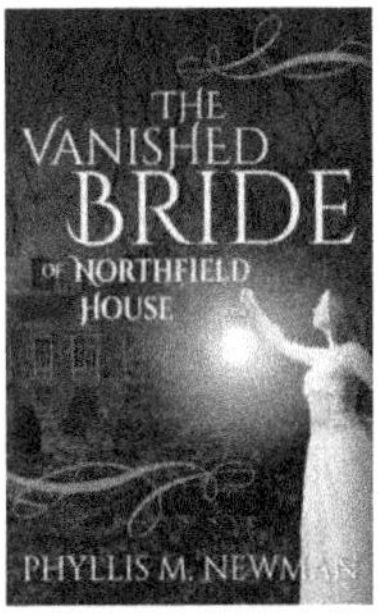


Young Anne confronts not only mystery, mayhem, and romance in this Gothic novel set in England, 1922, but she also encounters spirits. One death after another leads to discoveries related to a thirty-year-old disappearance and the ghost of a missing bride.

Orphaned Sonja desires a life of meaning as she struggles during the Great Depression, a time of deep economic and social turmoil. Instead, she's stuck with a cranky old woman at exotic Moorcroft Inn. Set in Baton Rouge, this Southern Gothic mystery concerns labyrinths, otherworldly strangers, and missing girls.

Kat Carson is once again in the center of the action. A treasure hunt involving Edgar Allen Poe's The Raven provides clues leading to the solution to theft, murder, and human depravity in this noir mystery set in the grand homes of Florida's wealthy class.

Phyllis M. Newman is a native southerner. Born in New Orleans, she spent formative years in Florida, Iowa, Mississippi, and on a dairy farm in Ross County, Ohio. After a long career in finance and human resources at The Ohio State University, she turned her attention to writing fiction. She published a noir mystery, "Kat's Eye" in 2015, a Gothic mystery "The Vanished Bride of Northfield House" in 2018, and the suspense thriller "Clearing in the Woods" in 2019. Today she lives in Columbus, Ohio, with her husband and three perpetually unimpressed cats, none of whom venture far from home.

You may contact/follow/like her at www.readphyllismnewman.com, @phyllismnewman2, or on
Facebook: https://facebook.com/ReadPhyllisMNewman/